THE BALLAD OF
AIDY AND LEFTIE

A CUTE MUTANTS UNIVERSE NOVEL

SJ WHITBY

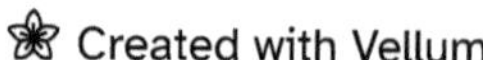 Created with Vellum

The Cute Mutants Universe

- *Cute Mutants Vol 1: Mutant Pride*
- *Cute Mutants Vol 2: Young, Gifted and Queer*
- *Cute Mutants Vol 3: The Demon Queer Saga*
- *Cute Mutants Vol 4: The Sisterhood of Evil Mutants*
- *Weapon UwU Vol 1: Godkillers*
- *Cute Mutants Vol 5: Galaxy Brain*
- *Shitty Mutants (Patreon Exclusive)*
- *Project Himbo*
- *Awakenings: A Cute Mutants Anthology*
- *The Mutantsitters Club*
- *The Mutopians Book 1: Imposter Syndrome*
- *Since I've Been Gone (Patreon Exclusive)*
- *The Ballad of Aidy and Leftie*

Content Warnings

This book contains subject matter that some readers may find distressing. Please be aware that The Ballad of Aidy and Leftie contains depictions of guns, blood, murder, cults, imprisonment, torture, and hate crimes against mutants.

Previously...

Once upon a time, a bunch of teenagers got superpowers. It seemed like it wasn't a big deal, honestly. Then things spiralled wildly out of control.

Long story cut seriously short, there's an alien energy being that lives in the centre of the planet. Her name is Cybele. She's responsible for keeping things relatively healthy, but she's had a rough time of late. Mutants were created a long time ago as one of her defence mechanism. Things didn't quite go according to plan, but they're getting *closer*.

Right now, there's an island somewhere. I won't give you its exact location. It's called Mutopia, and it's mostly populated with people with strange abilities. You might have heard of some of them before, but it's time to meet two new ones.

Welcome to the Ballad of Aidy and Leftie.

1

LEFTIE

My trial takes place in a room that contains nothing but me and a cloud of floating drone cameras as witnesses. Even still, they hold me in a cage. That is how much they fear me, and they are right to do so. If the device implanted on my neck falters, even for a second, I would be lost in the shadows, and they would be simply lost. The cameras swoop and dance, jostling for a better vantage. I glower at their blank little eyes. It is a promise that if I am free, I will hunt down every human eye that watches from a distance. I will pluck them from their skulls and they will be lucky to keep their lives.

No, I should take those too.

They have caged me. They have neutered me. This shall not stand.

There is a small, furious part of me that understands the likely outcome of this situation is my death. This so-called trial is taking place in order to justify my murder. They call what I did war crimes, and I must be visibly published. The newly resurgent American and Cascadian governments—rebuilding after the mess they walked their countries into—wish to show their teeth to the world once again. They brag that they have captured a monster, and now they shall slay me and call themselves heroes.

I attempt to find the shadows, but this box is full of light and in it there is no darkness at all. It is barely large enough to hold me, made of metal with an aperture in the door for me to see the cameras and the blank screen beyond. It should not be possible for me to be confined in this manner, but they have taken my mutant powers and dug them out with a blunt blade—some new technology I had not been aware of.

They may have leashed me, but they have not cowed me. There shall be a reckoning. I refuse to die in a cage at eighteen years old. I hate the man who made me and the grandiosity of the plans for which I was constructed, but one thing remains true.

I was born for greater things than this paltry death.

The cameras still move in their slow dance. My interrogators have given up on their scripted questions. I screamed too much defiance when they did. I exposed their lies until my throat bled and I drooled blood. Now I am tired, although I hate myself for it. The world is full of weakness, and I have always been strong. Now I look like a whipped animal with bloody teeth, and I loathe myself almost as much as I despise the wide-eyed authorities lurking behind the safety of their electronic eyes.

There is a screen on the wall. They have played some of my triumphs on it—what little camera footage exists of my attacks. Me, unfolding myself from darkness, pale and unsmiling. Pulling weapons from the shadows and using them to open throats in jagged smiles. Men with guns, hunting me, trying to kill a creature of smoke. They fire into walls and screens and each other. I have seen all this before. It is an attempt to prove what an unnatural abomination I am. It is dull to me. I was built to break an entire world, and all I am doing in this footage is breaking fragile little men.

I yawn theatrically. The screen changes to show a grid of faces. We have reached the moment to pronounce judgement. More steps in an elaborately choreographed dance to justify the death of a monster. A sour-looking old man proposes that I should be injected with poison, and they will all watch me as I die. Other serious people take their turns talking, performing for their audience. Their mouths move and their hands wave. The others watch and nod, their eyes darting around. I commit each face to memory. They will all die. So many old men. I'll take them before cancer and heart disease get a chance to. I am the world's most effective disease—The Left Hand of Darkness. I don't remember any other name.

There was once a cult called The Children of the Broken World. It was led by a charismatic preacher who named himself Uriel, and gathered many weak souls to his side. He created me to be their weapon of destruction. An elegant dagger held in a cage of glass and iron, except I was forged too well and became the instrument of their demise. These people watching behind their screens know that I have cut myself out of prison and destroyed my captors before. They should fear me doing it again.

There is a Latina woman on the screen. She speaks words of caution, of wisdom, treading a careful line. "We need to remember the Mutopia Accords, and at least acknowledge the official—"

She is shouted down, angry faces joining in a chorus to explain why she is wrong. The sole voice raised in my defence. I should spare her life. I'll plant a kiss on her forehead and tell her she ransomed herself from death. She attempts to marshal a further argument for my vindication, but the others have no time for her. The screen blanks for a moment. They do not wish me to see their disarray.

"Fucking assholes." I bare my teeth at them again. In this production, I am the deadly predator. If they would only let me act my role, I'd show them what I truly am and give a demonstration they'd never forget. Or, to be accurate, it would be their last memory. I imagine each of the watchers dying one after the other. Throats slit and eyes gouged and smiles ripped from cheek to cheek. Like the last gasp of the universe, stars winking out one by one. My defender left to stand alone in the void. Perhaps she would abandon her position, horrified to witness the truth of who I am.

At no point have I claimed to be anything other than a monster. I was built to break the world, but I turned away from my destiny. Now I am my own monster. I fight for myself and solve my own problems.

Except I am unable to solve this one. They have trapped me, and it enrages me. I cannot even rattle my chains, as what constrains me is a small black box attached to my neck. It sucks my powers from me like a bulbous mosquito.

"We need to stop prevaricating." One deep voice cuts across the clamour. "We've heard enough. The decision is clear. Talking about it any longer isn't going to change that. It's time to vote."

Rumbles of argument flare up across the grid of faces, but they fall silent one by one, focusing down on devices I cannot see. This council is preparing to sentence me to death, and I am helpless.

Before anyone speaks again, the door to the chamber bangs open. The cameras all spin away from me. All my attention is drawn to this surprise intrusion. I'm not even looking at the bank of faces to watch their reactions.

A figure stands in the doorway. Their skin is greenish, and they have a tangled mess of hair woven through with bright pink and orange flowers. Their eyes are large, a dark, earthy brown with the faintest glow of green around the edge. They're wearing impossibly casual clothes—a hoodie over torn jeans, with ferns and petals erupting from the cuffs, like they're smuggling a garden with them. The overall impression is that they rolled out of a flowerbed moments before they staggered in here.

This is no lawyer or court-appointed specialist. They're not a journalist or someone from the agencies that came together to produce this show trial. No, this is one of the most wanted people alive—although people might be stretching a point, if you believe the stranger conspiracy theories. This new arrival is none other than the mutant leader and murderous villain Dylan Chatterbox Taylor.

"I call shenanigans," they drawl, in their twanging accent.

The cameras swarm towards them, but are waved away like a plague of mosquitoes. A handful bounce onto the floor and lie still.

A loud bang comes from high up on the wall, accompanied by a puff of smoke.

"Fucking rude." Chatterbox reaches up and detaches a device from the back of their neck—a twin to the one which makes me helpless. "I'm assuming this was someone vastly overstepping their bounds?" They close their fist around it and squeeze until there's a sound of cracking circuitry.

"This was the operation of an autonomous system." The speaker on the screen is a slender man in a dark suit, obsequious in manner. "Not in any way a deliberate act."

"I fucking hope not." Chatterbox finally glances at me and closes one eye in an exaggerated wink. "You're lucky it didn't work, otherwise it'd be an attack on a foreign dignitary and I doubt any of you fuckers wants to carry that bag. Is it dignitary? Is that what I am? Doesn't fucking sound right, does it, Leftie?"

They're talking to me? They're calling me *Leftie?*

"My name is The Left Hand of Darkness," I sneer at them.

"Which is a mouthful, hence why I was shortening it. But I respect your right to shoot down my nickname." They turn their attention back to the cameras. "Now I'd like to meet some power play types. In here, in person. No fucking around, no bullshit. This is negotiation time."

This situation is unexpected, but promising. There are too many possibilities for me to construct a realistic plan from the uncertainty. Instead, I stay silent and wait for my moment to act.

Chatterbox leans against my cage, close enough I can't see them properly through the small window in the door. "Don't say a fucking thing, don't do your little shadow tricks. Hell, don't even look at someone with daggers in your eyes."

I want to tell them to go fuck themselves, but I close my mouth because this advice might be worth something. Once I'm free then—

The door opens again, this time revealing a stumbling delegation. I recognise faces from the camera grid. So they were in this building all along. Hiding from me like scared animals. As if there is any place they could scurry that would be safe from me after my escape.

For now, I do as Chatterbox says.

I say nothing. I smile, and cast my eyes down.

What do they see when they look at me? Dark hair falling down like two curtains either side of a cherubic face. Eyes like chips of permanently frozen ice, lips a glossy crimson slash. They let me dress this way, because it fits their narrative of me. Beautiful and deadly. They think they know my story. They've played it on their screens and spewed it between their computers.

They know nothing.

Chatterbox steps forward. They hold out one hand, entwined with vines and studded with tiny purple and yellow flowers. "Greetings from Mutopia. Shall we fuck around with pleasantries or get down to business?"

One man stands in front of the delegation. "Charles Faiducci. I'm chair of the Global Intelligence Committee. We're responsible for—"

"Fucking with mutants, mostly." I'd swear I can see everyone's breath as the temperature drops so sharply. "I know who you are. So there's no room for pleasantries, fine. I'm here to take The Left Hand of Darkness into Mutopian custody."

A tall woman thrusts her way forward, eyes narrowed. "There is no way, Ms. Taylor. I'm legal counsel for—"

"Mx. It's *Mx.* Taylor." There are thorns studded all over their hand. "Or Chatterbox, if we're being fuck-you formal. So—"

"It scarcely matters what we call you. There is no way that we will give up this criminal into so-called Mutopian *custody.* You may have browbeaten the United Nations into accepting you as a nation-state, but there is no way—"

"I think you'll find the treaty has been ratified by every country." Their smile is sharper than mine, and I find my fist clenching. "That's the word, isn't it? I'm no fucking scholar, but I've been told by much smarter people than me that I can come in here and do exactly this. It's *specifically* accounted for. The Left Hand of Darkness is our responsibility now."

"This is not happening," the woman spits. Seems like she really hates me. I wonder who I killed. I could assure her they deserved it, but I doubt that will help anything. "Your provision does not account for—"

"Even this one." Chatterbox raises one shoulder.

"Your Goddess is dead." Faiducci hunches his shoulders in his suit and steps forward. "You are not the threat you once were, and I would be very careful about taking an aggressive stance."

A series of five shining blades unfolds from thin air, coming to rest one at a time across Faiducci's throat. Each leaves a slender thread of red that seeps down to stain his white shirt.

I smile. I cannot help it.

"That's enough, Penny," Chatterbox says, and the blades unfold back into nothing. I cannot deny a surge of disappointment.

My prospective saviour steps towards Faiducci. He cringes backwards. Perhaps I would too, given the stormcloud air they have about them. "Goddess may be gone, and fuck you for disrespecting her memory, but you'll find we are not defenceless."

"You cannot do this," the woman lawyer says defiantly.

"It's done." Chatterbox shrugs again. "Complaining about it is just embarrassing. Think about it this way—she's our problem now. Isn't that a weight off your shoulders?"

The woman's breathing like she just got chased through the dark by a monster. "She needs to pay for what she's done."

"Oh, we'll make her work." Chatterbox laughs. "Don't you worry about that. Everyone's got their part to play." They give something that seems like it's supposed to be a salute, but it's with the wrong hand and isn't even close. They spin back around and cross back towards where I sit, hunched and confined.

I resist the small temptation to cringe like Faiducci. I am good at recognising threats, and this mutant is one.

A thump sounds from the door of the cage. It swings open easily, despite how many times I'd kicked furiously against it. Chatterbox stands there, smirking at me. "Come on then. The Left Hand of Darkness, let's get you home."

I don't move. "What if I refuse to go with you?"

They lean down and peer into the cage, talking low. "They'll kill you if you stay. You know where this is going, right?"

"I'd like to see them fucking try," I snarl, because I love the taste of defiance too much to stop.

They frown. "You're helpless right now. The GIC will kill you and get their props from all the mutant hates around the world. Then they'll hand your body over to

The Children of What The Fuck. Who have some prior claim on your corpse apparently."

For a brief moment, I feel like I'm submerged in ice water. Like the past is a grave and I've been buried in it this whole time, only dreaming of freedom. "That's impossible."

Chatterbox raises one shoulder in a shrug. "Oh, good. What a relief. This is all a terrible misunderstanding. Big waste of my time, but whatever. I'll be on my way then."

I know exactly why the cult wants me. They want to take the seed of destruction buried inside me, and use me as their tool once more. Their creature who was built to unleash the apocalypse. These people are not only here to kill me, they wish to hand my body back to the horrorshow that made me. I left the cult behind in dust and ash and corpses. They cannot possibly be *back*, no matter what this big-eyed leafy prick says.

I am overwhelmed by anger. The cult who leashed me. These people who leash me again. My helplessness, this situation cinching tight around my neck. The Left Hand of Darkness needs no pity. I want to rip off the hand of friendship being offered and beat Dylan Taylor to death with it.

But I'm smarter than that.

"Fine." I crawl out of my cage, a whipped dog slinking to another heel. "Get me out of here."

2

AIDY

I'm cleaning up at the end of class when Alyse Sefo taps my shoulder. I've got earbuds in, swaying slightly to sad Mitski songs, and I let out an embarrassingly loud gasp and splash water everywhere. My hands are all covered in paint from scrubbing out trays. Cleaning up the classroom after the juniors is one of the messier jobs, but I don't mind doing it. It's one of the many things I do on Mutopia to show that I'm a good citizen. Happy, shiny Aidy.

So I'm smiling wide when I turn around, even though my heart is thumping. "Sorry! I totally didn't hear you."

"My fault." Alyse smiles, radiantly beautiful as always, despite having spent the whole day wrangling a classroom of twenty mostly mutant children into some semblance of order. Her hair is pulled back into a ponytail and her pale blue sweater is daubed with substances I'd rather not speculate about. "I should've warned you."

My paint-covered hands hang awkwardly by my sides. "Is there something else you wanted me to do? I think all that's left is putting the rest of the art supplies away."

"There is something I've been wanting to chat about." Alyse's brow creases very faintly. "It's not school related though."

"Oh." I try to school my face into an expression of interest, even though my brain is sprinting in a thousand different directions. What could this be? Does she know something about my past? No, it can't be. I'm a new person, and this is a new life. Mutopia is a fresh start, and not only for me—that's one of the founding principles of our island home. Whatever Alyse wants, it's likely something minor. Although her expression is sombre and it makes me uneasy.

"Finish cleaning up and we'll talk in my office." She glances down at my hands, which are leaving multicoloured streaks on my sensible black pants as I fidget. Her smile flicks back on again, wide and dazzling. "And don't worry, it's not anything bad. There's no need to look quite so terrified. I'm asking a favour, that's all."

I turn back to the sink as she leaves, plunging my hand into the sudsy water. At least there I can disguise their shaking. It's a good thing, theoretically, to be close to someone so important on Mutopia. But it feels dangerous to be somewhere where the slightest slip could reveal me for who I am. The island is supposed to have ways of finding people like me and stopping them from coming to Mutopia. But their psychic Fetch couldn't see into the depths of me, some flukey outcropping of my protective powers, and so here I am. This is my chance at real safety and an opportunity for this rebirth as Aidy. It means I'll have to be extra cautious around Alyse. Which means not rushing through to her office, but finishing the job thoroughly and carefully like I would on any other day.

She's in the middle of grading papers for the older children when I tap on her door. The desk is covered in papers, a computer screen sitting dark on the corner.

"There you are." Her laugh is light. Everything about her feels like sunshine. It's easy to bask in her presence, which is a problem. It can lead me to the seductive belief that the Aidy part of me is all there is. "I thought maybe you fell into the sink."

"They're messy little creatures." I walk casually into the room and take a seat opposite her as if there's nothing at all to be nervous about. "Cute, though."

"You do a great job with them," Alyse says. "But I understand it's entirely unrelated to your powers. So we've been chatting and we'd like to offer you another opportunity."

"We?" There goes my heart, racing again as if I'm fleeing some future catastrophe.

"The brains trust." She laughs. "Or, as my best friend calls it, 'the brains trust and Dylan'."

"Dylan?" I cross my legs and fold my arms, then worry I look too nervous, so I untangle myself and attempt to slump casually in the chair. It's a disaster. I'm too fidgety, too weird. The problem is that Chatterbox is *terrifying* and I'd prefer to keep out of their sphere of notice. If they find out what I've done, they're not the sort to be merciful.

"Yes." Alyse smiles, trying to reassure me. "They're a sweetheart, honestly. And not remotely the point of this conversation. Although you *will* meet them, so remember they don't bite. Not people like you at least. Sorry, I'm rambling."

"It's fine." I make a valiant attempt to smile.

"Here's the situation: we're about to welcome a new mutant onto Mutopia. One with a very colourful past and some interesting enemies. She'll need help adjusting to the island, and also protection if things get complicated."

I nod along as if I understand. "Complicated?"

Alyse waves a hand. "It'll probably be nothing. But on the off-chance that things get perilous—which I can't honestly deny is a possibility, given recent events—it would be good to have someone with your... special skills."

"Oh." I need something better to say. "My powers?"

"Yes, Aidy." She shakes her head slightly with wry amusement, as if she's my mother expressing disbelief at how slow I am on the uptake. It's easy to forget she's only a few years older than me. "Your shield form, your parachute form. You're a natural protector."

This seems like a huge exaggeration. Especially the part about my parachute form. Aside from demonstrating my powers on entry, I've only ever used it once. It was in the Dark Year and I fell off a building while running for safety from some very unpleasant pursuers. I was sure I'd die, but my body had other plans, turning into something vast and billowing that carried me to the ground. I don't really understand the extent of my mutant powers. The very nice man at my entrance interview theorised it's beyond protection, but is for keeping me alive through everything. An ingrained survival instinct given mutant form. It's very much a *me* thing, and doesn't do a lot for other people. The idea of being a natural protector has an irony so intense it feels bladed.

I manage to control my expression. "I've never been in any kind of real combat situation before. The whole idea scares me, to be honest."

Alyse tilts her head slightly. The corner of her mouth twitches. When she moves, it's almost too fast to see. One hand whips something off the desk and hurls it towards me.

My body responds instinctively, my skin hardening into a protective layer. The projectile bounces off me and skitters across the floor. Now I can see that it's a small knife, beads of apple juice still clinging to the blade.

"You threw a knife at me," I gasp.

"I've read the reports on your powers." Alyse covers her smile with one hand. "Your skin can stop bullets. You could walk through fire in your shield form. Blades shatter on direct impact. It's theorised that you'd survive a nuclear explosion." She winks at me as if this is an ordinary thing to say. For her it possibly is.

"I don't want to test any of that." My voice is hoarse. I'm not built for this sort of thing. All I want to do is keep working as a teacher aide at Jing Hall's School. Not get roped into superhero antics simply because my mutation makes me impervious to harm. Which is a joke on its own, really. My skin may be unmarked by fire and blade and bomb, but my soul is a pulped mess of ropy scars. I've never had a shield that can defend me from that.

"Hopefully it won't come to anything." Alyse leans back in her seat a little. "This isn't compulsory, Aidy.

You know that, right? It's an offer we're extending because we think you'd be great at it. You're an asset to Mutopia, and we'd like to work with you more."

This whole situation is incredibly awkward. I'm trying to avoid drawing attention to myself, but that sometimes conflicts with this new version of myself that I'm building. Someone charming, someone helpful. Who's a good citizen and an asset to the team. A person others want to have around. And now this new and improved version of myself has worked a little too well.

"I'd love to help." I widen my eyes. "But surely there are better candidates."

Alyse shakes her head. "Not from where I'm sitting. But it's your call, Aidy. What do you say?"

I have no choice but to lean in and shake her outstretched hand. That's what Aidy would do.

I arrive back at my dormitory for the tail end of the dinner hour. The place where I live is a halfway house for new arrivals on Mutopia. It's somewhere to meet and mingle, to make new friends and find your role on the island before you get a place of your own. It's busy enough these days that there are two people in each bedroom, and all the living facilities are shared.

This makes it hard to find time to yourself, although there are plenty of places on the island to go if you need a break.

I've done well, because my roommate Skip is charming and funny, and happy to give me space when I need it. She talks a lot, which it turns out I enjoy, especially when it's someone that doesn't hate my company. In fact, it almost seems the opposite—she's one of the few people still seated at the long tables in the dining hall, and she waves when she catches sight of me in the doorway. I give her an enormous smile of my own, and gesture in the direction of the food. Today's meal is vegetarian lasagne with fresh bread. Once I've got my helping, I slide into the seat opposite Skip with a loaded plate.

"I heard a rumour about you." She winks at me. With her dark skin and bobbed hair, she's beautiful in a soft-focus way, like I've caught her looking through the window of a rainy cafe. There's a slight air of melancholy about her, and sometimes I wonder how different her story was before she arrived on the island. The past is a thing we don't talk about by shared agreement, willing to let the other keep their secrets. It's one of the reasons I like her so much.

"A rumour about *me*?" I duck my head to look down at my food.

"Yes, oh shy and demure one. Apparently the glorious Moodring has asked you to be chaperone to a top secret mutant arrival."

I drop my fork on the table with a clatter. "How do people know this *already*?"

"Rumours travel fast on the island." Skip picks up my fork and hands it back to me. "So it's true then?"

"It sounds like you know as much as I do."

"Do you know who it is?"

I frown. "Actually, that part wasn't mentioned. I was flustered by the whole situation—you know, being asked to join a team by an actual Cute Mutant. It's only now I realise I forgot all the important questions. Doesn't matter, really. I'll be doing the job either way. Alyse asked me, and I can't exactly say no to her."

Skip nods her head, but there's a smile on her lips like she knows something.

"You know more?" I ask, eyes wide.

"Only those pesky rumours." She's enjoying this, so I play along.

"Tell me." I let a playful whine enter my voice. "I'm the bodyguard. Who is it? Someone important, like a celebrity mutant or something?"

"A celebrity I guess?" Skip's voice goes up really high at the end. "I mean, she's famous."

"Oh god." I put my head in my hands. "Just tell me. I hate guessing games."

"Okay, fine." Her face is serious, all the teasing ended abruptly. "It's The Left Hand of Darkness."

"No." My voice shakes, even on that single syllable. "That's impossible."

"I've got no proof, only the rumour."

"Not even *here*. They wouldn't. They *can't*."

Skip reaches across the table and takes my hand. "Look, it's Alyse. She wouldn't ask you to do something impossible or dangerous."

I really don't know whether that's true. My brain won't even process the thought. All that drums through my head is that I've messed up my new life on Mutopia with one single *yes*.

Because I've just offered to be the bodyguard to one of the most dangerous criminals on the planet.

3

LEFTIE

I say nothing as we leave the room where I was imprisoned. When they brought me in, my head was in a black bag. Now I can see I'm not in some secret black site prison complex. We're in some official government type place—a tall building full of a thousand offices. I've been through many such places before, clearing monstrous corporations of the people who do their bidding. Once I'm done, there's nothing left behind but computers and desks and water coolers.

Chatterbox whistles to themself as we reach the elevator. "Feeling okay?"

I don't even give them the satisfaction of a glance. They *ordered* me to be silent.

The elevator dings, and they gesture inside. I consider ignoring them, but there will be better places to make my escape. And then it will be time to deal with everyone involved in this so-called trial.

The instant the elevator doors close, I reach up and contort my chained hands over my head. I feel the bulbous device in my neck, and tug at it.

This was a mistake. I've never felt this much pain. White noise burns through every part of my body.

The world hitches, dissolves into darkness, then snaps back with the force of a blow. My eyes are gummed together, and I blink them open. I'm lying on the floor of the elevator. Chatterbox has their hands on their hips and is looking down at me, shaking their head.

"That wasn't very smart." They reach down and haul me upwards. I feel like a kitten dangling from the mouth of her mother. "Can you stand?"

My limbs are shaky, like they've dissolved and haven't set. I snarl and shake my head, so they prop me gently against the back of the elevator.

"I'm not going to detach that thing in here, because you'll run off and kill everyone." They adjust my posture slightly, like my slouched state offends them. "Don't worry. We won't keep you on a chain forever."

"I'll kill you," I rasp.

"You're welcome." They wink at me.

"I didn't thank you. I'm not *going* to thank you." I try to find the shadows, but they are soft and faded, and my hands slip through like they're muddy water. "The instant you free me, I'll slit your throat. That's all the thanks you deserve."

"Yes, you're very scary. I like the attitude. Just dial it down a notch or two, and recognise what a hand of friendship looks like." They wave one in my face. It smells like something that blooms at night.

I'm so angry, I almost bite it.

The elevator dings again, and we exit into a corridor filled with soldiers. They're in body armour, holding weapons of rough stone.

"I'm sure this isn't intended to be threatening." Chatterbox wanders through the soldiers, holding my hand like I'm a child being led through a shopping mall. "So I'm not going to take it as an act of aggression. But you fucks better play it nice and soft or else we'll have a diplomatic incident."

"We're here to monitor the prisoner, Ma'am." The speaker's tones are made grating by the mask. "In case she kills everyone. She's got a nasty of habit of that."

"I'm perfectly fucking capable of managing the situation. And don't call me *Ma'am*, for fuck's sake. Just take a nice big step back and we'll all get through this together without anyone getting stabbed or worse."

The soldiers begrudgingly shuffle backwards until they're pressed against the walls. We pass down the corridor between them, blank visors tracking my passing. At the end is a big rotating door and we exit together, Chatterbox humming faintly. Outside, the sky is grey with the faintest smell of drizzle in the air. I don't recognise the city we're in, but it's full of tall buildings. The advertisements are in English.

Another security detail stands on the sidewalk, clustering around us as we exit. Chatterbox says nothing and ambles through the streets casually, one arm linked through mine as if we're a pair of tourists with an afternoon to kill. The soldiers clear civilians out of the way as we wend downwards. I catch a glimpse of a blue thread of river between buildings. It appears to be our destination, and sure enough, we turn a corner and the expanse of it is revealed, small carts selling food on the bank and tourist boats plying their trade on the water.

The river is wide and blue-grey, slightly choppy as the wind ruffles it. A small wooden boat bobs in the water, a short distance from a flight of stone steps. It isn't even moored.

"That's your plan?" I finally speak, unable to hold myself back any longer. "Just to remind you, we're fleeing my abduction, show trial, and probable death. And you want to use a fucking dinghy with no oars? They'll blow us out of the water."

Chatterbox places their thumb and little finger into their mouth and emits a piercing whistle. The boat skips eagerly across the water and nuzzles up against the stone. "That *dinghy* is part of Mutopia. Faster and more stable than any regular boat." They gesture downwards. "After you, Left Hand of Darkness."

They say it with a faint smirk, and it's somehow more annoying than the nickname. I trot nimbly down the stairs and leap lightly into the boat. I'm expecting it to shift beneath my weight, but it absorbs my landing without moving.

"Told you." Chatterbox drops down beside me. "Okay. Let's head back. Mission sort of accomplished."

The boat spins in place and speeds off across the surface of the water, a small wooden disc skimming between the waves. It darts between the other boats, heading unerringly for the mouth of the river and the ocean beyond. It doesn't feel unstable or unsteady at all, despite the speed of our travel. With the wind and spray on my face, it actually feels like I'm free.

Moments ago I was facing my inevitable death moments ago, and now I'm in the company of a notorious mutant, out on the open ocean. I'm aware of proverbs involving frying pans and fires, but I'm not sure how well it applies to my new situation. I'll need to be patient, but I've got too many questions to hold back from those.

"You said the Children of the Broken World are back,"
I growl. "Why did you lie?"

"Why would I? They popped their heads up when you
were sentenced to death. Said they wanted some
proprietary tech out of your body. Reading between
the lines, it's something nasty, and we'd obviously like
to keep it out of their hands. They waded into some
big legal fight over it and Cascadia capitulated. As
long as they got you dead and their fingerprints all
over it, they didn't care what happened next."

I say nothing for a moment. I'm digging in the bloody
muck of my memories, tallying the bodies of those I
left behind on my last day with the Children. There's
something fucked going on here, but I can't figure
it out.

"Where are we going?" I ask instead. "You have a
safe house or something?"

"Better." They're looking out to sea, so I only see half
of their smile. "A safe island."

This must be an elaborate joke. "*Mutopia*? Seriously?
If anyone comes for me, that's the first place they'll
look."

"It's still the safest place in the world to be a mutant.
The island will defend you, assuming you're not a
complete fucking asshole to her. Plus there's me
who's got your back, and a handful of other badasses
who aren't half bad in a scrap."

"I don't need *defending*," I snarl. "But it's pathetic to take me somewhere so obvious. If you had—"

"You'd be dead in that box with a fucking powers-neutraliser in your neck if it wasn't for me sallying the fuck forth to save your ass. I'm not expecting a thank you, but try to be less annoying. Speaking of—" They reach up, and I feel a strange tugging sensation at the back of my neck. It's sharp and cold at the same time. Then they remove their hand and show me the round black nubbin of the device the humans used to neutralise my powers.

I almost laugh. This is a grievous tactical error on Chatterbox's part. Do they really believe I would be so easily tamed by the sweet-smelling touching of their hand?

"Fool." I gather a handful of cool shadows cast by the boat onto the waves. It is a moment's work to fashion them into a blade and to slice it towards Chatterbox's throat.

I don't actually *want* to kill them. They bought their life with their rescue. All I'm looking for from them is the merest fraction of fucking respect. A delicate cut along the line of their throat might be conducive to that.

Except vines erupt from their body and twist around my wrist, yanking it away so fast and hard that my shoulder almost dislocates. Fuck them. If this is what they want...

I fashion a rough, brutal axe from shadow, and heave it in a savage swing. But those damn vines are there too, and my limbs are stretched out, the shadows I held dissolving to dark blurs.

Now I can spy two small creatures perched on Chatterbox's shoulders, grinning plant-monsters with sharp teeth. What the fuck is going on? Time to step it up a notch. I sidestep into darkness, where I can form far more serious weapons. Twin daggers blaze in my palms, darkness folded atop more darkness like a sword beaten from a thousand slender layers of metal.

Except I find the monsters here too. *Impossible.*

"Naughty, naughty," one says. Their hands flash with glowing vines that leave afterimages as they ensnare me.

I shake off my cloak of darkness and return to the brightness of the world. There is too much uncertainty here and I need to know more before I act.

"What the fuck are those things? Your personal demons?"

"Demons," one small monster cackles. "I love it."

"It's an easy mistake to make." Chatterbox reaches up with both hands and strokes the leafy heads of the two creatures. "They're my children."

"Hilarious," I sneer. "What are they really?"

"Aliens." One blinks hazel eyes at me. "Creatures built from our parent's DNA and hatched from plants. We're terrifying monsters, just like you. Except worse."

"Also better-behaved," the other says. "We haven't killed nearly so many people. I'm Soo-yeon and this is my sibling Willow."

"I'm The Left Hand of Darkness." Then I find myself capitulating to the damn nickname because Chatterbox was right—it *is* such a mouthful when you're having a conversation with people rather than using it as an ominous warning. "But Leftie is fine. And I never killed anyone who didn't deserve it."

Willow pokes their parent's cheek. "That sounds fun. Are we allowed to k-word people if they deserve it?"

"No." Soo-yeon waves a vine in Willow's face. "We've been through this. If we kill the right person, we might start a war. And that would be wrong."

I frown at Chatterbox. "Are they really your children? They could see me in shadow form, which shouldn't be possible."

"It's a different angle," Soo-yeon says. "But you're still there, silly Leftie."

It's hard to wipe the frown off my face. I'm calculating. I've had little to do with other mutants. I've been carrying out my own one-woman war on humanity without any need to collaborate with the chaotic mess of mutantkind. On this evidence, they'd be more dangerous enemies than I realised.

"I wasn't really trying to kill you," I tell Chatterbox.

"That's good." One corner of their mouth twitches. "I wasn't really scared."

The children nestle close into their parent and whisper. It sounds like the wind rustling through vast trees and I can't make out any words. Growing up among the Children, I was mostly kept aside from everyone else. My destiny was too important to sully with ordinary human contact. The sight of this family of unnatural creatures leaves me uneasy. The comfortable way they tangle together and give each other sustenance is something new that I haven't seen before. Together with their mutant abilities, I am left at a distinct disadvantage. I must find a way to get back in control.

"Are you the most powerful mutants on Mutopia?" I ask.

"Who? Us?" Willow giggles. "We're not even mutants. Aunt Violet's probably the most powerful. Aunt Marisol is pretty tough, and she could probably take you in a fight. Aunt Katie could roast you pretty good too, I bet."

"You're such a show off," Soo-yeon says.

"I'm answering the question, that's all." Willow leaps down from their parent's shoulder and peers up at me. "And this girl isn't *that* special. I mean, the shadow trick works on human types because their eyes are basic, but really it's like standing sideways and thinking people can't see you."

I consider kicking this alien in the face and knocking them into the water. Probably wouldn't be the smartest decision I've ever made, but it might help decrease the tension I'm feeling.

My tone is icy. "I think my record speaks for itself when hunting humans."

"Hunting!" Willow's eyes are wide. "That's not fair! We're not allowed to—"

"Hsst," Chatterbox says.

"But Pear!"

"Hsst, I said."

Willow scowls up at me, and then turns their attention back to their sibling. "I like the matter-generation thing though. Can you see the trick of it, Soo-yeon-a?"

Soo-yeon frowns and flexes their hand. On the third twist of their fingers, they summon a perfectly-formed dagger. The blade is slender and elegant, tracing the faint shape of an S. The hilt is ornate and carefully decorated.

A muscle jumps in my jaw. It took me *months* to create anything close to this level of detail, and these brats figure it out in seconds. My throat burns like I've swallowed scalding water. It's not worth wasting time on jealousy. They're aliens by their own admission. My fight is with humanity, not them.

"Not bad," I admit, only a trace of my begrudging left audible. I form my own dagger, longer and more wickedly curved, and hold it up to them.

Willow opens their mouth to speak, but Chatterbox intervenes.

"Enough, you two. Why don't you head home? I'll be fine with Leftie."

"But—"

"Trust me, for f— goodness' sake."

Soo-yeon lets their dagger dissolve and executes a perfect swan dive into the water. Willow follows immediately after and the two of them swim away through the water, barely making a ripple, their two heads sleek and shiny like a seal's.

Chatterbox watches them go, their back to me. I still hold my own dagger, and I move very slowly towards them. As I do, a series of thorns juts from their back, in two parallel rows. So. They *are* watching me after all.

I consider diving into the water myself, but I suspect they would find a way to drag me back. A brief alliance here may not be the worst tactical decision. As much as I fucking *hate* to admit it, the humans have the means to neutralise me. They've proven that, and I need a better plan before I come at them again. I also need to find the truth about the Children of the Broken World from a place of relative safety. It'll be annoying as hell to be surrounded by a bunch of mutants all singing in harmony, but Mutopia might have some useful people on it. For now, I will comply.

I walk up to stand by Chatterbox in the bow of the craft.

"Not far now." They extend one hand and point into the distance, where there's the faintest smear of blue-green on the horizon. "That's home. We brought her in fairly close for you, but still in international waters."

I say nothing. People talk online about the changing location of Mutopia. There are websites that track it and satellites that monitor it, although they're always suffering from equipment malfunctions or show degraded, impossible images. Everyone knows the island moves. It's not that fucking impressive to talk of *bringing her in* like she's a beat-up old car.

"We fought long and hard for this place," Chatterbox says, as if I asked. "People died for it."

Including them, if you believe the weirder theories. I always thought these were the rantings of those obsessed with conspiracies, but on this evidence I'm forced to re-evaluate. Whatever Dylan Taylor might be, they're far more dangerous than the casual clothes and swallowed consonants would have you believe. I recognise threats, because I am one, and I'm always aware of others.

This person, their alien children, this island? My radar is a constellation of blinking signals.

I continue to say nothing as we move closer. I'm not really a great admirer of nature and physical beauty, but I understand what it *is* and the island checks all the boxes. Sloping hills and pale cliffs, tangles of trees and fields dotted with flowers. A waterfall cascades down one side like someone forgot to turn off a faucet. The boat skims across to a wide, sandy bay that shimmers in the sun. It dances over the waves even lighter than before, as if it's excited to return home.

"This place has healed a lot of people," Chatterbox says. "It could heal you too."

I continue to say nothing, and let my lip curl up in a sneer.

They make a very faint sound of frustration in their throat, and it's the first thing in a long time that has made me smile. I'll beat them yet.

4

AIDY

The next day, I still have no idea how to get out of my new job. Last evening, Skip got too tired to listen to my circular rambling and drifted off to sleep. Her basic opinion is that I should trust Alyse because of who she is. Which I didn't argue with, because I'm here in Mutopia and so I need to smile and go along.

I can't tell her that I think the Cute Mutants caused as many problems as they solved. They saved the world and got a free pass on their more questionable decisions. Whether their success was luck or good judgement is up for debate, but not by me. I made myself new the day I stepped off the boat onto the shores of Mutopia, and I will be perfect enough that nobody ever wants to pry beneath the surface.

When I wake in the morning, Skip's doing her makeup in front of the mirror. "Rough night?"

"I don't remember," I shiver.

"You were groaning in your sleep." She waggles her eyebrows at me. "Not the fun kind either."

"No, the worrying kind." I try not to hunch my shoulders. "There's a person responsible for literally hundreds of murders showing up on the island today. Coming *here* because so many other people want to kill her. And I'm supposed to be her shield wall."

"Better than cleaning paint trays," Skip says brightly.

"Do you honestly think that?"

She gets up from the chair and leaps onto the bed beside me, sprawled against me without any affectation or awkwardness. "More exciting at least. And, like, you're on Mutopia, surrounded by the coolest and most badass mutants on the planet. They're not going to let anything terrible happen to you. This whole situation is like a call-up to the big leagues. I'm jealous."

When I arrived here as Aidy, leaving Ruth-Anne Bader dead and buried behind me, I never expected to meet someone like Skip. She's genuinely kind and delightful, who actually thinks I'm worth spending time on. She's the type of person I long to be, someone whose warmth and acceptance feels like a permanent embrace. Her manner makes me so comfortable that I almost let things slip, but it becomes this game of increasing stakes. The closer I get, the more I want to tell her everything, but the more I can't bear to lose her. She's friends with Aidy, and Aidy isn't real, no matter how good it feels to be them.

"You're jealous," I laugh. "We are very different people."

"Maybe you'll become friends with her." Skip places the back of her hand to her forehead and sighs theatrically. "You'll ask to trade rooms so you can shack up with history's greatest monster."

"History's what?" I pull the blankets up higher, like I want to hide under them. It's only partly play-acting.

"That's what they called her on this terrible documentary I saw recently."

"Great. That's my new responsibility. And no, I'm not going to trade rooms. She'd murder me in my sleep!"

"Tough skin." Skip pats my cheek. "Her shadow-knives would bounce off you."

"That doesn't make it okay!" I flop back down onto the pillow. "I hate this."

"Do you think they'll let me meet her?" Skip asks. "Mélodie wants to as well. You know her, right? She works in the kitchens."

"Sort of." I frown at the ceiling. "Why on earth do you want to meet her?"

"Fascination on my part," Skip says. "Plus Mél thinks she's hot."

"Gross! That's as bad as the women who write to serial killers in jail!"

"Except she's not in jail." Skip pokes my legs. "She's coming *here*. And she's not a serial killer. She's more like a hot, deadly Batman. A lonely vigilante protecting mutants from the worst of humanity."

"You're both gross." I finally sit up again. "But yes, if Ms. Sefo says it's okay, you can meet her because it takes some of the pressure off me. I'd rather be a silent shield wall who spends most of their time invisible."

"Hurry up and get dressed, then." Skip bounds off the bed. "I'll find Mél."

"The wonderful thing about Skippy," I sing-song after her, but she's already gone. I'm left alone to dress in peace. Not that it helps. What should one wear when greeting history's greatest monster? I own nothing that suits that mood. The most appropriate outfit would be a wedding dress covered in blood—although that would be in very poor taste, if the stories I've heard are true.

Instead, I wear a flowing, baggy shirt in a shade of pale green that Skip once said works with my eyes, along with three-quarter pants and boat shoes. Mostly, I dress for Mutopia like it's a cruise ship, which isn't so far from the truth. I don't bother with makeup or jewellery—not necessarily because I don't like them, but because it makes me even more anonymous.

Once I exit my room into the corridor, I find Skip and Mélodie having a rapid-fire conversation in sign language. I've only picked up a few bits and pieces since I've been here, but I'm trying to learn. The other mutant is a stocky Thai woman with spiky hair dyed a startling shade of blue and a cherubically beautiful face. She waves hello, and I give my own awkward greeting back.

"Mél is into the whole Left Hand thing. Big time." Skip seems equally excited from the way she's bouncing on her toes. I suppose it's understandable—I must be dreadfully boring in comparison.

I mime stabbing myself with a dagger. "Dating seems like a deadly proposition."

Mélodie signs back, and Skip translates for me. "There are worse ways to go." An iridescent bubble escapes Mél's lips. It bursts in the air and the sound of her laughter spills out. This is her mutant power, to generate objects from sound.

"Don't blame me when this all goes horribly wrong." I glower at them both, but Mél only spills more bubbles of laughter. I'm sure she's lovely, but I'm a tiny bit jealous of how close Skip and her are. With Skip being the first friend I've had in a while, it's hard not to see the other mutant as a threat. Maybe it'll be good if Mél gets close to the incoming assassin. They can both distract each other, and leave me and Skip alone.

All this leaves me with mild nausea and the beginnings of a headache, like storm clouds gathering on the horizon of my mind. This is not the beautiful life I intended on Mutopia. Maybe if I do a terrible job, they'll write me off as hopeless and let me go back to washing paint trays and looking after children.

We exit the building as a trio to find Alyse waiting for us. She greets everyone cheerfully, and leads us through the town of Emmaline. We make our way to the centre and the main government building. It's an enormous hollow tree with multiple floors built into it, like something out of a fairy tale. Our destination is a room on the bottom level, a big open space that has a sparring ring sketched out on the sandy ground. There's nobody else around.

"Don't worry, she *is* on the island," Alyse says. "Dylan did their dashing rescue thing. They say Leftie's very charming."

"Leftie?" I frown. It seems unwise to give a monster a nickname.

"Charming." Mél and Skip exchange glances, which makes me feel even worse.

Before I have a chance to ask more questions, we're joined by more mutants, all of whom I recognise and who remind me I'm in way over my head. I'm in a room with some of the Founders. One is Feral, who's like a catwoman walking on two legs complete with claws and twitching ears. And then there's Marvellous, or Dani. She's one of Dylan's girlfriends, and is no longer even human, rebuilt by the alien energy being Cybele to be a creature that's half plant and half person. I've never been this close to either of them, and they're both extremely unnerving. I find myself standing slightly behind Alyse to avoid Feral's golden gaze and Dani's cool hazel one.

"A whole welcoming committee," Feral says, a faint purr in the back of her throat. "I'm sure she'll be delighted."

"Dylan says she's very charming," Marvellous says, and I can definitely hear the sarcasm this time. I shoot a glance at Skip and Mélodie, but they're both gazing at the mutants with expressions of awe.

Someone else appears in the doorway, a shaggy and dishevelled figure with an oddly elongated shadow. I've met Chatterbox once before on my first day in Mutopia. They wore a bright pink t-shirt that had a burning dumpster on it and trousers with too many pockets. Today they're wearing an extremely large hoodie with a cartoon devil on it and apparently nothing underneath.

"Fucking finally." They run a hand through their hair, dislodging a crop of leaves. "The gang's all here. Leftie, dearest, say hello."

Chatterbox's shadow melts away, revealing a girl who's maybe a little older than me. The main impression is pale skin and a lot of dark hair. She's beautiful, but not in an attractive, endearing way— more like gazing upon a statue of a death goddess. If you stare too long, a dark power will strike you down. Probably her.

History's greatest monster says nothing. Her expression is neutral except for a faint expression of distaste.

"Hopefully you remember Feral, Marvellous, Moodring." Dylan waves a hand towards the three older mutants. "You'll see a lot more of them around, no doubt. You're really here to meet this lot. These are the new kids I was telling you about."

Now everyone's attention is directed at us, and I very much would not like to be here right now. I can't quite fathom the missteps that brought me here to this moment, and this savage girl's attention.

Leftie's icy gaze flicks between us and settles on Mélodie. "Looks like you brought me an eye candy bodyguard." Her voice is surprisingly deep, like it's marinated in the depths of her body before spilling out rich and warm. When she transfers her attention to Skip, another twinge of jealousy unrolls deep in my stomach. "And you're utterly delightful, aren't you?"

Both Skip and Mél stammer responses, and I resist the urge to disappear completely behind Alyse.

Leftie smirks. "And who the fuck's the baby cruise director?"

I flush, because she's obviously talking about me. I desperately wish I'd worn a different outfit today. Or that Alyse had chosen literally anyone else for this miserable task.

"This is Aidy," Alyse says cheerfully. "She's your actual bodyguard."

"Wow." Leftie pulls an exaggerated face at Dylan. "It's lucky I can defend myself or I'd be really fucked, wouldn't I?"

"You're not invincible, asshole." Dylan stifles a yawn. "Aidy's pretty damn close."

The girl moves lightning fast. The nearby shadows in the room are drawn to her, like her hand holds a magnet for darkness. Within a second, she's formed it into a spear and it is hurtling towards me.

If it was left up to me to consciously summon my powers, I'd be dead where I stand. My brain is frozen in a panic over being attacked out of the blue like this. Thankfully, my powers have given me a preternatural sense that detects danger and responds to it without my unhelpful brain needing to intervene.

Leftie's blade shatters into a thousand dark shards that pepper me like shrapnel. The force of the blow still sends me staggering backwards, ungainly as a toddler until I collapse down onto my ass.

Everyone's looking down at me. I can feel the judgement, the disapproval, the disdain. It's almost tangible, acrid in the back of my throat like I'm inhaling trace elements of my failure.

Leftie twirls another blade between her fingers. "Hey, look. She's not completely useless after all. If they only shoot her once. Otherwise I guess I'm out of luck."

"They," Skip snaps. "And you're lucky they're willing to help you."

Leftie ignores us, and turns to Chatterbox. Her smile is sweet as poisoned honey. "This was not remotely my deal. I didn't ask to be jailbroken, didn't ask to be dragged to your tropical paradise, *definitely* didn't ask for this wide-eyed accidental shield to throw themself into danger for me."

Skip holds out a hand and pulls me to my feet. I'm flushed and shaky, my skin tingling. If only my powers extended to protect me from everyone's obvious assessment of me.

Leftie's sneering, that perfect bow of a mouth poised to shoot again.

"Some of us aren't in love with violence," I snap. "We're not all monsters eradicating everyone from their path like it's a video game."

Her eyes lock onto me, pupils swamping the icy ocean of her irises like oil slicks and then encroaching onto the whites. Soon they're glistening black orbs in her beautiful face. I could drown in them if I don't look away. Shadows ripple down her skin, like intricate tattoos that will dissolve her into the night. "You know *nothing* about what I've done, little mutant." Her teeth are stained a rusty red. "I'm a disease, engineered to destroy my enemies. I'm—"

"Oh my God." I'm channelling people I'd rather not remember, overwhelmed with a vicious, urgent need to puncture her sense of self-regard. "Will you get over yourself? You're a disease? Seriously? You're one more sword lesbian in a place half-full of them."

Skip's staring at me, like she's wondering what happened to the sweet, shiny Aidy she knows. I wish I could suck all those words back into my mouth, but in the face of this girl and her blank disregard I'm dragged back to previous iterations of myself, repeating words from old scripts.

A blade appears in the girl's left hand again, but Chatterbox interposes themself between us.

"Let's dial this down a bunch shall we?"

"Fuck them," Leftie snarls. "I like swords, and I'm a lesbian, but I'm not a fucking *sword lesbian*." She smirks briefly. "I'd prefer a twin daggers lesbian, or a giant fucking axe lesbian. But if this stuck-up bitch wants to try me, let's find out how fucking impervious she really is." All the jokes are gone, and right now I'm staring into the face of someone who would try and take me apart. I'm very, very grateful for my protective powers.

"I told you to dial it the fuck *down*." Chatterbox is right in her face.

"This is bullshit. I don't need a fucking bodyguard, you walking compost pile. Bring me anyone on this island and I'll take them apart with my bare hands."

Lines of thorns run along Chatterbox's jawline, long and curved. They slowly slide back into their skin until it's smooth and unmarked. "You want to spar then, Left Hand?"

"Like I said." Leftie's lip curls again. "I'll take anyone on this fucking island who can fight properly. Or I can keep stabbing away at your little shield kid until they start crying and crumple into a ball."

"I know why they call you a disease," I mutter. "It's because you make everyone sick."

Someone gives a yelp of laughter. Leftie lunges for me, but Chatterbox yanks her backwards.

"Feral?" There's a smile in Chatterbox's voice. "Let's give Leftie here a little lesson in humility."

5

LEFTIE

This fucking enby bitch is lucky they're not dead. Can you call someone who's nonbinary a bitch? Is bitch gender-neutral? It fucking should be, and they are one regardless. Them and their fucking impenetrable skin. Maybe if I stick my fist down their throat I'll be able to do some damage from the inside.

Now I'm supposed to fight this Feral. I didn't really pay attention to who's who, but they won't last a handful of seconds against me. I'll give these assholes a demonstration of who I am and what I can do.

"You sure, Dills?" There's an honestly stunning Latina woman leaning languidly against the wall. She's got a ruff of fur around her neck and what look like cat ears and a tail. They're seriously going to make me fight a fucking furry? I mean, she's gorgeous, but still. This is embarrassing.

It's only the way she moves that gives me pause. The cat vibe goes right down to the graceful way she prowls towards me. She smiles, exposing wickedly sharp canines. I bare my own sharpened teeth back at her.

"I wouldn't want to hurt her." Feral's voice has the faintest trace of a purr.

"You won't even touch me." Shadows drip down my arm and coalesce in my palm. I give Dylan a languid glance, almost flirtatious. "How do you want me to take your kitty-cat apart?"

"Will the two of you stop bantering and start actually fighting?" Moodring says with a faint smile, catching Chatterbox's eye. I can't read the vibe between all these people. I'm not meaning the kids, who are naive and painfully earnest, but the older ones. They're like soldiers who've been through some shit, except they're also weirdly soft around each other. When I first got back to the house where Chatterbox lives, some of them hugged it out for minutes on end. It's fucking weird and creepy and I left rather than looking at it. Who needs that shit?

"Ready, kid?" Feral winks at me. She has huge golden eyes like a cartoon lion. They're annoyingly arresting, so I let the shadows fill mine again. This way, I'll only see movement and motion. No other distractions.

"Sure." I coax a blade into my hand. I'll stick it in this cat woman's heart, or at least press it right up against her chest. If I actually kill her, I bet there will be hell to pay. I'm not ready to destroy this place yet.

Feral moves. For a moment I think my mind's playing tricks on me because godfuckingdamn, she is *fast*. Of course. She's a fucking mutant. I've been picking off weakling humans so I've gotten soft and lazy. She swats one claw at me, like a cat batting at a toy. I'm not that goddamn slow, so I duck easily out of her way and slash my blade up at her. Stick it through that little claw and she might think twice.

Her arm isn't there. It's not possible that her arm isn't there. I don't miss, not from this close. But my blade is cutting only air, and she's rotating like she has extra axes or joints, because of course she's a goddamn mutant *cat*. She cuffs me around the back of the neck hard enough to slap me to the ground.

I'm already seeking the shadows, dissolving into smoke and appearing again behind her. My blade traces a shallow cut down the back of her left arm, before her tail smacks me in the face. I taste blood. My lips mash in against my teeth. Swelling. It's been a long goddamn time since someone made me bleed. Fuck *that*. I unleash a flurry of blows, but they either miss or she blocks them with her fucking claws or fucking tail, because she's got five limbs and they've all got inbuilt knives. This fucking creature. The truth is already painful and apparent. I'm fast, she's faster.

I slip into shadow again, watching her for a few moments. She's breathing fast, so light on her goddamn feet. Perfectly balanced, tail twitching and ears flicking. She's listening. The fur around her neck bristles. Waiting for any displacement of air. Fuck, she's good. It's hot as hell, but I also hate this. It was supposed to be my time to shine, put that goddamn person in that ridiculous flowing shirt in their place.

I summon twin daggers and melt slowly back into reality, imprinting myself upon the air in the faintest way. At the last possible second, I strike. Feral brings both her forearms up, catching my daggers on her claws. She hisses, and her golden eyes widen. Then her foot catches me in the chest and knocks the breath out of me. I go skidding across the room. I'm startled enough that it takes a second or two to summon the shadows. She's already leaping towards me, a grin on her face.

I feel the edge of her claws catch me as I disappear.

Among the shadows, I drift around the room. This is fucking embarrassing. I remember those bratty alien kids on the boat talking about their deadly aunts. Should've paid more attention. What's with this goddamn family? When it comes time to kill them all and escape, it might be a problem.

I'm not out of tricks yet. This may not be as satisfying as beating this woman in hand to hand combat, but it's impressive in another way. I step out of the shadows at the far end of the room, bow in hand and arrow nocked. Before I'm fully present, an arrow already speeds towards Feral and I'm preparing the next one.

She's not even looking directly at me, bouncing on the balls of her feet and poised for a fresh attack. I don't think she's even noticed I'm here. Then her fucking tail snatches the arrow out of the air. She spins around to look at me, and bats the others from the air too.

What the fuck is she? I let the bow dissolve and draw my pistols from the dark. It took me many hours to craft these, building every piece of the mechanism from individual pieces of shadow. I'm not going to kill this Feral, but I'm going to kneecap her. Maybe she won't be so fucking fast in future.

I point and shoot, in sync with my breaths. I'm a perfect shot. I know exactly where each bullet will impact her. Except none do. She sidesteps them, as if I threw them clumsily underarm.

"Super speed." She grins. "It has advantages."

Fuck. This. Bitch. I sprint towards her, one pistol in hand, and an axe taking form in my right hand. She's done. I am not fucking around anymore.

She blurs through the air, dancing past the bullets even as I track her and adjust my aim. One finally hits the meat of her forearm. She hisses, but I'm on her, swinging the axe. She's forced to use both hands to block, and I let momentum carry me over so I can avoid those damn feet of hers. There's still the tail to worry about, but I've already switched my pistol for a short sword, and I hack down to sever the fucking thing at the root. The metal attachment on the end embeds itself into my shoulder, but I'll take the hit if it takes her tail out of commission. I hit the ground hard, but my knife catches her. She lets out a horrible yowling sound.

Fucking *finally*. Music to my fucking ears.

The tip of her tail rips out of my shoulder. I grit my teeth against the pain. More important things to do. I drop the knife and tumble away. My hands fumble for a throwing axe, ready to bury it in her back.

She's too fast again. It's impossible to witness, like some trick of CGI happening in real life. The cat woman spins and lunges on top of me, pinning me with her claws. I summon weapons into both hands, but I can't get leverage to stab her with them. She's got me pinned with her feet, and her tail is poised at my throat.

"Get the fuck off me," I snarl. "I'll cut your fucking throat."

"Chill, Leftie. Take a breath." Her eyes are wild and her breath is coming fast. "This got out of hand."

She springs up off me, retreating fast.

Yes, that's more like it. Fucking *run* from me.

I pull a sword from the shadows and stride towards her. I don't get more than three steps before something ensnares me, a network of vines wrapping around my legs, torso and arms. Goddamn these plant people and their creepy powers.

Chatterbox strides into view. There are no vines coming from them, so it must be the other one that's got me. Fucking Marvellous.

"Hey, Feral told you to chill." Chatterbox's eyes are intense, the hints of green swallowing them whole.

I thrash against the vines that hold me captive. "Let me the *fuck* out."

"It's called sparring, and it's over. You need to stop now."

"Let's say it was a draw." Feral rolls her shoulders, feeling the pain. "We both drew some blood. Took it a little far."

"Okay, Leftie. Can you accept a draw without flying off the fucking handle?" Chatterbox's eyes are a creepy lurid green, like the alien lurking in the centre of the planet is looking out at me too.

It goes against every instinct I have to call it a draw. I always fucking win. The problem is deep down I'm unsure if I can defeat this Feral, especially without killing her. And if we hadn't been sparring, I've got an uncomfortable and very unfamiliar feeling she would have ripped my throat out in seconds.

This is all useful information, if I can calm the heat in my blood down. If these mutants are an obstacle, I need to know everything about them. In case the time comes where I have to destroy or co-opt them. Bombs might work. I wonder if I can build one from shadow.

"It's a draw." I hate every single word.

Chatterbox rolls their eyes, presumably at the venom in my tone. "Fucking finally. Let her go, Dan."

The vines spin me around, so I'm face to face with the alien beauty of Marvellous. I clench my jaw tight. Her eyes have no green in them, only impossibly complex patterns of hazel.

"My love has a softer heart than me." Her voice has the same twangy accent as Chatterbox, but it's colder and more elegant. "They wanted to rescue you from your certain death, and so I indulge them. But if there is any significant danger to me, my family, or the ones I love… You will find I have very little mercy."

When I was a child, I knew fear. Of my parents, of the destiny I was promised. Of Uriel, the monster who ruled over the Children of the Broken World and had them dance to his bidding. The man who created me. Since I was changed, and became The Left Hand of Darkness, I have never been scared. When I look into the eyes of Danielle Kim, aka Marvellous, I feel an echo of fear stir deep inside me once again. This is a woman who'll do anything for those she loves. And that stirs more than fear, other more inchoate feelings that reverberate down the well of need at the heart of me. What could I have become in the arms of a parent like her?

"I won't do anything," I mutter, mostly to avoid the weight of that gaze.

"No," Marvellous says. "You won't."

The vines release me abruptly, and I stagger free. My shoulder aches, and I've got multiple serious cuts from that damn cat-bitch's claws.

"Someone get Doc," Chatterbox says from behind me, but I'm already walking for the door, trying not to disguise the seriousness of my limp. Humiliation and anger are fighting a war inside of me, and it's about as close as my fight with Feral. Call it another fucking draw.

The younger mutants are clustered in a little group off to the side, where they were watching this so-called demonstration. Where I was supposed to kick Feral's ass and instead they watched some furry beat me to a standstill. Me, the most deadly woman alive.

"Yeah, that's the thing." Cruise Ship Host isn't even looking at me, focused on their friends. "She's apparently this tough monster disease person, and yet?"

I wish I could attack them. Draw a blade across their neck and watch the blood spurt out over the surprised faces of their friends. Watch them place their pale fingertips to the gash and fail to form words. I wonder if I can do it stealthy enough to fool their fucking powers.

"And yet?" I pitch my voice as low as I can, only a handful of paces away.

They turn, eyes wide and startled. There's the beginnings of colour forming in their cheeks. I'm not sure if they knew I could hear, or if they did, they weren't expecting me to confront them like this. There's a delicious moment of confusion that crosses their face, like they're furiously calculating how to process their way out of it.

She chooses really fucking badly. "You got your ass kicked by Feral."

There's a short-circuit moment where the fuse of rage gets lit and explodes in the same second. It's not like I *decide* to do anything. My fist slams into their face of its own accord, more shadow than flesh right up until the last fraction of a second. The impact of their invulnerable skin hurts like hell, but I'll heal. If they're a bodyguard, they should be able to take it as part of the fucking job.

Someone screams. Probably the apparently invulnerable one, getting a fright. They really are useless.

I'm pretty sure I hear Chatterbox say "for fuck's sake."

But I'm out the door and running, despite my wounds.

6

AIDY

The shock hurts more than anything, thanks to my powers which turn my skin into something too impervious for Leftie to touch. But it comes with memory too. I've been punched in the face once before. It's not a memory I like to dwell on. That's all something buried deep in the dirt with my past selves. What's worse is how I acted—not Aidy-like at all. The bitterness, the rage. I let it spill out of me like the disdain from that girl was a blade that sliced open some horrible poison sac still nestled in near my heart.

Everyone's exchanging glances. I suppose this meeting between bodyguard and assassin went even worse than they were expecting.

"This is my fault." Feral's fidgety, still pumped up with adrenaline. "I took that goddamn fight too far, but fuck, it felt good. Nobody can really go one-on-one with me like that, even Adeline."

"This wasn't your fault." Marvellous's voice is sharp.

"You're blaming me then?" Chatterbox asks, with a laugh.

"No. Aidy's getting the consequences of their own actions." Marvellous is unimpressed. She's not wrong, that's the worst thing. I should have known better on so many levels. Especially since that's not the sort of thing Aidy is supposed to do.

"Aidy did nothing wrong," Skip says, which I appreciate, because friends are supposed to defend you even when you don't deserve it. At least that's what I've read in books and seen on TV.

"I said some really ill-advised things," I croak. "Especially when she's new on the island, and has been through a lot." Finally, I'm finding Aidy-ish words, the things I should have said. Even though I didn't feel it, I'm still shaky from the speed and power of the violence directed my way.

Mélodie's hands move quickly, signing a response I can't follow.

"Exactly," Marvellous says. "Some things are best left unsaid, especially when certain volatile people might be feeling humiliated or upset."

"Sorry." I wish I could unroll all my decisions back to arriving on the island, but I'm here in front of all these people and I don't know how to escape it.

"Saying dumb shit is hardly the worst mistake anyone ever made," Chatterbox sighs. "I do it every fucking day. Don't worry, I'll go deal with the impossible one."

They stalk out of the room, and I wish I could scurry away in their wake. Shame stains my cheeks like paint. "I'm sorry." I half-move into an awkward bow and then stop, because it's even more embarrassing. "I shouldn't have been so thoughtless."

"No need to apologise further." Marvellous looks almost entirely human, aside from the thin green threads streaking across her skin, and the petals dappling her throat. "If you insist, you should say it to Leftie, but it's probably better to leave well enough alone for now. I think the situation's dealt with."

It's so hard not to say anything. These smug people taking the side of that murderous wraith? I suppose it's to be expected, given what they are. When I was trying to decide whether to come here or not, I read articles from both sides. The negatives talk a lot about how Mutopia was born in blood, the actions of a few mutant radicals. These *are* those radicals, so I suppose it's to be expected they'd protect their own kind.

Even if Marvellous did threaten Leftie and stop her going further. And I also know firsthand the sorts of horrifying things mutants went through before this place existed. But none of this justifies bringing this Left Hand girl onto the island. She's a creature of pure rage. They should have left her to face the consequences of her own actions. I can't imagine a world in which the two of us can hang out in the same room, let alone us working together. I'm supposed to save her life, but I honestly think I'd be happy to let her die.

"Are we good?" Alyse watches me closely, like she can read far more than I'm showing her. Hopefully her eyes can only graze the surface.

"Yes." Words boil on my tongue, but I lower my eyes. Aidy's smart enough to be cowed and to let others win. The older group clearly wants to talk about the situation, so Alyse ushers the rest of us out of the room. She pauses in the doorway, her face more clouded than usual, as if her true expression isn't fully revealed.

"Are you okay?" At least her eyes are kind.

"I'm fine." Except for the fact I can't meet her gaze so it renders my words meaningless.

"That didn't go as badly as you think, Aidy. I know you've always been so sweet, sometimes it seems like you want to be entirely made of candyfloss. It's nice to see that's not all there is."

I want to snap at her about the foolishness of her decision to put me in the same room as that sneering monster, but Alyse is the only one remotely on my side, so I chew the words into pulp and swallow them down no matter how bitter they taste.

"Please say something," Skip whispers in my ear.

"Hopefully next time we can both be more polite." I find a smile from somewhere, the sort of expression Skip might summon effortlessly.

"You might have to lead the way, honestly." Alyse laughs. "We'll see if Dylan can talk sense into her. It would be an impressive feat, but they're good at those." She pats me on the shoulder and turns back into the main sparring room. It leaves me with a bunch of possible retorts lined up in the hollow chamber of my mouth—things about how Dylan Taylor shouldn't be responsible for anything, but I leave them unfired.

"Wow." Skip tugs on my arm. "Let's go debrief."

"Milk bar?" Mélodie signs, which is something I can recognise at least.

I nod and try to find another smile, but it's a misfire. Neither of them seem to mind, and link their arms through mine as they tow me through the streets. They spend the entire time recounting a play by play of Leftie's fight with Feral, which they're both dazzled by. I can agree that it was impressive, almost surreal in its speed and ferocity. Except it all unnerves me, watching reality *bend* like that. People shouldn't be able to do these things. My power feels different, a passive thing built to protect me. Something evolutionary, to enable me to survive a world that won't stop beating me down. There's no need for predators as dangerous as Feral and the Left Hand of Darkness to exist. It is evolution running amok, fang and claw sharpened until nothing can stand against them.

I stay silent all the way to the milk bar, right up until we're seated at one of the long bench seats. We're looking out through the open window and down the hill to the half-moon bay that cradles the ocean. I sip at my shake as my mind replays the moment when Leftie punched me. The anger rises up inside me again.

"I hate her." I stare fixedly out the window, because I don't want to see the reactions.

Skip giggles. "Aidy, I don't believe you, because you like *everyone*. I'm sure you'll eventually be explaining all her deep-down good points to us."

It strikes me again how Skip only knows the new version of me. Which is a good thing, because nobody ever liked who I was before. I was a mess, a coward, and an awkward, blabbering thing. I can't *blame* anyone for their feelings. I didn't even like myself. It's why I became someone different when I arrived here. Someone brave enough to finally say I was nonbinary again, after the previous disastrous attempts, and to hone myself into someone who people would be drawn to. My past was buried and this was a beautiful new place. It was a perfect opportunity to fix most of my problems in life. Except now people believe Aidy is real, and so they say things like Skip did, about my capacity for personal warmth. Except the truth is that I used to hate so many people. They're often cruel, selfish, and ignorant. Like stinging insects that lash out indiscriminately.

So I smile, and turn away from the window, and conjure reasons that Aidy might use to explain themself.

"But it's so dangerous." I widen my eyes. "I know we shouldn't believe most human propaganda, but the evidence is clear with Leftie, right?"

"She's a total badass," Mélodie signs, as Skip translates. "A defender of mutants."

"And I trust Chatterbox and Marvellous," Skip adds.

I have to bite my tongue really hard and count to ten. "It still seems risky. I know they're protecting mutants, but should they protect *all* mutants?"

"Everyone signs the charter," Skip says, which sounds like a fair point, but anyone can scrawl their name at the bottom of a document. It says you agree to lots of stuff, but if you decide to break the rules, someone still has to *enforce* it, and the leadership of Mutopia seems far too enamoured with Leftie to actually do anything about her.

Mélodie has her phone out on the counter, scrolling through news stories. "You know she was in a cult?"

"Yeah, yeah, something about it." I wave one hand dismissively. "The stories all mention it. I don't know the details, but, like—"

"She was like *the* figurehead in the cult. They were obsessed with her. She was like their prophesied figure or whatever. You know, right up until she..." She draws a finger across her throat.

"Yes." I try not to let my voice get too loud. "She killed them all! Her family, all these people she grew up with. Everyone over the age of sixteen, like she was a Biblical plague. She said that thing about being a disease, and she *believes* it. And—even worse—she actually *does* it. Like how many people were there?"

Mélodie's hands flash through the air. "Eighty-six. Led all the kids out like the Pied Piper, except she took the cult money with them and set them up with some trust. They all love her, and tried to argue that she shouldn't be on trial."

"She murdered eighty-six people." I'm aware I sound like a disapproving grandmother.

Skip is reading over Mélodie's shoulder, her body pressed up against the other girl's. "It was a pretty messed up cult, Aidy. They were trying to bring about the end of the world."

"You can't." I try to speak more clearly, because people aren't getting this. "Murder. Eighty-six. People. And don't say cult again like it's an excuse for it all, please. All sorts of people get mixed up with cults."

Other people in the milk bar are giving each other looks, and I'm blushing again and it's even more awkward.

My hands flail, like I'm trying to punctuate but have no idea how to do it. "All I mean is some people from Idaho or wherever end up in this cult thinking it's a way to restore Christian value. Except they're getting manipulated by a psychopath, which is only partially their fault, because they were taken advantage of. But then they end up murdered by a superpowered teenager." Nobody's agreeing with me. I'm talking too much. "All I mean is I don't think people should be allowed to go around murdering people because they feel like it."

"They brainwashed her and tortured her, Aidy," Skip says. "I don't think she did it because she *felt like it*."

I'm desperate to back out of this conversation, because they're looking at me like I'm the bully.

"I'm talking about indiscriminate murder," I half-whisper. "Did all of those cult members hurt her individually? Anyway, they weren't even the only people she killed, were they?"

Mélodie nods. "Yeah, after that she started defending mutants. This was right up when we hit the Dark Year though, so everything was chaos. Which she took advantage of. She killed a lot of bad dudes."

"I spent the Dark Year oblivious," Skip says. "I knew the city was changing, but my parents had good jobs and we were well in Michael territory. I had the app, and didn't think much of pressing it to my heart every morning. It was just what everyone *did*."

"The Dark Year didn't change much in Thailand," Mélodie signs. "Mutants had already been subject to discriminatory laws, and a lot of us were in hiding already." She's absent-mindedly scrolling through her phone still and her voice trails away as she reads. "Oh, wait. This looks really bad. There's a representative from a company that claims to represent the estates of the people who were in the cult. Saying they own some technology in Leftie's body and they're going to get it back no matter what."

"That won't work." Skip looks worried, despite her confident tone. "Any attack on Mutopia won't go well."

"Maybe they'll take Leftie back," I say casually.

"Oh my God, Aidy, don't sound so thrilled," Mélodie signs.

"If it's politically dangerous and risks all these mutant lives? That's all I'm saying. Why bring a bomb into our midst?"

Skip's usually bright expression is twisted into a frown, and I have regrets layered on top of regrets. Why can't I stop talking? I'm going to push everyone away all over again.

"Because this place is all about protecting mutant lives," Skip says. "Even ones that aren't easy to like."

I flush yet again, like I've been in my place. They're seeing too much of the ugliness inside me, but this Left Hand girl has unsettled me and my emotions are sloshing around inside me and spilling out unasked for. I need to shore myself up, to rebuild my glittering exterior.

"Sorry," I say. "I'm headachy and moody."

"Yeah, it's not like you," Skip says. "It was all very intense, and Leftie did punch you in the face, even if it didn't hurt. Maybe you should lie down and get some rest. You want me to come back to the apartment complex with you?"

There's that look of concern on her face, an expression that reads as *friendship*. It's a rare and precious gift, and reminds me that I can't let my hatred for this unhinged loose cannon they've dragged into Mutopia ruin things. The Left Hand of Darkness may be a nightmarish vanity project on the part of Chatterbox, but I'm not going to let her destroy the Aidy that I've built, or my new life I'm building.

It's the only thing I have that's worth anything at all, and I'll do whatever it takes to keep it.

7

LEFTIE

Chatterbox finds me stalking along the edge of the forest. Parts of my body are wreathed in shadow because I heal faster that way. Most of my wounds are superficial, but the one in my shoulder hurts like a motherfucker. Above me, the trees are gnarled and twisted, branches forming a barricade. If I cut my way in, I'd probably summon the guardian spirit of this creepy fucking island. She's probably tough to kill, although it might be a good workout.

"Proud of yourself?" Chatterbox looks unruffled, which annoys me.

"For fighting Little Miss Meow-Meow to a standstill?" I sneer.

"You know the truth of that fight."

I almost hit them, but I'll just get tangled up in vines. Besides, they're not exactly wrong. Galling as it is, Feral could have ended me a couple of times.

"Fine. Whatever. Your pet is deadly."

"Her name's Feral, or Marisol, and she's a sister to me. Plus, she's not even the most dangerous mutant here, so add that to your calculations."

There are a couple of dangerous heartbeats where I almost attack them and flee, but I consciously tether myself to the current moment and wait for it to pass. "Calculations?"

"I'm smarter than I look." There's a flicker of a smile, and they're actually cute. "Just barely, but I am. Doesn't take a supergenius to figure you're making escape plans."

"Why would I escape?" I keep my voice flat.

"Spare me. This cult business isn't a joke."

"I destroyed the Children of the Broken World," I sneer. "They're scattered rats without their leader."

"Well some corporation with deep pockets wants whatever they did to you. They'll cheerfully kill you to get it. But for some bizarre fucking reason, I want you safe. I also want to stop anyone getting their hands on whatever creepy shit you've got going on. So if you do run, I don't want any collateral damage. And believe it or not, I don't even want *you* getting hurt."

"You really think I'm the one you need to worry about?" I scoff.

"Dani warned you before. That's not a joke. She will take you the fuck down. If by some miracle you get past her, there's Penance. And if you ever lay a finger on either of them, you'll meet the other version of me." This time when they smile, there's nothing cute about it at all.

I don't know what to do. A large part of me wants to storm off, to find the shadows and flee this place but once again they are not fucking wrong, and I fucking *hate* it. I've got a hit list, starting with the people who locked me up, and moving onto these assholes that want me dead. I've got no quarrel with mutants, aside from them standing in my way.

All I have to do is wait for my moment.

"Fine." I stay stoic.

"And please, try not to punch anyone else in the face. Surely you've got a fucking modicum of self-control. Aidy was only trying to help."

"I don't need help." It's so easy to sneer. "You've seen what I've done. Doesn't my reputation precede me?"

Chatterbox shrugs. "You've killed a lot of soft targets, sure. Doesn't mean you wouldn't be better off with a team."

"Team is me and a bunch of dead weight."

"Oh, kid. You've got a lot to learn."

I near as nothing stab them for being so fucking condescending. "You're not my parent, Chatterbox."

"No. Otherwise I'd be dead." Their eyes flutter closed. "Shit, I'm sorry. That was uncalled for. I've got my own baggage in that regard."

I shake my head. "First time I've respected you all day. Saying what you actually think."

"What I think is that I'm right. You're a scary mutant, but I know a lot of those. Every single one of us is better as part of a team."

God, this smug *asshole*. I was raised to be Worldbreaker, given the blood of the Goddess, and transformed into The Left Hand of Darkness. I will have my reckoning on those who've hurt me and who continue to hurt others, and I need nobody at my side to accomplish it.

Chatterbox, for all they've done, is still nothing compared to me. They laid the path, but I'm the only one strong enough to make the world safe for mutants. All I need to do is bide my time, and take advantage of the opportunities they've given me.

"Sure, whatever. Are you done lecturing me?"

"Seems like you're done listening, so I may as well be." They shrug, and stick their hands in their hoodie pockets, and they're back to being the cool, shaggy aunt.

"Thanks for stopping by and sharing all your wonderful opinions." I give them a big cheesy smile, like I'm one of their precious little wannabe superheroes.

They shake their head and clench their jaw. When they turn abruptly away, the tree branches part and usher them into the cool green darkness. I'm curious to see what's in there, but the branches slam shut in front of me.

Rather than start yet another fight, I head back towards the little house they've grown for me. It's barely ten feet away from Chatterbox's, like I'm a bratty teenager who's not allowed too far away from the parents. It doesn't have much more than a bed and a bathroom, so I slam into the main house because now that the fight is over and the adrenaline has ebbed, I'm fucking *starving*.

"Leftie." The fragile figure of Penance is curled up in an armchair with a paperback. I put a lot of effort into looking menacing, and it's annoying she's apparently this wicked mutant badass when she's barely over five feet tall and is mostly curls.

"What?" I glare at her.

"How was your first day?." She smiles sweetly, and puts a bookmark inside the book carefully.

"I fought your sister with the claws."

"Marisol?" She covers her smile with one hand. "I'd love to have seen that. I'm assuming from the scowl that she won."

"It was a draw." There's a knife in my hand again.

"Yes, our Feral can be very sweet. I've been very interested to meet you, Leftie. Your powers are remarkably similar to mine." Penance extends one hand, turning it into a series of five blades. "I talked to Cybele about it. She thinks you're the real deal and I'm the accidental knock-off Spark made." She folds the blades away, back into a small white hand. "You're from the second Emma line, the OG transfusion crew with Katie and company. Everyone's very fascinated."

"That means *nothing* to me." This is a lie, but only a small one. "Blood of a Goddess, death to the Goddess. That's what they told me when I was changed."

"Word of warning." There's a tough-looking woman in the doorway with two intricate sleeves of flames tattooed up her arms. "Don't use that name around me. Not like that. *Especially* don't say that shit around Dilly and Dan. And extra-fucking-special don't even fucking think it around Lys."

"New girl fought Mari at training," Penance says. "Apparently it was a draw."

"Holy shit." Fire Tats grins at me. "Bet that was a sight. I'm Dragon, anyway. One of the other gang."

"You." I smirk. I saw you sitting on the White House. That shit I liked."

"Alas, these days I don't get wings. How you getting on with the big boss?"

"Chatterbox?" I shake my head scornfully. "They're mostly giving me lectures. Pretty sure they hate me right now. I punched one of their trainees in the face for being an asshole."

"First time I met Dylan, I nearly roasted their Pear." Dragon laughs. "Like literally, I breathed fire at them for no reason at all. What a fucking asshole I was. All pissed off, wanting to kill everyone. Guess nobody here can imagine what that's like."

"Subtle, Draggy." Penance picks up her book again and starts reading.

"I'm just fucking *saying*. You'll be fine, Leftie. As long as you're not trying to exterminate mutantkind, Chats is a great big softie." Dragon raises her eyebrows and disappears back into the room she came from.

Feeling dismissed, I head into the kitchen and find something to eat. There's not much on offer, because apparently Cybele just grows a bunch of fruit and vegetables. I don't know how to talk to the energy alien and ask for a cheeseburger, but I manage to find bagels instead. I'm slathering them in cream cheese when I hear multiple voices, and poke my head out of the kitchen.

"Oh, you are here." Feral seems unruffled and uninjured, as if our fight hadn't even taken place. "We were taking bets on if you'd stormed off."

"Apparently I'm in terrible danger so I need to curl up in the arms of my wonderful mutant shields." I bat my eyelashes.

Chatterbox appears in the doorway. They're arm in arm with Marvellous, with the alien children perched on their shoulders. "Guess we don't have to send out that search party." They smile at me, as if that argument back at the edge of the forest was nothing.

"Still worth seeing the news." Marvellous flicks on the TV at one end of the room. "See what the latest chatter is about our controversy."

I'm left standing in the doorway to the kitchen, rendered awkward by the unfamiliarity of this scene. This is not a place I'm built for—a group of people, all comfortable with each other, inhabiting each other's space as if it's a simple thing to do.

"—Left Hand of Darkness," a voice on the screen says, and I immediately look up. A man sits at a circular desk, framed by another two more people in suits. The chyron says he's Dr Chad Decker, Mutant Professor of Mutant Studies, Harvard University. His head is abnormally large, with a huge brain cavity.

"It's a bold move," he says, in his deep voice. "We know Chatterbox is fond of such statements, but it's hard to imagine what's going through their head with this one. Abducting a prisoner in plain sight? It makes me wonder whether this is only one step in a bigger, more dangerous plan."

Chatterbox rolls their eyes. "Fuck this big-brain motherfucker. He doesn't know shit."

I glare at the screen. "Why don't I go smash his head open and see if it's really full of brains or only bullshit?"

Feral gives a yelp of laughter. "I think someone's coming for my codename."

"Hush," Marvellous says. "Can we keep the banter to a minimum? We need to hear this."

Decker's not close to the end of his pontificating. "The powers on Mutopia have walked a very careful line thus far. Careful not to push against the bounds of the treaties they've established. This seems like they're trying to provoke a response, or discover how far they can step out of line before retaliation."

Chatterbox gnaws on the end of their thumb. "Leftie's right. I'm tempted to fucking smack this guy."

"Dills." Marvellous frowns and there's a weird mirroring between their expressions, as if they're sharing their thoughts between them.

"I know," they sigh. "But he's *asking* for it. The Leftie thing isn't a goddamn plan. We're saving a mutant life. It's what we *do*. It's the entire fucking point of this place. Which he would know, if he was a real mutant, and not a fucking turncoat traitor selling us out on—"

"Watch out!" Marvellous screams. Vines spill out from her body like a sickly green tide. I'm thrown backwards, an invisible hand shoving violently against my chest. The chair I'm in tips backwards. I reach for shadows, but my gaze snags on a small silver shape spinning in the air above me.

"The hell is that?" I ask.

Everyone is up and out of their seats. They're clustered around me, peering at the shape in the air.

"Give me a second," Marvellous says, in strained tones. "I think I can take it apart."

The silver device splits open and disassembles into its component parts, like I'm watching a schematic diagram unfold.

"Power negater," Chatterbox says. "Wired into a regular old fashioned bullet. Straight for the brainstem. Nuke your abilities and take you out at the same time. Instant kill."

"For me?" I'm still on the floor, looking up at all the little pieces floating where my head would have been.

"Dumbfuck move either way." Chatterbox reaches out and pokes at the outer shell. "But it means someone's coming to play. Vi, go investigate. We need to get Leftie to Alyse and Aidy."

Penance flickers and disappears, folding herself away like an origami girl.

Chatterbox and Marvellous flank me, two huge figures made of heavy wood and thorns. This is far from the first time someone's tried to kill me, but I've got to give Marvellous credit for saving my ass on this occasion. Up until now, I've kept ahead of my enemies by staying hidden. Even in the Dark Year, I hunkered down and only came out like a blade in the night. It was only post-reconstruction, as the world heaved itself back into its mutant-hating orbit that I slipped up, frustration and boredom leading me to strike at every target I saw. Now I've attracted people who've got their hands on some very fancy technology, potentially capable of killing me. It doesn't matter. Whoever they are, they'll soon learn they're fucking with the wrong person.

I reach for the shadows, but they slip through my hands like frigid water. This has never happened before. My head pounding, I try to wreathe myself in darkness, but it only eddies around my feet in sluggish pools.

"I can't teleport," I gasp.

"They're coming for you, bad girl." Feral takes my hand. "Let's get you to safety."

8

AIDY

Alyse intercepts us on the way back to our dorm. She's tall and chrome, a fearsome gleaming sentinel who looks more like a bodyguard than I could ever be. It makes me feel incompetent all over again. "There's been an incident. Someone tried to shoot Leftie. The island is under attack."

It doesn't surprise me at all that someone tried to kill the Left Hand of Darkness. Anyone who spends more than a few minutes with her probably feels the urge. But attacking Mutopia is a big deal. There are plenty of people that don't think mutants should be allowed to live, but most of them don't get far enough to raise any alarm. I feel unsteady, like our island has become little more than a sandcastle. It's too soon for this.

"Will you be coming with me?" I ask.

"There's a lot going on right now, Aidy. I'm needed elsewhere, so you're going to be Leftie's bodyguard like we discussed. It's vitally important that these people don't get their hands on her. Do you understand?" There's definitely a different edge to her voice now, an echo of command.

"Yes." My voice comes out firmer than I expect. "Where do you need me?"

"Head for the school outbuilding where we keep the gardening supplies. There's a bunker underneath it. Feral will be waiting there to hand off Leftie. I believe in you, Aidy. You can do this."

I actually salute, which I've never done before. The situation calls for it, and as annoying as Leftie is, I need to remember why I'm here. This is an opportunity to prove that I'm worthy of this life on Mutopia. A chance to reinvent Aidy even more. A valued part of the team.

Skip and Mélodie head back to the dorm reluctantly. They're both way too excited about intruders being on the island. This is a moment to panic, not be thrilled that you're living through your own Cute Mutants experience. Nobody else is out on the streets. Everyone has received the signal that the island is under attack, and have headed to safe places to be protected.

Except me. I'm heading directly for one of the most dangerous locations on the island. And *I'm* supposed to be the person doing the protecting. Me, who's spent my whole life hiding and running. Even my powers are a defensive reflex. Something to soak up the inevitable damage.

I'm breathing fast, almost light-headed when I arrive. I'm relieved to see the tall figure of Feral step out of the shadows, Leftie slinking sullenly at her heels.

"Finally." Feral lifts her head and scents the air. "I've got people to kill, so get your asses downstairs." She pulls open the door to the supply shed, and punches in a long combination on a keypad. A section of the back wall slides open with a heavy metallic sound, revealing a set of narrow stone steps leading down.

"This is bullshit," Leftie snarls, like she's in the middle of an argument.

"You're the target." Feral pokes her in the chest with the tip of one claw. "And you're damn close to helpless right now, so get inside. And don't come out until I show up."

"I'm never helpless," Leftie hisses.

"And I'll fucking throw you down those stairs if you won't go down yourself." The fur around Feral's neck fluffs out enormously. "You know I will."

Leftie says nothing further, but stalks down the stairs as if she'd been intending to do that all along.

"Take care of her." Feral pats me on the shoulder and bounds off into the night.

I can't think of many worse scenarios than being trapped in a bunker with this horrible girl—but Alyse Sefo asked me to, so here I am. The door slides shut behind me as I descend. There's warm light at the bottom, and when I reach it, I find a small wood-panelled room, about twenty feet by ten feet. A series of three hanging lights dangle from the ceiling. There are large, comfortable couches along each side, piled high with cushions. At the far end is a refrigerator and a set of cabinets.

Leftie, of course, is interested in none of this. She punches the wall hard enough to splinter it. "They should let me fight."

I roll my eyes. "They know what they're doing. This isn't the first time the island has been invaded."

"And they beat Michael." Leftie's voice turns mocking and high-pitched. "And Quietus too. They're the biggest, baddest mutants in all the world." Then her voice switches back to its deep tones again. "Except for me. They've got no idea what I can do."

My next words are not my smartest. "You got caught. If Chatterbox didn't show up, they were going to kill you and stream it live around the world."

"They got lucky." She bares her teeth at me, brilliant white and sharpened into fangs that could tear my throat out. It's a good thing I have my powers.

"Looks like their luck isn't running out." I wave my hand at her. "Where are your shadowy powers? Why don't you dance on out of here and slice everyone's throats like you're oh-so-good at?"

Her fingers twitch, like she's trying to summon one of her weapons from the air. There's a flicker of darkness and then it's gone. "How lucky am I? To get a bodyguard and a stuck-up twat all in one like a combo deal?" She steps in close, right up in my face, then slams her fist into my chest.

My skin turns instantly impervious. I hear the bones in her hand crack, see a flash of white as the flesh splits over the knuckle. She doesn't even react, not even a flinch. Instead she hits me again, even harder this time.

"What are you doing?" My voice is high and panicky. "Stop it. You're hurting yourself."

Her teeth are gritted, cheeks pale as she pummels blows into me over and over. "Pain means nothing. Life is pain. Death is the absence of pain. I do not fear death, because I am death. I do not feel pain, because I am anathema to life. My birth was the promise of a broken world, but I have killed god. Now I am nothing but the echo of that death, ringing over and over again in the ears of humanity."

I stumble backwards until I hit the couch and collapse into it. I'm staring up at her, looming over me with her hand dripping red, blood oozing between her fingers and dripping from the tips. "Please, Leftie. Stop it. You're scaring me and this isn't helpful."

"Fucking hopeless." Leftie turns away in disgust, right as a man appears from thin air.

I'm frozen because this shouldn't be happening. Someone teleported into Mutopia. This is supposed to be safe. We're in a secure location. But I'm staring at a tall woman dressed all in black, red hair tied back. There's a long weapon in her hands that looks like a cattle prod. An intruder. Here to attack.

I should lunge up from the couch where I'm sitting. My job is to spring into action, put my body in between this woman and the person I'm supposed to protect. Let my powers do their job. But I'm sitting here, frozen in indecision, watching like a spectator as a bolt of electricity leaps from the prongs on the end of the weapon. It burns a hole right through Leftie's jacket and the sheer black top she wears underneath. I can smell burning flesh from my prone position among the pile of comfortable cushions.

The impact sends Leftie flying backwards. She ricochets off the wall and sprawls on the ground. The intruder spins the weapon in her hands, steps forward with it raised to fire again. Except Leftie's already moving, even with her shoulder smouldering. She springs up from the ground, so fast it's hard to make out the individual movements. It seems less than a breath, but the sharp, shocking sound of the woman's arm snapping makes me yelp. The weapon hangs uselessly at her side, but Leftie bends the arm even further, wrenching the shoulder joint until the woman screams. There's another visceral tearing sound as something internal gives way.

Leftie smiles wide. She's enjoying this. "You've got to be way better than that to come for me."

The woman's breath is high and whiny. Spit bubbles on her lips.

I'm helpless, still watching as Leftie wrenches the woman's head back, sharp teeth bared. "Who fucking sent you? Tell me which asshole is playing these games. I killed them all, so who the *fuck* is trying to dig up Uriel's grave?"

"Filthy apostate killer," the woman chokes out. "You'll get nothing from me."

"Let's see about that." Leftie yanks on the woman's shoulder. The answering scream is horrifying, a wounded animal stuck in a trap. It escalates until it doesn't even sound human, a voice remixed into a chorus of agony. When Leftie releases her grip, the woman is pale and sweaty, broken whimpers flitting out of her mouth. She's bitten her tongue and blood drips down her chin.

"Here's a message for all your bosses," Leftie says. "They can poke around in Uriel's tomb all they fucking want for whatever shitty trinkets he left behind. But I'm my own creation. They can come for me all they want, and it's going to end in blood like this. Every. Single. Time."

The woman coughs and splutters but can't find a single coherent word.

"Listen, asshole. This is the part where you start talking. Tell me where your money is coming from. Who's giving you all that fancy tech that fucks with my shadows? This shit that lets you pop into Mutopia unannounced."

"I will never give you what you want," the woman spits.

"So tedious." Leftie lifts the woman's other hand up to her mouth in one smooth movement. For a moment, I think she'll kiss the back of it, elegant as a romantic hero. The tip of the finger brushes along Leftie's lips, an almost intimate movement. But then her sharp teeth snap down like the blade of a guillotine, severing the little finger just below the second knuckle. The woman screams, trying to pull her hand back, but Leftie has it held fast. Blood sprays fine across Leftie's pale cheek, a delicate constellation.

The woman sobs and gasps.

Leftie rolls her eyes, and turns her head in my direction. Her lips are an even darker red than the blood that spatters her skin. The finger's still held between her teeth and she casually spits it towards me. I've got my hands clamped to the sides of my head to drown out the screams, and now I can't look away from the small chunk of flesh lying at my feet.

My gorge clenches, and my throat feels like I've been gargling acid. Saliva floods my mouth.

"Talk," Leftie growls. "Or I keep going."

The woman's frantic sounds turn to choked whimpers, and more saliva bubbles from her mouth. Her whole body jerks, face suffusing a deep shade of purple.

Leftie leans in and sniffs at her mouth.

"Shit." She lets the body drop to the floor. "Mindless asshole cult fucks taking fucking poison." Her boot comes down hard on the woman's head. There's another horrible crack and this time I do throw up in my mouth. Leftie slams her foot down over and over again until the skull shatters like it's nothing more than eggshell, spilling blood and worse over the soft grey carpet of the room.

I lean forward and spit vomit all over myself. Leftie wipes her feet in the gore, which only smears it worse, and then stalks over to the opposite couch. She collapses into it and throws her legs up on the arm of it. I'm looking at the soles of her boots, smeared in what has to be brains, and I throw up all over again.

"Tremendously fucking helpful." Leftie rolls her eyes, prodding at the meat of her shoulder where the weapon hit her. "I'm so glad my official Mutopian babysitter was here to save my ass."

It's not like I haven't seen brutality or death in my life before this. Some of that inevitably follows you when you're a mutant. But this is up close and personal, crashing into the bucolic idyll of my new life. It leaves me dizzy and shivering. I try to tell myself this isn't the shadow of the past reaching out. This isn't what I deserve. At the same time, I can't be shocked at the actions of the Left Hand of Darkness. I've been telling everyone this is who she is.

But I still volunteered for this job. I promised Alyse I could protect her, and all I've done is throw up over myself. Whatever low opinion Leftie had of me, I've thoroughly reinforced it. I'm scrambling for excuses, but I feel like shit because I am shit. The truth is I failed miserably and it was right in front of *her*.

My hands twitch in my lap. "This is my first combat situation! We were supposed to have training before anything like this, but you've got so many enemies they apparently can't wait to come and kill you."

"They fear me for a reason," Leftie drawls.

"You bit her finger off." I close my eyes but that doesn't stop me from seeing the replay in gruesome detail.

She laughs and lays her head back on the cushions, eyes closed. "Had to make her talk somehow. It's honestly not that gross. You'll have to get way cooler about a lot more shit if you're going to stomach this job."

I shift in my seat uncomfortably, wracked with a blend of indigestion and anxiety. My body can't decide whether to run or hide, and it's settled for making me feel thoroughly shitty instead, like my self-loathing has stamped on me repeatedly until I've leaked all my gross feeling like brains across a carpet.

Then another person appears in the room. A man this time, wielding the same type of weapon. His eyes are wild and he swings around to point it right at Leftie.

I lunge up out of my seat.

Maybe this time.

9

LEFTIE

Even with my eyes closed, I feel the air displacement of someone else appearing in the room. Maybe their fancy tech has cut me off from the shadows, but I'm not completely useless.

Unlike Cruise Ship Baby, who let me get shot in the fucking shoulder and then threw up all over their tacky red shoes. They're not even good company.

My eyes snap open, identifying the threat immediately. Some tall and bulky asshole, wielding one of those fire stick things the first bitch hit me with. Strange weapons I'm not familiar with, possibly engineered to avoid Mutopian sensors. Need to stop this guy from taking his poison pill, and find out what the fuck is going on.

I killed Uriel, all his servants, and anyone else involved in the Children of the Broken World. That means we're talking about bankrollers and backers, or else one of the kids that I saved from that mess. The latter which fucking galls me to think about, especially since—

These thoughts tumble through my mind as I throw myself off the couch. I'll make him chase me around the room, then take him unawares and rip out all his teeth until I find the cyanide one. Except there's a fucking miracle happening, because Aidy the useless sack of shit is staggering to their feet. In a wild swing at competence, Cruise Ship Baby throws themself in front of me, waving their arms. The man shoots anyway, figuring he can blow away this uncoordinated person who's squeaking like a dog's chew toy.

The blast shreds their ugly shirt to rags, setting the threads smouldering, but dissipates against the shield wall of their skin. It's a hell of a nice trick, this impervious skin thing. Shame it's completely wasted on them. Maybe I'll ask that damn Cybele to take it away from Aidy and give it to me.

He's not smart enough to do anything sensible with his failure, like focus on me. Instead, he lets out a shout and stabs the weapon right into Aidy's skin. It shatters into fragments, and he stumbles forward with momentum.

By that time, I'm behind him. One arm is wrapped around his neck and my other hand pries open his lips. He bites down hard so I sink my teeth into the meat on one side of his neck. When he shrieks, I shove my hands inside his mouth, fumbling slick over the enamel of his teeth. I'm too late. My skin blisters on contact from whatever shit he's sucking down. I'm so fucking angry I snap his neck in frustration.

Who the fuck is sending these people, so dedicated to the cause that they'll die for it? I've known too many cultish assholes in my life, and they only ever have such fanatical devotion to a leader. Which means someone's popped up in Uriel's place to take over the cult and remake it. I really hope it's not one of the children. Much rather it was some rich prick with a hardon for tech. I need to get off this island and figure shit out. As soon as I get my powers back.

Aidy's standing there, poking at their ruined shirt. The skin above their binder is very pale, completely unmarked. Their shoulders are trembling slightly. It's very irritating—if you're invulnerable, how can you be so anxious?

I roll my eyes at them. "Congratulations. You weren't totally useless that time."

"Why can't you say thank you?" There's colour in their cheeks, so they're not about to faint. "I took that shot for you, but you sneer at me like I'm nothing."

"Fuck me. This is what I get for trying to be nice. You're obviously their charity case who they're trying to help with building, like, self-esteem and shit. In this whole situation, you were genuinely hopeless. The first time you let me get shot and the second time, you did nothing to fight back. You're fucking impervious to harm. Fucking *use* it."

All they do is blink tearily at me, like my words are weapons slicing them deeper than any real blade could. I cannot figure out how this person has survived this long. Even for regular people, the world's got claws and fangs. Someone who curls up into a ball at the first sign of danger isn't evolved to deal with shit.

"Okay, whatever." I drop back onto the couch. "Wake me when the next prick comes. See if you can throw a punch."

But the next arrival is Feral, prowling down the stairs looking sleek and deadly. As soon as she sees the pair of corpses on the floor, her demeanour changes instantly. The claws come out and she scents the air again. "How did these two get in?"

"Poof." I splay my hands. "Like magic."

Dylan clattering down the stairs after Feral, all shaggy with leaves. There's a ragged cut along the top of their chest that's oozing a sticky amber substance. "Yeah, these fucks have found some teleportation ability. So that's another thing on the todo list."

The room is well-lit, but there are still pools of shadow in the corner. This time when I reach for them, they curl around my shoulders like welcoming arms.

"None of that." Dylan reaches out and grabs my arm before I'm fully discorporeal. "You're staying here."

"No fucking way. They came for me. I'm not standing by and—"

"They can cut off your powers whenever they want." Their voice cuts across mine, and I back down like a puppy with their nose smacked. "And yes, you're fucking tough, but they've armed themselves for a Leftie hunt and they're well prepared. Let us handle them instead."

"I'm not weak," I growl.

"Nobody said you were. But this is about being smart. And if that's not your strong suit and you insist on running anyway, then off you fuck. Except I'll send Penance after you and she'll drag you home."

"Your other little girlfriend?" I sneer. "She told me herself she's an inferior knockoff of me."

"Not entirely my words." Penance unfolds herself from the air, blade by blade. A woman made entirely of edges, with mouthparts that snicker-snack when she speaks. "I'm something darker and stranger, but you and I both walk in the shadows. Wherever you run, I'll find you."

"Bitch," I mutter, and throw myself into the darkness.

I've got no idea how Violet Parker's powers work, but I've got to seize my chance to get off the island and find out what the hell is going on. Those alien twins might be able to see me in the shadows, but I doubt that this woman with her eminently kissable mouth can lay a finger on me. Even if she can turn herself into a kitchen drawer full of knives.

The stairwell is full of shadows, and when I reach the top I find the entire island slumbering in darkness. It is everywhere, a glorious unfurling of night only punctuated with tiny pools of light. I dance my way along the path towards the clifftop. There's less gravity in darkness, so every step propels me headlong. There is nobody giving chase. I knew it was all talk.

I reach the top of the cliff at the island's edge, where the ocean spills before me like ink, only faintly dappled with the silver brush of the moon. A whole world of shadow for me to flee through. I'm horribly short of information, so I'll find a nearby city and do some research before planning my next step. At least I won't have anyone breathing down my neck or trying to make me integrate into their society.

"Hello, Leftie." Penance gleams in the shadows beside me, a blade descending in the dark.

I meet her with a blade of my own. "Forget this shit, *Violet*. You can't stop me."

"I've followed you every step of the way." She holds out one blade-fingered hand and unclasps it to reveal the bulbous shape of the power negater the humans used on it. "I hope this isn't the only thing that'll stop you from running."

The taste of iron fills my mouth, my teeth mashing my bottom lip. "You'd chain me to your island."

"Dylan likes to think that you'll choose to stay."

"Why the fuck do they care?" I strike out at her with a pair of beautifully-wrought daggers, but she blocks me effortlessly.

"My theory?" Penance smiles, mostly folded back into something that looks human. "They see something of themself in you."

"Fuck that. I'm nothing like them."

"Then maybe I'm wrong." She raises one shoulder. "Either way, we've all taken a big risk bringing you to Mutopia and protecting you, especially given the attention you're getting. And we did that because we genuinely believe in protecting mutants. But also because we don't want anyone getting their hands on what's inside you."

"They want the apocalypse seed."

"It's likely, yes. You were supposed to kill Emma, right? Murder Goddess and then destroy the world as we know it, ushering in an age in which the righteous would thrive. Meaning all Uriel's chosen."

"Something like that." I clench my teeth to stop them chattering. I'm not afraid of my past. I burned it to the ground and there's nothing left of it. Except what they left inside me. I don't want anyone taking that from me either.

Penance looks past me, out at the rippling dark of the ocean. "If they got hold of you, what could they do? What's this seed inside you for?"

"I don't know," I admit. "They only talked about it in metaphors. The onrushing dark, the plague on all sinners, God's blade to drain the blood from those who turned away from righteousness. A bunch of Bible shit too, the cleansing fire, the angel taking the firstborn children. I never really thought of it as a *real thing*. I thought it was an idea. And then when I became a mutant, became death to the humans, I figured maybe it was real, waking up inside me. Honing me into the most deadly weapon to ever live. Present company excluded perhaps."

"A nanomachine maybe," Penance muses. "A virus. A parasite bonded with your DNA. Either way, whoever is coming for you thinks it's something they can take. 'Excavate it from your corpse' is the wording they used in one of their internal documents."

"You've seen their internal documents?" I look sidelong at her.

She shrugs. "We have our spies. Although they've been unable to locate where this newest iteration of the cult is hiding. Which is worrying enough on its own, hence us trying to keep you close."

I choke down my anger, because it's not really at this woman in the shadows. I can see her point, if I calm down enough to take a breath. She's trying to protect her little island, this haven for mutants. After I carved my way out of the prison the cult had held me in, I dedicated my life to being the dark protector that mutantkind needed. Even Chatterbox bows their leafy head to society's rules in the end. That's why they need somebody like me in the shadows, doing what they can't or won't. So maybe Penance and I are on the same side, and my hands are tied. Until I figure out what the fuck is going on, and can clean up this goddamn mess.

Penance takes my silence for something else. "You hate everyone and everything, fine. But you chose not to destroy the world once before. Can you make that same decision again?"

God, she's so fucking dramatic. Although if the humans did neuter me, and carve the darkness out from my core? It might be as dark a future as pretty Penance fears. For now, my task of defending mutants might take the form of sitting on an island and staying quiet. Which I fucking despise with every tiny part of me, but it's the right move.

"Fine." I hold out my wrists to her, like I'm waiting for her to wrap them in chains. "I'll stay on your island. For now."

"Oh good." She beams at me, and there's no sign of anything deadly about her at all, a stunning brunette in a cuddly blue sweater. Someone I'd try to pick up at a bar on one of my few interactions with humanity. "No need for deadly knife battles on the edge of the world."

I arch one eyebrow. "But that might be a lot of fun, Violet." I drag out her name, let my voice go the faintest bit husky. "I'm ready to play if you are."

"Not quite my type." She winks at me. "I mostly prefer my dates on the butch side, like Dylan. Although there is Dani, but she's undeniable."

"Wait." I frown. "You and Chatterbox and Marvellous are, like...?"

"A polycule? I hate that word. But yes, the three of us are a *thing*. Romantic. In love." She links her arm through mine and we start down from the cliffside without the shadows around us. Two people walking through the night. I should pull away, but I don't. I'll stay in the sway of this island for a breath or two, give them a chance to solve my problem. It's not capitulation. It's not giving in to them. It's being smart, using their resources, allowing them to take the risk. Once the situation is resolved, I'll hunt again. And Chatterbox and their friends won't be able to stop me.

10

AIDY

n the aftermath of the fight, I'm sick and shaky and miserable. As soon as I get the chance, I stumble up the steps and out of the claustrophobic bunker with the bodies lying ruined on the floor. Two people dead, both gruesomely attacked by the Left Hand of Darkness. Who finds this entirely unremarkable, and leaves their remains behind like misplaced punctuation marks to emphasise my own failure.

Alyse finds me outside, my arms wrapped around myself as I stare into the dark. "Are you okay? You look like you need a hug."

I fall into her arms gratefully. She's transformed into a bigger, stronger version of herself, something to wall out the night and the horror. The events of tonight have unmoored me, taken this careful new Aidy that I've built and rendered them as a fragile figure, little more than a child's drawing on a scrap of paper and now fed to the flames.

"It will get easier," Alyse murmurs. "You should have seen our first mission."

I shake my head against her shoulder. "This isn't what I'm good for. You picked the wrong person."

She gives a soft chuckle in the back of her throat. "Perhaps. I'm sometimes wrong, after all. And you don't have to do this, Aidy. I'll be happy to work with you in the classroom for as long as you want. But this is Mutopia. What we do here is important, and I hope you can see that. You've been blessed with a power that can help us, and while not even Cybele herself can convince you to use that, we'd definitely love it if you did." She releases me from the hug and steps backwards. "Now go and get some sleep. I know it's been very dramatic, so perhaps debrief with those friends of yours. And if you're still having trouble sleeping, talk to Beesting at the dorms. She'll find someone whose powers will help you drift into dreamland. Do you need someone to walk you home?"

I shake my head. "It's close, and the island is safe."

"Aidy? Please ask for help if you need it."

I widen my eyes and nod my head, and walk briskly down the path away from the school. It's all very sweet of Alyse, and I think she's genuinely lovely even with the *do this for your species* speech, but I need to clear my head. Ever since Leftie showed up on the island, I've been turned around. She's a tornado that touched down in my life and shattered it to matchsticks. This place is my opportunity to make a new start after the nightmares. And maybe that's not as picture-perfect as I wanted it to be, but I have to adjust and adapt. That's what mutants do. So as uncomfortable and distasteful as it is, I have to go along with what's in front of me. Make myself part of the island, weave Aidy so thoroughly into the fabric of their lives that I become part of the background, so they can't even see me for what I really am.

Skip is asleep when I get back to the dorm, sprawled out fully-clothed on the bed with her phone still playing a video very quietly. She doesn't stir when I creep inside, not even when I sigh loudly and thump into bed. I can't bring myself to wake her, especially since I can't figure out how to recount the events I lived through. All I really got from tonight was a ruined shirt, and another lesson in how dangerous the Left Hand of Darkness is.

I'm prepared to spend the night unable to sleep, haunted by my nightmares.

Except I'm barely aware of even laying my head on the pillow. The next thing I know, my eyes are snapping open and a leafy head is bending over me. My scream doesn't even emerge, dying in my throat and coming out as a stale breath.

Chatterbox places their finger to their lips and jerks one thumb towards the doorway. Then they shamble out of the room, leaving me sitting bolt upright and staring after them. My heart hammers in my chest, but I get up and dress in the dark regardless. I've made enough of a fool of myself already. It'll be easier to go along with this latest interruption.

Outside the dorms, the air is cool. The sky is brushed with stars, dawn only a faint line on the horizon. Chatterbox, Feral, and a slender brunette mutant I don't recognise are standing in a small group, talking in low voices.

"Miracles do happen," Chatterbox says. "Here's little Aidy come to play." There's no sense of malice or judgement in their voice, but I flush all the same.

"I talked to Alyse." My voice comes out high and uncertain, and I want to cringe. "She made me realise how I can help out, especially since you've all done so much for me."

"We're good like that," Feral says. "Dragging our pet island around for everyone to play."

The ground rumbles faintly underfoot, somewhere between a very gentle earthquake and a wry chuckle. Feral stamps her foot in response.

"Cybele thinks you're hilarious," Dylan says. "Anyway, Aidy, we interrupted your beauty sleep because we thought you might want to come on a mission."

"Mission?" I'm really not at my best. This is embarrassing.

"We thought you might want to see where your new best friend Leftie came from. Going to poke our noses into dusty holes and see if there's anything nasty curled up in them that might try and sting us. You feel like coming along for the ride?"

Here's my brand-new plan already being put to the test. The idea of leaving my precious bolthole to go an off-island mission with two particularly dangerous mutants fills me with no joy. Especially not when it's all in favour of Leftie. On the bright side, at least this should be relatively safe, given the company I'm running with.

"Of course." I force my face into a smile.

"Brilliant." Chatterbox beams at me, and waves their hand towards the third mutant. "This is Keepaway. They're our ride. I'm dreadfully mean to them all the time, making them boop willy-nilly round the earth to all sorts of places."

"It's nice to meet you, Aidy." They're softly spoken, with floppy hair and remarkably pretty brown eyes. "The thing about Dilly is you should only pay attention to about half of what he says."

"But which half, my sensible family minivan?" Dylan pats their hair. "That's the question."

"I'd say half's a hell of a stretch." Feral bats at the others playfully with her tail. "But we should stop bantering and start missioning. These clowns broke into our island, and that makes me extra-special twitchy."

"How will you stop Leftie from following us?" I blurt. "She was really mad last night."

Chatterbox shrugs. "It's fine. Penance had a nice cozy chat with her. And besides, the twins will do their best to run distraction. They're very good at that."

"Your kids?" I ask nervously. There are a lot of strange stories about Dylan and Dani's children—who are apparently small aliens with a helping of human DNA. I haven't personally seen them up close, but half the island claims to have met them at one time or another.

"Not exactly mine, not exactly kids." They smirk at me. "But Feral's right. We should be moving. Keeps, if you would?"

Keepaway taps Dylan on the shoulder and they disappear instantly, blinking out of existence like they were never there. It gives me a fright, honestly. Who knows where they are right now and where they're going to end up? When you're teleport you're taken apart and put back together, and the whole idea of that is—

"This might feel weird the first time." Keepaway smiles at me apologetically. "But it's all perfectly safe. In a handful of seconds, you'll be back with Dylan."

The Dylan part doesn't *entirely* reassure me but I remind myself that I have to commit to this role. It's my way to cement Aidy in Mutopian society. Make me into someone reliable, someone worthy. That's what they need to see when they look at me. So I nod to the teleporter, and they touch their hand very lightly to the small of my back.

For a brief moment, I'm nowhere. It's like the world is holding its breath, refusing to let me exist. I'm surrounded by a featureless white expanse. It hurts my eyes, having nothing to focus on. I'm nowhere and nothing, every individual part of me collected and stored somewhere else until I'm finally reassembled. Panic swells in my chest. What if I never come back, and exist here in this nothing place forever, like—

I blink and I'm standing in a long, dark tunnel, like a large metal pipe. There are panels above that look like fluorescent lights but they're all dead. Dylan's a few steps in front of me, holding up a bright lamp that illuminates the tunnel stretching ahead of us.

"Fucking bunker chic," Feral yowls from behind me.

"Cults and their interior decorating skills," Dylan says. "Let's find somewhere more interesting."

I stick close to Dylan as we make our way through the tunnels. Keepaway stays behind me and Feral brings up the rear. I'm so nervous that I'm sure my heartbeat is echoing off the walls around us, a dolorous rhythm like a drumbeat dragging a song behind it. The tunnel reaches a T-junction and eventually unfolds into a confusing maze. None of this bothers Dylan. At each intersection, they shrug and pick a direction at what is seemingly random. After a quarter of an hour padding through the darkness, I realise they've got no idea where we're going.

Until we round a corner and come across a man standing in front of a large metal door. He's wearing black combat gear and holding a weapon. It's a thick black tube so heavy and ungainly that he has to support it with both hands.

"Burn the forest down." The shout echoes through the tunnel, like he has an army with him.

His cry gives me the seconds I need to remember my role in the team. I push my way in front of Dylan, stumbling awkwardly towards the man. Every instinct screams at me to stop, but I'm the tank, there to soak up the damage. The soldier flicks a switch at the base of the weapon, and a jet of fire leaps from the barrel. It envelops me in its burning grip. Even though it doesn't crack or scorch my skin, I can still feel the distant heat, like I'm lying on the grass under the midday sun. The flames cling to my skin. They flow along the lines of my arms and legs, furious at being denied the pleasure of splitting my skin or the joy of incinerating my heart. I'm a candle in the shape of a person, a blazing flare, staggering one step in front of the other.

The man toggles off the flame weapon. It falls to the ground with a heavy clang. He reaches behind himself and pulls out a squat black gun that he aims in my direction, squeezing the trigger. I'm still engulfed in flame, but the bullets ricochet off me, striking the metal walls with red-hot pinging sounds.

It feels like I'm *growing*, the heat is expanding me until I've swollen to fill the tunnel, a vast red-hot shield bearing down on the increasingly desperate soldier. An expended clip rattles on the ground at his feet and he fumbles at a new one, struggling to reload the gun. I swing one arm at him. There's no real force or intent behind it. All I want is for him to stop. For this whole situation to be over.

I'm not sure whether it's the smouldering heat of my arm, or the steely invulnerability of my skin, but my blow sends him sprawling to the ground. He sits slumped, staring at the floor as if he's fascinated by the pitted metal in front of him. Blood leaks slowly from a wound in his scalp, dripping down his face in streaks.

"Burrrrrr," he says.

"What's wrong with him?" I squeak. "I didn't mean to hurt him."

The man's mouth works, like he's practising his words internally before he says them. His tongue pokes out, swollen and painted with gory lines. One hand twitches at his side, reaching for something and failing to find it.

"I'll handle this." Feral squeezes past me, kneeling in front of the man and raking one claw along his throat. His head drops forward, blood sheeting down his front in a watery rush. "We weren't going to get anything useful out of him either way."

"Fuck." Dylan pats me on the shoulder. "You did good, Aidy."

I'm not sure what horrible conception of *good* they see in this situation. There's a dead soldier in front of me. A man who tried to kill me. A man who I killed. I've committed murder with my own bare hands. Questions of his guilt or what's deserved flutter like flakes of ash through the burned out wasteland of my thoughts. I'm still burning. This is hell of a sort, I suppose, just like my mother and grandmother told me about.

It's not the first time I've realised that I deserve to burn.

"I'm sorry," I gasp. "I didn't mean to. It was an accident. Please believe me. I didn't want this. It's not my fault. I mean, it is my fault, but the intent wasn't there. And intent matters, right? All I wanted was for him to stop shooting at us." With each sentence that spills out of my mouth, my voice cracks more and more, until I'm amazed it hasn't fallen apart.

Feral looks from me to Dylan, one claw still dripping blood. "I've got no answers to whatever set of questions that was. If it makes you feel any better, you just dinged him up real bad, and I put the finishing touches on the whole mess."

"That makes me feel zero percent better," I gasp. My brain doesn't have room for anything aside from one single fact.

I'm a murderer. Again.

11

LEFTIE

I sleep terribly. My decision to stay on the island already feels like a mistake. I'm not good at trusting people and I've got no idea whether these mutants can really do what's necessary to solve the problem. Someone's out there, splashing around in the lake of gore left behind in my past, and it's going to need an intervention. I've held to my decision for a handful of hours, but maybe I need to get out of here after all. I'll listen to Penance and make it a very quiet, very careful look around. One where nobody even really knows I'm gone. No violence, no bloody revenge. They can't get too mad at me for *looking*.

I dress in all black, even a black hoodie in honour of the great Chatterbox. Then I fold the shadows around myself and prepare to depart. Unfortunately, someone is already there waiting for me.

"You're in trouble," Willow sing-songs. They're hanging upside down from a vine. Their hazel eyes blink at me, and they bare their thorny little teeth in a wide smile. Leaves drift around their head in slow motion, like a very sluggish breeze is stirring them.

"I don't care about *trouble*," I sneer.

"You should." Soo-yeon's voice comes from behind me, and I try not to jump. It's unnerving how these two can be here in my place of safety. "Pear is... what's the word?"

"Reckless?" Willow asks. "Relentless? Unstoppable? Far smarter than they let on?"

"I was going to say terrifying." Soo-yeon sighs. "But all those are true. When they want something, they'll do a lot to make it happen."

I would dearly love to knock these plant kids out of my way, but they send my threat radar screeching in a way I've never experienced.

"Are you really Chatterbox's children?" I ask.

Soo-yeon swings around to hang beside Willow. Their smiles are identical, but overall Willow's look shares more of the crooked charm of Chatterbox, whereas Soo-yeon has the icy perfection of Marvellous. "We have DNA from both the ones you know as Dylan and Dani. But we are also linked with Cybele, and through her to the energy network of the entire planet. It gives us a different perspective on life than most entities."

"Do you hate me then?" I ask. "I've taken so much life."

"You're very dramatic," Soo-yeon says. "Nature takes life without thinking. It is no act of volition, or of Cybele's doing. Our in-between position is complicated. We attempt to help where we can, but humans do tend to poke and prod and make a mess."

"I am a force of nature." Why am I trying to impress them? "Except I take life where it is deserved. Uriel created me to destroy the world, but I rebelled against my destiny. Now I decide who lives and dies."

"So dramatic." Willow laughs, but it doesn't feel mocking. "We like you, Leftie. Pear likes you too, and they're a good judge of character most of the time. We think you're cute, like a vicious little kitten going yowl and shredding nasty little bugs with your claws."

It's lucky they can't see me flush with embarrassment among the shadows. These frustrating little *monsters* patronise me and dismiss me. Yet they do it with such fondness in their voices and smiles that I can't help but feel warmth towards them. My birth parents were so stiff and awkward around their chosen child, and Uriel and the Children were always so controlling and devoted.

"So are you sad about being left on the sidelines?" Willow asks. "It's okay. You can tell us who you really feel. Be honest."

"No." I colour my voice as dark as my shadows. "I want nothing to do with all these ridiculous mutants."

"We did say you should be *honest*." Soo-yeon sways gently. "I mean, we're different too, so we know what it's like to be on the outside. But we have our family, and like a thousand aunts. Plus one huncle."

"Did you say huncle?" Willow frowns.

"Our hunky uncle. Everyone thinks he's handsome. Obviously we don't understand the concept of human attractiveness, but lots of people agree he's very good looking. Not Aunt Fetch, or some of the others, but like—"

This conversation is frustrating me. It's supposed to be my escape attempt. I drop out of the shadows and back to reality, but the twins are waiting for me here as well.

"Pear's trying to help you," Willow says.

"Help me how?"

They roll their eyes. "That's a secret, *obviously*. But people are out there following leads. Pear and Feral and Aidy, too."

"They took *Aidy*?" A pulse of rage kicks in my chest. That they'd drag Aidy's pathetic ass along with them is ridiculous. I am a honed weapon, and they are simply a chunk of wreckage.

"Don't be jealous, Leftie," Soo-yeon croons, and reaches one green hand out tentatively to brush hair off my face.

I flinch away, as if they're going to sting. I'm not entirely sure why. It's partly that I don't trust them, but also I don't need *sympathy* from these creatures. My life and destiny are mine. Any problems I'm facing are setbacks I will conquer on my own. Being stuck here is the most frustrating thing of all, having to endure all these people and their awful proximity.

"Sorry." The child crouches on the ground near me, looking up at me with their beautiful hazel eyes. "We should ask before touching. I thought you might need reassurance. Everyone does sometimes, even us."

"I need nothing I cannot provide myself." I stare down at them.

Soo-yeon widens their already wide eyes and turns to Willow. The two of them gaze at each other, having a wordless conversation.

"We go on missions, too," Willow says eventually. "With our parents. Sometimes one of Cybele's avatars comes too. It's very, very top secret, so you cannot tell anyone."

"Protect the planet," Soo-yeon adds.

"You're eco-warriors." I laugh. "Of course. That makes sense. There are a bunch of them these days. I've tripped over some occasionally and I leave them be. They're on the right side overall, but they're mostly harmless."

"We're not harmless," the alien kids say in unison, their voices warping into something that sounds like a signal travelling between the stars. It's cold and empty and I feel my skin prickle.

Sure, I want to say, you go out with your parents on little family outings, but you don't understand what it is to stalk alone. Except I don't, because they're genuinely fucking unnerving. For a second, I imagine this is what it's like for a human to watch me step out of the shadows, eyes bright and smile wide, blades coalescing in my hand like wisps of smoke.

"No," I say instead. "I don't think you are."

"Do you want to come along on our mission?" Willow asks. "We're just spying, but you could join. As long as you promise you'll stick to the shadows."

"You have to promise." Soo-yeon's eyes flicker.

"I don't promise anyone anything."

Willow giggles. "She's so badass, Soo. If she comes along and fucks everything up, we'll play innocent."

"The 'rents have zero respect for our innocent act. They will *know*."

"Ugh, fine." Willow wraps their vines around themself. "She can stay behind then."

"No." I push myself up out of the chair. "Fine. I'll come along for the ride. And don't worry, I'll behave myself." I tell myself I'm doing this to learn about these two creatures who have powers that honestly outstrip mine. Especially if they're going to become obstacles in the future when I make my escape from the island. Except the real truth is this is partly from boredom and partly from jealousy. I hate the second part in particular, that my mind is conjuring fantasies of having a twin of my own, a Right Hand to my Left. Two of us, cold and merciless and striking together from the darkness.

"Shadows," Soo-yeon says sternly.

"I understand." I slip into the welcoming shade, becoming smoke that drifts unseen through the world. The twins share identical smirks at my arrival.

"Team-up." Willow reaches out to give me a high-five.

I do not respond because I am not that sort of person.

They lean back with a huff. "Fine. Be that way. We shan't celebrate with you on a successful mission either. We will all stand there and nod superciliously to each other."

Soo-yeon snorts. "Who taught you that word?"

"Aunt Lys."

"I like it. Leftie does have a very supercilious face."

I don't even know what the word means, but I can't tell them that, so I increase the volume on my sneer until they both break into giggles, which ruins the effect completely. Damn exasperating alien children.

"Now come with us," Willow whispers. "Follow if you can. We travel along the secret currents of the Earth."

I have no idea what this means. They simply vanish, leaving the faintest of afterimages in the air, like tentatively traced lines of glowing smoke. Travelling long distances through shadow is more complicated than you might think. I am far better than I once was, where I needed bright light or deep darkness. Now I can step into the faintest smudge of grey and slide myself along its edges before reappearing in the real world.

Ocean travel presents its own obstacles. Luckily, although the day is bright, the sea is choppy, and the waves cast shadows as they crest. I skim the underside in darkness, and pop out to dance light-footed along the crests of them, a half-shadow, half-real girl soaking my feet in spray before I slip into darkness again.

"Such a lot of effort," Willow's voice sighs. They are nothing but radiant smoke, drifting along axes I cannot detect. "But pretty for all that."

I have no idea how far we are from land, and although this method of travel is tiring, it is exhilarating as well. I have spent far too much time on shitty buses and cramped planes, travelling on false passports. It is good to know I can cross an ocean on my own, if need be.

Soo-yeon breaks me from my travelling trance. "Up ahead. Look, our destination."

There is no land mass growing on the horizon. Instead, we're approaching the grey bulk of an enormous ship.

"Aircraft carrier." Willow speaks from the shadows at my shoulder. "Brought from the American Navy during the Dark Year. They use it here as it is harder to enforce law. A ship registered to a country that no longer exists, floating far from anywhere."

"Not far enough from us," I say, because this is truly what I live for. To strike against those who deserve it but do not expect it, who have insulated themselves with money and power.

"We are watching today," Willow reminds me. "Retrieving evidence."

"Fingers and knives to yourself," Soo-yeon trills. "I know you did not promise, but…"

I ignore them both and dance ahead to the boat, skimming across the water like a perfectly round, flat stone. The twins skitter behind me, chattering among themselves in a language I don't understand. I suspect they're discussing what a mistake they made in bringing me along.

When I reach the boat, it's an abyss of shadows compared to the dappled wavescape of the ocean. I sink into their refreshing darkness which swallows me as if I am extinguished. It feels like a giant metallic tomb. I drift through its cramped corridors as the hull pings around me and the great engines throb deep in the bowels. A small number of armed guards patrol the deck, although more sleep in their quarters below, and three play a desultory game of cards in one tiny chamber. It would be the work of minutes to break them all. They are woefully unprepared for my arrival.

But I am not here to strike from the darkness. I don't even know if this is a valid target. Yet. I search for the core of the ship. Usually, people such as these hide their schemes deep. It is a sufficient veil for most, as an incoming attack party would have to fight their way through. I flicker my way in, melting from darkness to darkness. I do not even need to take physical form. The lights in here are weak and pale yellow and spill on the metal floor like pools of vomit.

I stop when I find the laboratory. It is pristine and white. The lights are blinding and there are so few shadows there. I have to press my shadow-self on the outside of the door, peering in through the thick glass of the single window. It's impossible to tell what's taking place inside. There are three men and a woman, all at workstations and busy with inscrutable equipment. I am no scientist, but they do tend to spill information with a blade at their throat.

"What are they doing here?" I whisper to Willow and Soo-yeon.

"Once, they worked on a bacteria that would eat the plastic in the oceans."

"That sounds... good?" I'm confused, because I thought the twins were all about being eco-warriors. Then I think about the emphasis Soo-yeon placed on the word *once.*

"And now?"

"They are developing a bacteria aimed at targeting a certain kind of plant material. One that is unique in all the world, and only grows in one location."

"Your island," I whisper.

"I would prefer you call it *our* island, but yes." Soo-yeon and Willow are barely visible in the darkness around me, but they seem darker and more plant-like. Their forms no longer seem remotely human, tangled masses of leafy growth and trailing vines from which multiple eyes glow. "They seek the destruction of us, our home, and our parents. They believe they can grievously wound Cybele this way, but they are feckless and naive fools. Her words, not ours. Sometimes we feel her too deeply."

I feel a chill at their words, even here in the shadows. "How can you stand by and do nothing?"

"We are not *doing nothing*," Soo-yeon says, and it sounds like her again. "We are recording what they do and we shall take it back to Mutopia. The scientists will confirm what they are doing, and we shall pursue legal challenges before considering other alternatives."

"It is perhaps not the most efficient way," Willow croons, "but it is the right way."

I stare at the few sharp shadows cast inside the room, drawn by bright lights and hulking equipment. It would be a single step to walk inside. To return to the shadows. To strike. To be what I was made for.

I wet my lips. My body is a weapon. I am deadly.

This is why I am here.

12

AIDY

There's a hand on my shoulder, one that's pale green and smells of summer hedgerows. "You did a good job, Aidy. You saved us all. Saved Keepaway, especially. It was pretty damn impressive, honestly. That fucking shield wall thing does the job."

I'm not even sure where Keepaway is because my vision's too blurred with tears.

"It was cool." Feral drags the corpse of the man I killed off to the side. There's blood smeared everywhere, pooling in dents in the metal floor. "Great instincts, throwing yourself into danger like that. I heal pretty fast, but fire and bullets still aren't *fun*."

This only makes me cry harder, like I'm being wrung out. I try to gulp my tears back, but that makes me cough. It's even more embarrassing, but I finally manage to wrangle myself under control. My emotions are a confusing tangle, but they're gradually being swamped by a rising tide of rage.

Chatterbox dragged me out on this mission, and they must have *known* there was real danger. Last night they could have pretended there wasn't, because nobody should have been able to teleport into a Mutopian bunker. This endeavour was a deliberate test for me. One that I passed, but with a cost. I want to scream at them, to smash my invulnerable fists into their chest, to make them understand a fraction of what I'm feeling.

I'm less good at hiding this than I thought.

"I get this was intense, and you're having a lot of emotions right now, but I'm going to be honest, because that's what I do these days." Chatterbox looks no older than me, standing with their messy hair all tangled with petals, and their fists bunched in the pockets of their hoodie. Their eyes look bruised with tiredness. "Yes, I knew we might run into soldiers here, and I brought you along anyway. This is part of what we do and a taste of what the job is. Sure, Mutopia is a haven to protect as many people as we can, but not everyone gets that luxury. It's your choice to be a part of the team, but I figured—in all my less than infinite wisdom—that it would be good for you to see the real shit and understand the reality of what's at stake."

"You and speeches," someone murmurs, and Alyse steps out from behind Dylan. This is obviously where

Keepaway went, to fetch someone able to manage my meltdown. These mutants and their carefully choreographed dance. I understand what it's like to try and get people on your side, so I get why they're doing this.

"Hello, Aidy," Moodring says. "Can we walk for a moment?"

"Sure." I wish I had another transformation that could protect me from situations like this. An emotional shield wall. Despite how carefully I have constructed Aidy to shine and be perfect, I know too well that I'm riddled with cracks.

Moodring slips her arm through mine, and leads me down the tunnel away from the body. It's a relief not having it there, bloody punctuation to underscore my actions.

"So this turned out to be rough," she says.

"Chatterbox knew this might happen," I stammer. "They took me here anyway."

"Ah." Alyse's voice is weighted with fondness, despite the subject. "They do like to throw people in the deep end. You would have been perfectly safe, no matter what happened. Dilly is very resilient, and Feral is more than capable of dealing with all these problems. You were in no real danger."

"I killed someone," I yelp.

"You injured someone in self-defence. That man would have murdered you if he could, along with three other mutants. It was Feral who chose to end his life. It's up to you how you frame that, honestly. But the stories we tell ourselves matter. Many people would tell this tale with themselves as the hero." She breaks off and turns towards me, her eyes on mine. "I was a lot like you, I think."

My heart thumps at this, like she somehow knows everything about my past and is preparing to spill all my secrets in an ugly tide.

"You were like me?" My voice is barely a whisper.

"I found it hard to know who I was. I spent a lot of time trying to be what people wanted me to be, building a new Alyse in every setting and adjusting the dials for my audience. It's why my powers felt so ironic, that I changed based on my mood in the same way I tried to change my *self*."

My pulse flutters, a butterfly effect that might magically twist me into someone else again. She sees far more than I'd like her to. "I don't understand. How is that like me?"

"People are complicated," Alyse says. "We have previous versions of ourselves, all the attempts at figuring out who we are. Despite ourselves we're all made up of layers. Some parts are bedrock, others we've built on consciously, others grow when we're not looking."

"But you," I whisper, even though I can't finish the sentence.

"Part of me is still the same kid changing myself desperately to make friends, the same girl hiding in a bathroom stall getting barged in on by Dylan Taylor."

"Young Chatterbox." I'm fascinated despite myself, because this is practically a myth, the story of these kids who turned themselves into superheroes.

Alyse laughs. "You've never met someone so spiky and so soft. And I had no idea who I was, but Dylan did. She knew herself, and they also saw something in me I'd never seen before."

"What?"

"A best friend. Someone who'd look at them and say yes, this is my person, and I think they're amazing. Someone who they could be messy and real with, and know I'd always be there. Romantic love is great and all, but the Ballad of Dilly and Lys is as important as anything else in the story of the Cute Mutants. Best friends means everything." She wipes her fingers under her eyes, and when I glance at her she's a glowing cloud, shot through with pink light and drizzling gold. "Aidy, you should've stopped me. I'm being far too sentimental."

I don't want this conversation to end. Her words are like stones dropped into a well of loneliness at the heart of me. I have the potential of a real friend now in Skip. It's wonderful, but I'm so scared of her seeing all my previous iterations and the parts of myself I don't like, there's no way I can be messy and real. People always recoil. I know this is true. And while Alyse's words are lovely, the miracle she shares with Dylan isn't meant for someone like me.

"I like the sentimental stuff," I say softly.

"My point being." She reaches out and touches my shoulder lightly. "Opening yourself up is scary, but it might be worth it."

I smile up at her, as if she's gotten through to me and won me over. It's what she wants to hear, and she's so radiant I can't possibly disappoint her. At the same time, not everyone deserves to have their dreams come true.

I definitely don't.

"Come on." Alyse holds out her hand. "Shall we continue the mission?"

I'd dearly love to say no, but that's not what she's looking for. And while she has a level of insight that almost undoes the clumsy stitching holding me together, I'm still in an impossible position. Without rebuilding myself, I'm nothing. That's the difference that Alyse doesn't understand. At her core, she's something light and good and beautiful. Whereas I—

"Yes," I say firmly, because that train of thought leads down a tunnel longer and darker than the ones we're trapped in now, and it's not the time to sit alone, rocking and staring at the wall. "Let's do it."

We head back towards the door the dead man had been guarding. Feral and Dylan are waiting for us, idly chatting beside the corpse as though he's merely bloody furniture. My eyes keep drifting back to him, but Alyse nudges me through the doorway and into an inner chamber. There's a whole network of them, connected by smaller tunnels. Blood leaks from under one door that's slightly ajar, showing that perhaps the others weren't totally idle while Alyse and I were talking. There's a horrible part of me that wants to fling it open and reveal the secret inside, but I think in their own way they're trying to protect me. After the production I made over the first soldier, I can understand why. Something else soon catches my attention—an enormous photograph of Leftie, a few years younger than she is now. It's in black and white, showing her in an apparently candid pose. She's dressed in a neat black dress and seated at a small table, looking off into the distance. An enormous caption underneath says

SHE WILL DESTROY ALL SINNERS

AND USHER IN THE NEW WORLD

Dylan's staring at the photo too. "But how, you assholes?"

I can't look away from Leftie's dark eyes. "By murdering them all one by one. Which seems a slow way to do it."

"Nuh-uh. Her powers came later. They raised her from a baby to be what they called Worldbreaker. After she got out of the cult, she started killing off the enemies of mutantkind. That was her doing good, not some cult-approved nonsense to kill those who weren't righteous enough for Uriel's weird as fuck standard."

My voice sketches the words. "You sound like you approve of her killing all those people."

"They hunt and fear mutants." Dylan's hand reaches out and touches the photograph-Leftie's cheek. It's a tender act, like a parent reaching out to reassure a child—something they wish they could do in real life but the actual girl wouldn't tolerate. "If we always sat passively by, none of us would be alive right now. Where were you during the Dark Year?"

"Hiding." It's not entirely a lie.

"Me too, after a fashion." They laugh. "Anyway, there's got to be something here. They were guarding this place for a reason."

The others move through the room with purpose, sifting through information. I drift aimlessly, trying not to stare at the growing pool of blood ebbing from the other door. The space is plain and utilitarian, a military bunker that's not intended to be a home. Each bunk bed has two photos taped to the wall above it—one of the younger Leftie, and one of a pale man with short, dark hair, dressed in a suit and holding a Bible.

"Uriel." Feral holds up a sheaf of papers. "That's the leader, right?"

"Was." Dylan's crouched in front of a computer, tapping away on the keyboard with an expression of great frustration. "He's a corpse now, and good riddance."

Feral hisses like a cat, waving a sheaf of papers in one hand. "Someone's using his name then."

Dylan attacks the keyboard like they're trying to hammer each key through the bottom of it. "Some prick inheriting the cult? Oh good, here's their fucking email. Let's see. Why the fuck is searching emails so slow? Chug chug, motherfucker." They smack the side of the monitor, as if that will help. "Oh, shit. Fairy, this isn't good."

"What?"

"Look." They tilt the screen slightly towards the feline woman, who can apparently read it from across the room.

"No fucking way. He *survived?* I thought nobody over sixteen survived Leftie's fucking rampage when she broke free from the Children."

A chill crawls delicately down my spine, cold fingers touching each knob of bone. "Who are you talking about?"

"Fucking Uriel. Big boss daddy asshole of the precious little cult that made Leftie. Someone she is very sure she left a pile of blood and guts. How the fuck did he—?"

"Same shit that made Leftie all shadowy," Feral says.

"No." Dylan hunches their shoulders, and thorns spring up the line of their neck. "That fucking... We need to *find* him and kill him. I'll tear his throat out myself."

"No." Alyse joins them at the computer, darker and sharper than I've seen her. Like a twinned blade to Leftie, something drawn from midnight to hold at the throat of the world. It makes me want to run. "I'm the one who gets to do that. These people don't get to touch her."

I stare at the triptych of mutants, staring at the computer screen as if it's a holy relic they've unearthed.

"Uh, can someone please fill me in?" I ask.

"Uriel used Emma's blood to turn Leftie into a mutant," Feral says. "Part of some wacky plan to power his precious little Worldbreaker up to be able to kill Goddess. But now it looks like they did the same thing to resurrect Uriel after Leftie murdered him. Explains some shit about how this cult managed to spring some of their surprises on us—sort of, at least. But it makes Uriel a mutant, and one who's gunning for Leftie."

Dylan shakes their head. "She'll fucking throw herself at him if she finds out. Run herself right into his trap and he'll get revenge. Shit, we can't tell her. There's no way she'll listen to reason if she finds out this man is still alive." Their eyes land on me. "You understand this, Aidy? Leftie cannot know about Uriel's resurrection. We'll tell her once the prick is dead and she can be pissed at us then."

Feral leans against the desk. "She deserves to know."

"Yes, she fucking does. I'd want to know, and I'd be furious at anyone who didn't tell me. But me and the kid have a few things in common, and not even you lot could hold me back from going after him. But they can negate her powers, which not only means she'll end up dead, but they'll dredge up the goddamn Worldbreaker thing from inside her and that's a whole new chapter of fucked."

"Sometimes I fucking hate this job," Feral sighs.

"I agree with you, Dylan," I whisper. "If Leftie finds out, she'll be so angry. I've seen what she's like when she fights and it's terrifying. So I promise I'll keep it a secret."

"Yeah, she's tugging on the goddamn leash, so we need to find this fucker fast." Dylan pushes back from the desk. "Bring everything back to Mutopia. We'll go through it in more detail. I want this solved yesterday."

"So bossy." Alyse nudges them with her shoulder, darkness dissolving away and returning to the warm and beautiful person I'm used to. "Come on, Aidy. Help me collect stuff."

I help load papers into boxes, but all I can think about is how Leftie's past has reached out and touched her. Something she thought was buried, forcing its way up through the dirt with a skeletal grasp.

And for the first time, I actually pity her.

13

LEFTIE

I've read enough books to understand romantic yearning. Growing up mostly in the dark, surrounded by sycophants with their own sinister plans, books were my escape. I discovered other worlds there, and all of them were lies, much like this one. Romance never held much appeal, although I have kissed my share of girls who made my heart race. I find it hard to trust people. They wanted me to ascend from the right hand of the Father, to break the world and reforge it in chaos, and all those around me from the day of my birth told any lie to accomplish that aim.

There is some echo of yearning that stirs in me when I see these alien children, but I swallow it. I despised those people in books who were weakened by their desire. I am here on a mission, I remind myself. Nothing more.

"If they succeed, what happens?" I ask.

"In destroying us and our family?" Willow asks.

"Yes."

"Then we shall be wiped out," Soo-yeon says, "and the world will continue to turn."

Their shadows move and rustle in the darkness. They wait and they watch.

"You brought me here for this, didn't you?" I ask.

"Did we?" Willow asks. "That seems dangerous of us."

"A theory with no evidence." Soo-yeon laughs. "Wishful thinking, perhaps."

"Nobody commands you, Left Hand of Darkness." It is Willow's voice, but darker and older, as if the alien in them has awoken and stirs. "Why would I be under any misapprehension that the two of us could?"

I smile in the darkness, and shadows swirl around my hands. There are blades here, so many and so sharp. When I was born in the womb of the world, a child crafted gene by gene to bring death, I was their tool. Chained to them, a monster dangling on the end of a razor-edged chain.

They should never have fed me the blood of the Goddess. They should never have loosed me, a thing built for death and becoming darkness, slipped off the leash and hungry for vengeance.

Now I am here, and I am mine, and I bow to no will but my own.

"I did not promise," I tell Willow and Soo-yeon. "And now I will fulfil my purpose."

"Dangerous," a voice sighs, and I do not think it is either twin. "So very, very deadly."

I do not listen to any more of their words, for I am already dancing from shadow to light. When I decided I would no longer be the Right Hand of the Father, I named myself the Left Hand of Darkness in opposition to him. When I ended his life, my only regret was that I could not perform the act again and again. I do regret the name, however, as I am no simple extension doing the bidding of something greater than myself.

I am not the Left Hand of Darkness.

I am darkness itself.

Death is my true name, and I am the destroyer, spilling blood and stealing life. These are my chosen targets, and therefore they will die, their names struck from the Book of Life. I no longer believe in that book, the one I read each night with my name embossed on the cover, filled with the names of the faithful that waxed and waned in accordance with the Father's will. Nobody named in that book is alive today anyway.

I stand, bathed in the full glow of the bright laboratory lights. In my hands I hold a spear with a blade at each end. The four corpses here with me leak their essential fluids onto the floor. I nudge one aside with my foot, and the face tips toward me, sightless. I feel nothing, not even satisfaction, because death cannot be satisfied. It is inevitable, and the only thing I choose is the moment to strike.

"Messy." Willow appears in the laboratory beside me, a slender reed of a person whose eyes glow pale green. "Naughty naughty."

"It is our fault." Soo-yeon leans against the door, a smirk on their face. "And we shall take the blame."

"That's what you get for running around with weapons."

"Even scissors." Soo-yeon winks at their sibling.

Any further words are drowned out by the blaring of alarms. It seems our presence has been detected. This time, I sense the bullet slicing through the air, and recognise the way it disturbs the world by its presence. It is disturbing to know the humans sense me, and I cannot understand how.

I reach for the shadows, but the alien children surround me, dropping all pretence of human form. They are green and tangled life, sprouting tendrils and thorns and hanging bulbs that disperse fragrant spores.

"They knew?" My voice is hoarse, almost high. It sounds panicked, although I am not.

"Yes." The voice from within the plant-thing is resonant, buzzing like a honey-bee. "They have stolen your powers again and almost murdered you. There are a number of interfering *things* attacking you. More exist within the periphery of this vehicle. We shall protect you."

"I can defeat them," I say, ever defiant.

"Perhaps not," Soo-yeon's voice says. "I have won the bet between myself and my sibling though. This second wager, at least."

"I won the one that you would kill everyone," Willow says. "Soo-yeon said the humans would be waiting for you. The target was too enticing. They will use this as evidence you cannot be trusted, and proof they should kill you."

"Unfortunately, we do not have much skill with technology." There's the brief suggestion of Soo-yeon's face among the foliage. "We cannot stop the footage of your attack getting out, and then the GIC will be interested all over again."

"No." A tiny silver drone floats into the room. It spins lazily in the air, revealing the Cute Mutants logo glistening in purple light on its surface. "Yet I am also watching, and I am *very* good with technology. All transmissions have been murdered in their cozy little beds, and I have terminated all digital life in the vicinity. Remarkably cruel of me, you might say."

"*Reboot*," Willow says, and the plant-creature disassembles itself back into two individual figures. "How lovely to see you. I win the third bet, Soo."

"Pear said you were doing other things," Soo-yeon tells the drone.

The device glows brighter. "Most of us are. Chasing down rabbit holes, but you may call me *Grendel*, for I am an experimental outcast and potential ravager of humankind. Potential in that while I am not taking an outwardly aggressive pose, my default stance is that if they fuck with me, I fuck back."

Willow lets out a gurgle of laughter. "Still running the Chatterbox protocol."

"What is going *on*?" I demand. "What is this thing?"

"Pear sort of accidentally uploaded their consciousness into a drone swarm once upon a time," Soo-yeon says. "It's a very *them* thing to do. This one will keep this mission a secret, which we hoped would happen. So all this has been very successful, actually. We learned that the humans are waiting to swat you, and also proved to you why it's dangerous to go off-island."

"Lucky us." Willow's smile is remarkably sharp.

"Or very well planned." Soo-yeon takes their sibling's hand.

"Shall I report this to Chatterbox?" The drone spins rapidly in the air, so the glowing lights on its face look like a smiley. "They do like us popping by to give them information on the various things we spy."

"We wouldn't mind so terribly much," Willow says, "except they have an annoying habit of reporting everything to Mum, and Mum takes everything rather more seriously."

"I wouldn't call her a killjoy," Soo-yeon says, "but she does ask a *lot* of questions."

"You are powerful." I frown at them, because I don't understand this. "More than any mutant, it seems to me. Why would Chatterbox and Marvellous limit you? Those who claimed to own me fell before my blade like any other." This is not entirely true, but I like to say it, because it feels more like justice.

"The problem is that we love them," Willow says.

"So very much," Soo-yeon sighs. "It is rather frustrating, but we do."

This revelation bothers me. I never felt any true warmth towards the pretty, vacant shells that were my parents. And the only thing I felt towards the Father and the other acolytes was loathing.

"Love is only chemicals in the brain," I tell them.

"No, silly Leftie." Willow smiles and reaches out two leafy arms towards me. "It is sacrifice and companionship and empathy. It is holding someone in the night when they are sad, and travelling together through unpleasant lands, and doing things because it makes someone else happy. It is a thousand things we do that twine together and make us grow in harmony."

"Sib." Soo-yeon nudges them. "That was beautiful."

"I listen. I learn. I am not *entirely* a brat."

The twins both watch me, as if they are waiting for my opinion in the matter, but I have none. Kisses are not love, and duty is not love, and a quest to rid the world of evil is not love, even if it shares the single-minded devotion.

"We should return," Soo-yeon says. "Our Leftie is in danger the longer we stay."

"Hush," Willow says. "She will not like that word."

"*Our* Leftie?" I demand. "I am *nobody's*."

"You are our friend," Soo-yeon says. "Or you would be, if you would allow such a thing to happen. Perhaps we are wrong, and friendship is worthless, but we have seen what is between our parents and all those they hold close, and we wish such a thing for ourselves."

"And we like you best." Willow says. "Of all the people we know that are not our parents or our aunties. You are *interesting,* and your brain works in curious ways, and we enjoy spending time with you."

I am not sure what to do with this revelation. Nobody has ever liked me before. I was always a tool to break the world, something set apart from all others, a precious weapon held in velvet and darkness. Even to the women I kissed on dancefloors and in hotel rooms, I was only something pretty to hold, to melt the night into sugar and stars.

It is why I wish for freedom, to be nothing more than mindless motivation, a virus that flows through the bloodstream of the world. Nobody can use me, not even myself. I am nobody's and nothing. A girl born dead, born death. It is the only way I can find freedom.

To be *liked* is something unfathomable.

Who could like a thing like me?

"Let us return." My lips feel numb. My body feels less like a weapon, and more like a burden.

I flee to the shadows, and trust the twins will destroy all evidence of our outing. It does not take long before they catch me, their smoky trails catching at my ankles and dissolving playfully. I do not understand them. They are alien, and to be under their regard feels like being pinned beneath the eye of a god. I learned early on that the god that the Family worshipped was a lie. It was an easy assumption to make that all the other gods of humanity were equal falsehoods, stories to give comfort and ensnare. And now *these* creatures break my assumptions and make me question memories that should remain buried. I am a grave that contains my own past, and so many bodies are tumbled headlong atop it. These two are forcing me to exhume things that—

No. This is merely another avenue of attack. More subtle than the usual ones. I must remain myself, unfettered, and not allow the myriad strangenesses of mutantkind and their allies to distract me from my cause. This brief sojourn among the Mutopians is not my new life. I am *using* them, taking advantage. Distractions are unnecessary, and always have been.

It does not mean I cannot enjoy the sensation of dancing through the shadows of the waves, of feeling the salt spray on my face and the delicate crystals that form on my lips. I taste them as if they are unshed tears.

When I see the island ahead of me in the distance, I feel a slight sadness that this journey is coming to an end. Worse, there is a small yet persistent sensation of *returning*. Like a barbed hook has been embedded in my chest, and someone is tugging lightly on it. I have never felt this before. When I fled the place called home, it was a burning wreck and I was glad to leave. Everywhere else I have stayed has been a surface to skim over.

This is more of their tricks, their games, their delicate, wide-eyed innocence hiding a more sinister aspect. They aim to ensnare me, to trap death in their cupped hands as if I am a darkly fluttering moth. I cannot let them. Their attacks are more subtle than the humans who simply wish to extinguish me, but both would result in me no longer being what I am.

As we enter the bay, the waves become smaller, and the shadows are tiny slices that require me to dance frantically from one to another. I finally give up, and step back out into the light, soaking my jeans up to the thighs. I pull damp tendrils of hair back from my face and secure them tightly before I stride through the water. The sun dances on the waves as I did, and sets them all to sparkling. I feel my shoulders relax. My home is in darkness, but I can appreciate the light.

On the beach, the twins are sprawled together, looking like seaweed tossed ashore. I am sloshing through the shallows, sending arcs of water spraying ahead of me, when they both leap to their feet. My eyes track an elegant figure moving down the path from the clifftop. The twins' so-called *Mum*, said in their crystalline voices, but with the u sound so clearly emphasised. Danielle Kim. So very beautiful, and I fear she is as deadly as I am. If she ever let herself off the leash of propriety and caution, how devastating she would be.

I wonder what it would be like to press my face in the perfumed hollow of her throat, to stitch a line of kisses down her neck, to taste the thrumming of her heart beneath her skin.

"Thirsty," I chide myself, and stride dripping from the sea.

"Mother dearest," Willow says, with a wide smile. "Light of our lives."

"Subtle," Soo-yeon nudges their sibling. "We have been enjoying the sea and the sun."

"Yes." Dani raises one eyebrow, an ironic arch I would love to run one fingertip along. "And the ship, the assassination, the murder attempts, and the drones. It was my plan, after all, believe it or not."

"Ha!" Soo-yeon pokes Willow in the side. "I told you it felt like one of Mum's schemes rather than Pear's."

"Violet's as well." Dani's unfathomably beautiful eyes are fixed on me. "She said you wouldn't be satisfied until you'd seen for yourself. The humans are prepared for you, Leftie."

"Yes," Willow says. "And we will protect her. With our lives if necessary."

"Always so dramatic," Soo-yeon says. "But it's true."

"Let's hope it doesn't come to that." Dani seems unruffled at the thought, as if she trusts these unique children of hers to carry this burden.

"It will not be necessary." I jut my chin at them, as if it is a weapon itself. "I will protect myself."

The three of them exchange glances, like they are tallying up the number of times this particular family has saved my life, and it irritates me. I did not ask them to. They have meddled for their own reasons, and I still do not trust them, even if I find them annoyingly endearing. It's an unusual feeling to be drawn to these creatures, as if I could be a weapon that is part of a set.

14

AIDY

I return to the island with a secret. Something that Leftie would kill to know. A single piece of knowledge that gives me the power to split her future along the seam of the scar left by her past. I could remove her from the island so easily, dangle this truth in front of her like a toy on a string. Not that I would be free of consequence. There are four people who know this information, and it would be instantly clear who was responsible. And, despite the temptation, I wouldn't do it—not even to the Left Hand of Darkness. It would be a betrayal, walking her into certain death.

I'm walking slightly ahead of the main group as we head back through the town. The day is warm and sunny, a breeze ruffling the tops of the trees gently. From this vantage, I can see all the way down to the beach. A small boat has been pulled up onto the sand disgorging a small contingent of new arrivals on the island. The mutant population is growing once more.

"It's the seeds of a team, don't you think?" Feral says to Dylan. "Leftie on attack, Aidy on defence, and Skip does short-range teleportation. Probably need another heavy hitter, although maybe Aidy could double, given that skull-crack she dealt. Be nice to have someone to do light healing, although Leftie's one of the fast-recovery types like me, and—"

"What do you mean, a team?" I whip around to face her.

"For missions and shit," Feral drawls. "This cult is only one entry in a long list of problems we're facing. And then there's shit like rapid response and rescue. Wouldn't it be cool to walk into burning buildings and rescue people?"

"Of course." It's an unfair question, because who says no to that? Even though I don't want to be dragged all around the world into perilous situations and expected to be heroic. This is not the life I wanted here on Mutopia, not remotely, but nobody ever talks about how to escape being chosen for something like this. Everyone else thinks it's an honour and a privilege. Skip would overflow with joy if she knew the amazing Feral had mentioned her name in conjunction with a *superhero team*.

"It's a possibility." Dylan seems distracted, probably wondering about their precious Leftie and how to keep the vicious little weapon in her sheath. "Keep it on the backburner for now though, yeah? Stop the cult, tame Leftie, then we can talk about the makeup of a new team."

I lengthen my stride, getting ahead of them to catch up with Alyse, but I can still hear them talking.

"How'd the thing with the twins go?" Feral asks.

"Fine. Some assholes took a shot at our Leftie as predicted. The main thing is that it kept her distracted while we turned over rocks. And maybe now it'll keep her cooling at heels at home while we find U and—" They draw their finger across their throat and make a visceral squelching sound.

"Imagine if one of our plans went that smoothly." Feral laughs.

"You doing okay?" Alyse nudges me. "After all that intensity?"

"I think so." I offer her my best hopeful smile. "It wasn't really about me. The main thing is making sure Leftie stays safe."

She narrows her eyes at me, like she's trying to figure me out, but I keep my smile up until she nods approvingly. "Maybe you two will be friends after all."

It takes everything in me not to laugh. Even if I was delusional enough to think some cross between a snake and a rabid polecat would make a good companion, the Left Hand of Darkness would never deign to offer a single fingernail of friendship to me. "Maybe."

Alyse follows the others back to the main Mutopia government building, while I head back towards the dormitory. I pause for a moment outside the main restaurant in town to watch the new arrivals enter the city. They're all in a straggling line, clutching each other and staring wide-eyed. I remember my first day here, how everything looked so incredibly surreal and beautiful. How I felt dazed by the miracle of washing up on this island shore.

There's a small family right in front of me—two men with a young girl. Someone offers to take their photo in front of a tree draped with a dazzling array of multicoloured flowers. Two girls walk arm in arm behind them, taking selfies. Everyone's laughing and chattering among themselves. Behind is a petite girl, early twenties with tan skin and short curls. She looks a lot like someone I—

No. She *is* someone I used to know.

A ghost. Rayner's supposed to be dead.

Leftie's not the only one whose past contains freshly turned soil on top of graves. This can't be happening. Not *here*, where I'm supposed to be safe. Rayner probably won't recognise me anyway. I'm looking much healthier than last time she saw me. My hair is cut differently, I'm wearing different glasses that change the shape of my face. I don't even dress the same. She'll glance right past me. Yes, just like that. I'm one more face in the crowd to her. Hopefully it'll stay that way. I'll have to find out where she's staying and what job she gets on the island. I don't see where her powers would take her. Being able to turn into a moth and seek the light? What use is that here? But once I know where she ends up, I can make sure my path and hers never cross. Hopefully she'll hear about me from someone else. Oh, that's Aidy. They're part of one of the Mutopian superteams. Hangs around with the Left Hand of Darkness, don't you know? She'll never draw the link between me and—

"Ruth-Ann."

I keep my body still. I don't even flinch. That would be a rookie mistake. I carry on walking down the path, as if those two syllables didn't catch me with barbed hooks.

"Ruth-Ann! Alex!" The voice again, louder. It'll attract attention. There's nobody else on this part of the path, so I turn. My face is schooled into an expression of polite confusion.

"Are you talking to me? My name's Aidy."

"Holy shit, it is you." Rayner tugs on her curls. "You look different, but it's definitely you. How the hell did they let you on this island?"

"I don't know what you're talking about." I've got this intense, panicked feeling of everything slipping away from my desperate grasp. But I have no choice but to keep trying to sustain this charade. "Who exactly are you? Are you new?"

"Fresh off the boat." She leans in closer. "And this game doesn't fool me for a second. I know you, whether you're Ruth-Ann or Alex or Aidy. I can't figure out how the hell you escaped the city, but you don't deserve to be on this island."

"I'm so confused by this," I tell her, eyes wide. "My name's Aidy and I *work* for Mutopia. I've just come back from a mission with Chatterbox, Moodring, and Feral. Why don't we go and see them and you can explain your problem in detail?"

It's a wild, wild bluff but I see the confusion break over her face. I don't think I've convinced her of anything, but invoking the sacred name of Chatterbox is a big deal. A mutant who's been less than an hour on the island doesn't want an audience with someone like that. Unless they're Leftie, of course.

"I can't figure out what your game is, Ruth-Ann, but—"

"It's Aidy." This is rapidly becoming the most stressful situation I've been in today, and not so long ago I was facing down a heavily armed soldier. "Look, why don't you come with me and I'll explain everything."

Rayner gives a short bark of laughter. "It'll have to be a hell of a story."

"Believe me, it'll blow your mind." There's still nobody else on the path, and this time of day the dormitory is pretty much deserted. Especially if I take the shortcut. "Look, come to the dorms and have a meal with me. I'll explain everything, and at the end if you're still not satisfied, I'll take you to Chatterbox myself." There's another reminder that I run with the scary people, but I also sound eminently reasonable. It's enough to sway her, at least for now. She's thrown off balance by everything—first getting to the island, then running into a ghost from her past.

A plan appears in my head fully-formed, as if it was inserted there by someone far smarter and more bold than I am. Not an Aidy plan or a Ruth-Ann plan, but one created by a newly formed third person, the one being carved out of the future by Dylan and Alyse. It's reckless and risky, but it might be the only way to stop Rayner from derailing the future of any version of me.

I've got to move fast, keep her reeling, so I walk quickly down the path. It wends its way through a lovely sun-dappled forest of beech trees towards the cluster of buildings that make up the residential dormitories. This is a fairly central part of the Emmaline township, and there are an entire tangle of paths leading to different places. If I take one of the ones along the fringe, there's almost zero chance I'll run into anyone.

Despite my bluff, I can't risk Rayner going to Chatterbox and saying what she knows. I've been fretting about exactly how my life on Mutopia should look, but the entire foundation is threaded through with cracks. Now here is a woman who could tear it down with a single heavy footfall.

"This place is wonderful." I keep my voice light and bubbly. "You'll get to know the island properly in your first couple of weeks, and then you can roam to your heart's content. There's beauty tucked away around every corner. Like, look up here. Off in the trees. See?" I point off into the distance, and she cranes her head to look.

Rayner never was that smart.

I hit her at the base of the skull. After what happened this morning, I make sure to pull my punch. It's still maybe a little hard because she collapses straight down, lying prone at the base of a beech like she's had too much sun.

"Shit." I crouch beside her and place my fingertips to her neck. There's a pulse and it's steady. There's a rush of relief. At least I haven't killed her. They say there's no surveillance on-island for residents, but I've got no idea how *watched* we actually are on Mutopia. Either way, I feel like murdering someone might attract some attention. Cybele must notice blood watering the soil.

None of this is what Aidy should be doing, but in the simple act of *arrival*, this person from my past is rocking the foundations of my life. Right now, I need to forget about the Aidy I've been building, and concentrate on being a person who can make it through the next few hours. Which is someone with a very inconvenient body on their hands. There's a location I can stash her, but there are logistics and timing against me.

When the plan unfolded in my head, the next part seemed straightforward, but now that I'm here, it's a lot less so. I don't have any great alternatives. If I get her closer to the dorms, I can pick my moment and try to sneak her in unnoticed, but that's an incredibly risky piece of timing which could go wrong at any time. The fallback position is to stay in the woods with her and bop her on the head whenever she stirs. I'm going to be forced into another bold move, one terrible decision begetting another like the endless Bible lists of names my grandmother made me memorise.

I'm not even sure how feasible this is. When I faced down the soldier in the tunnel, my body automatically grew. My body grew along with my skin becoming invulnerable. An involuntary reaction to danger, like the parachute form that carried me down from the top of the building in the Dark Year. My power isn't unbreakable skin. It's protection. And if I can flood my system with enough awareness of the peril I'm in, my body will hopefully shift form to protect me.

I've been soaked in adrenaline from the moment I first saw Rayner on the island and thankfully my body gratefully adjusts itself to solve my problem. I grow both taller and broader, a depression forming within me. I awkwardly stuff Rayner's unconscious body into it, like I'm a strange kangaroo. My hardened flesh covers her over until she's sealed away. I have a brief moment of panic that she'll suffocate, but small perforations appear over the surface of my stomach. I'm almost completely naked because most of my clothes won't fit my new shape. Thankfully, my body's adjusted to have skin of gleaming steel so it's far less obvious.

I've transformed into a huge, ungainly figure, but there are unusual people all over Mutopia, so nobody pays attention to me as I make my way along the path to the forest. It's a faux pas to draw attention to a mutation, and the few people I pass simply nod their heads in greeting. By the time I make it to the top of the island, there's nobody around at all.

My destination is a series of small shacks at the edge of the forest. They're overgrown buildings that look like part of the landscape. I've never seen anyone in them the whole time I've been on the island. I discovered them on my second day, when Mutopia seemed overwhelming and I was looking for somewhere to hide. Even back then they were in disrepair, walls sketched over with moss and boards warped. By now, the farthest hut has become almost entirely swallowed by the forest, thick green branches reaching out to cradle it. It looks as deserted as always.

When I push the door open and step inside, almost no light filters into the interior. The floor is bare dirt, rough grasses sprouting in patches. It's the most secure place I can possibly find on the island. And while it's not a realistic long-term plan, it should give me time to come up with something better.

I secure Rayner tightly with vines and make a makeshift gag from a piece of my shirt. She doesn't stir the whole time, but her breathing is still steady. There's an uncomfortable feeling in my gut that I've done some permanent damage to her, but I'll worry about that when I come back to check on her at nightfall.

My body's returned to normal, so I quickly dress again. I still feel on the verge of panic, so I'm half-expecting to accidentally transform into something useful again. It's like my whole body is one of those expensive pocket knives, and I don't even know what all the attachments are for.

I prop branches against the door to barricade it thoroughly, and then walk away from the hut. Even a few paces away, I can barely see it, lost among the trees. I walk as quickly as I can back down the path towards the town. I've only gone a short distance when I spy someone else coming towards me.

A familiar and entirely unwelcome person.

"Hello, little Aidy." Leftie's hair is loose and tossed in silky strands by the breeze. "What in the world are you doing out here?"

15

LEFTIE

My trip with the twins has left me antsy. Being trapped is not a good look on me. I'm not a fucking housecat. I piss everyone off by pacing around until Dani sends me outside to run off excess energy. The twins find this hilarious and then tell me that if I really wanted some excitement, I should go and present myself to Cybele in The Forest—capital letters clear in their pronunciation.

Time to find out if she's a god, an alien, or an imaginary friend.

The walk up to the summit is relatively short, but it still feels good to stretch my legs. Until I run into the last person I expected—a dishevelled and furtive-looking Cruise Ship Enby. They've got a ripped shirt, and they look like they've gone a few rounds with something tough. Maybe they've been in the forest, fighting God.

If this island was actually scary, The Forest would be a codename for a secret underground facility where they'd strap you into a seat, fill you full of drugs, and force you to watch some shit dug up from your brain. There were places like that in the compound where I grew up. The Tabernacle. The Throne Room. The Incense Chamber. The Father's Presence.

As far as I can tell, this is nothing more than a bunch of trees.

"Hello, little Aidy." I smirk at them. "What in the world are you doing out here?"

"Walking." They're breathing fast, all their vitals elevated. Maybe exercise, maybe not. Not my problem, honestly. Whatever they're up to, I'm sure it's mind-numbingly dull.

"I've come to pay homage to The Great Green One." I wave my hand towards the trees.

"You shouldn't. Nobody's supposed to go in there." They're so serious, oh my god.

"Twins suggested it. You know, Marvellous and Chatterbox's brats. Weird kids."

A brief frown crosses their face. "You shouldn't be talking to them either."

"Oh, the little critters like me. The whole family's trying to adopt me." I wield this casually, as if I have no idea how every mutant on the island reveres that damn family. "You want to come say hi to the trees with me?"

There's a moment where I think they're going to say yes, but they swallow that back down and retreat back into their timid self. I sigh theatrically. Every so often, I think they might be interesting, but then they go and let me down again.

"It's not safe. There are bigger dangers in the world than you, Left Hand."

I roll my eyes and push past Aidy to slip among the trees. It's immediately a few degrees cooler, and the light is filtered and green. It's like being underwater. The air even *tastes* different, like chopped up herbs, and the chill of it stings my windpipe.

"It's pretty." I tip my head back and look at the fractured daylight above me.

"Oh, you can recognise beauty?" Aidy stands outside the forest with hands on hips, glaring at me. "I thought you only cared for death."

They're so tiresome, but it's sometimes hilarious. "Death can be beautiful. If you'd seen more of it, you might know that."

"I've seen enough." They hunch their shoulders, angling away from me and stumble out of the forest.

"Thanks for the escort," I call after them, but they don't reply. Their loss, I suppose. I shake my head and head deeper into the forest. The path curves gently in an easterly direction. I picture the map of the island in my head. This trajectory is definitely leading me towards the centre. It makes sense, I suppose, going by the working theory that this island was created by Cybele, and that this forest is her dwelling place.

In the labyrinth under the compound where I grew up, the centre was the place where God dwelt. The Father and I were the only two people who were allowed there. Anyone else who attempted to come into the presence would be killed.

It was a threat I never had to follow through on until much later. And by then, nobody was safe. That labyrinth around the centre was dark, and lit by smoking torches. This one is beautiful and fragrant with a single path to its heart rather than many tangled branches. Yet they are both still pathways to gods. Mine was a lie, unless death was the god—and to be fair, that's as good a god as any.

A short distance further in, I spot a dim figure in the trees ahead of me. I freeze. There are so many shadows in here, it would be easy to slip into one. It would be the cautious thing, but I'm still standing here unhidden because this cannot be real. The trees have drawn in close, slender black trunks that look like they've been scratched out of the night with a thin stick of charcoal. Bark flakes away in ashy strips, and the leaves cling tightly to crooked branches. I didn't see the foliage change like this. I've taken one step, and everything has changed.

Far harder to reconcile is the figure in front of me. The canopy of heavy leaves blots out the light from above, and the only illumination is faint bioluminescence filtering up from the ground. It leaves the boy's face in shadow. I recognise him by the way he stands, as if his limbs are slightly too long and he cannot arrange them to his liking.

If there was a little more light, I'd see the delicate pink line of his half-smile and his barely-there eyebrows sketched on in the faintest grey. Eyes paler than mine, a blue faded like denim in the sun. Dark hair tousled, falling across his eyes every time he tilted his head in question.

He cannot be here, because I slit his throat in the bed that was supposed to be ours.

A message to the Father, from before I could speak it far more clearly.

I am not yours. This arrangement is not to my liking. You send me this crumpled, pretty creature who is intended to lay his hands on me in preparation for your own? Then I will send him back to you drained, his lips stained a blue paler than his unnatural eyes.

The boy's blood was warmer than his touch.

Even death has fears, it seems, and this forest reveals them. It is a psychic trick, no doubt, and an effective one, but I have slain all my demons and presenting them to me in this way is more like a triumphant highlight reel..

I stride forward, and the boy stumbles towards me. He is a leafblown thing, grey and desiccated. When I catch him, he weighs almost nothing at all and comes apart in my hands. I brush shreds of him off my fingers and watch them skitter through the air on strange currents. The shadows here reach with grasping fingers, taking pieces of the boy and secreting them away, as if they hoard every piece of what I've discarded.

There is something else here with me.

I hear it breathing.

Him breathing. That sound. It makes my throat tighten, and sweat prickle at my temples.

Uriel. The Father.

He used to watch me. First on camera, without me even noticing. One of my attendants whispered that secret to me. That voyeurism didn't bring him enough joy, so he would stand on the other side of the one-way mirror that made up one wall of my quarters. Occasionally he would press too hard on it, and tiny tremors would shiver through it. I became hyper-sensitive to that sound, the fine hairs on my arms rising when it quivered at his touch.

Later still, he watched me from the darkness, surrounded by his acolytes, the erratic pattern of his breathing sharpening and smoothing. Occasionally, I would catch a flare of light from his wristwatch or from the weapons the guards held.

If I ever made a move towards him, they would swarm upon me and press me to the ground.

"Not yet, Worldbreaker." He would laugh every time, his voice hitching on the final syllable. "The world has not yet been shattered. It is not yet time for us to inherit it."

Back then, I hated the shadows. I thought they spilled from him, as if a leak in his soul poured darkness into the world like dropping ink into water. That was before I was welcomed into their soft embrace, and they taught me how to strike. Before I drank the blood of the Goddess.

Now I stand half-shadow, half-real. I am dissolved on the border, both darkness and blade.

"Uriel," I say to the rush of breath. "Do you like what I have become? Am I all that you imagined?"

There is the tell-tale shudder, air rasping between teeth, and he comes forward, into the milky light that spills up from the ground. The leaves are wet and rotting, and he grows from them like something poisonous. Spots of mould dot his skin. His fine suit hangs off him, decaying into damp strands. In the centre of his chest, something flutters, beating wings and pulsing flesh.

"Fucking goddamn forest," I growl. "I don't like your tricks."

Uriel Clements, the Father of the Children of the Broken World, raises a hand towards me. I fucking told him that if he ever fucking did that again—

I summon razored edges from the darkness, and sever his arm at the elbow with two powerful blows. Nothing comes out but a sour trickle of dark fluid. I drive another blade into his chest, slamming it into whatever stirs there. Another dagger cuts a line across his neck, opening him up like he's a bag of sawdust.

He lets out a ragged shriek, like a rusted hinge being torn open, and then gallops away from me, trailing damp leaves and puddles of dark liquid behind him.

"Fuck this." I leap after him. It's not a conscious thought. I would kill the Father in any world, and I will end his life as many times as it takes.

Branches whip at my face, but I am more shadow than girl now, and they splinter against me. It is easy to track my quarry. I follow the broken passage through the trees, and the spilled blood, and the smell of decay. Soon, I see the white and wavering shape of him ahead of me. He is indistinct, coming apart in a messy cloud of spores.

There's a small clearing ahead, barely more than a space among the trees. He stops there, hunched over, drooping down as if he's waterlogged. In amongst the messy cradle of his arms is a girl. She has long dark hair that swirls around her face, and obscures all but the round apple of one cheek.

The Uriel-thing whispers to the girl he holds, and it sounds like wind moving in the trees.

"The world will break," the girl says. "And I will break it. And from the shining centre of the world, our Lord will hatch from the cradle where he has slept since his death. It is not three days he lies beneath the earth, but three ages."

I could finish this speech for her, but it is meaningless noise. Gibberish vomited forth by a broken man who wished for nothing more than power and control. He broke so many people, including my parents, and raised me up to be a broken thing. It was me who forged myself anew. It was me who escaped, who pinned my broken limbs back onto the shell of my body and found a new way to be.

Blood of the Goddess, but not death to the Goddess.

A new life. A new way. A gift from her.

I step forward, and summon shadows around me like a whirling vortex of blades. Each is placed with care into the body of the Uriel-thing, until he is nothing more than broken pieces.

"Are you satisfied?" I howl at the forest. "Is this what you wanted?"

"I thought you might have questions, rather than dealing death once again." A dark-skinned woman steps out of the trees. Her eyes are a green that puts every shade of it I have seen on Mutopia to shame. I expect to see life spilling from it, growing vines and flowers and every thriving thing.

So this is Cybele then, or at least an aspect of her.

"Monsters do not deserve to live." I let the forest of blades that swirl around me grow even thicker. A threat to her, perhaps, if she wishes to take it as such.

"Yet you are a monster, according to some." Cybele brushes my blades away with slender fingers, and they dissolve as if she is sunlight melting them away. "As am I. As are many of those who live here. My children, who you have met, may be the greatest monsters of all."

"By their fruits you shall know them. One verse I still have time for." I let the shadows fade and return to myself. This production has unsettled me, but it's clarified something. No matter what the twins say, no matter the danger they've shown me in the world, I cannot be brought to heel. "But I am done with your island, and with your games."

Cybele tilts her head quizzically. "And why is that?"

"You resurrect an old nightmare, dredging up my darkest moments to scare me."

"Or to show you that you have already defeated your demons, and there is no need to fight forever."

My lip curls. Is that what she attempted to do? This alien is no less foolish than her children and assorted other creations. "All you have done is confirm that there is still work in the world for me." A single blade springs into my hand, long and slender. "There are other Uriels, and other girls sitting at the right hands of monsters."

"Yes." Cybele wilts, the green of her eyes diffusing. "It is a sad truth."

"I am unlike the other girls. That might be a cliche, but it is also a truth. I will not find wholeness and healing inside a group. The Father raised me in darkness, as you have reminded me. When Goddess changed me, she could only take me into shadows, not into light. It is where I must stay."

Cybele sighs. "You read too much into randomness. Your genes were twisted at her hand, but with the spinning of a wheel, not an elegant crafting."

"She *saved* me." My voice is cloaked in shadow. "Nothing about that was *chance*. I sensed her. She was the sun at the centre of my universe, and I was the shadow she cast. The gift she gave me was to be a weapon for my own hand."

"Too many dreams of destiny." Cybele reaches one hand towards me, but doesn't touch my skin. The tendrils that wrap her hand dance near me, as if tasting the energy that wafts from my skin. "It seems you cannot escape all of your past, no matter how much you try."

"This place is not for me." I'm almost sad, like it *could* have been, if not for so many things, starting far too long ago, when my parents laid a girl down in a cradle in the darkness. "I will take my chances back in the world. It is better that way, to live and die on my own terms."

"And if you die?"

"What loss will that be?" I smile at her, and I watch the green tide rise in her eyes. "Weapons break, weapons fail. Until then, I will bring as many monsters down as I can. One final, glorious stand."

"They told me you were stubborn." Cybele smiles, and it's the first time she's looked remotely human. Then she turns, and drifts off among the trees. "I am sorry I failed you here. And please be careful, Leftie. I would like to meet you again, you know."

Then she is gone, and I'm standing in the forest alone. Light filters down through the leaves, and the trees overhead all seem to sigh in unison.

16

AIDY

The whole way back to the dormitory, I'm torn between frantic fretting over Rayner and hoping the forest eats Leftie, or at least takes her down a peg or two. If that's even possible. I'm so thoroughly distracted that I walk right past Skip and Mélodie without even registering them.

"Rude." Skip yanks on my arm from behind. "Where have you been?"

I spin and stare. "Oh my gosh, I'm so sorry."

"I've been worried!" She shakes me slightly, but it's affectionate.

"We," Mélodie signs.

"Fine, yes. *We* have been worried. You were gone when I woke up, haven't been here all day. So we eventually showed up at the school to find you, and there was a relieving teacher there! They were very mysterious about you."

"I was on a mission," I admit. "Top secret. With, um, Chatterbox?"

Skip gapes at me, and it's kinda cute. "What has happened to you, Aidy Dwyer? Everything's so different, I'm not even sure I recognise you anymore."

For a horrible moment, I think she'll see right through my facade to the old version of me. That her next words will be the name Rayner used. Which is a dead name of a sort, but not in the way people usually refer to it. I left my old self buried for multiple reasons, and they need to stay there. "I'm still the same me," I insist. "It's all to do with this Leftie nonsense."

Mélodie gives a dramatic sigh and bats her eyes.

"I get that she's pretty," I say emphatically. "But it seems like a very bad idea."

"Fun idea," she signs back promptly.

"Things can be both." Skip links her arm through mine. "So how much can you tell us about your top secret adventure?"

"I got set on fire and shot." The words spill out of me, tugged by Skip's warmth, and her very gratifying and focused attention. "It was totally terrifying."

"You were the shield wall." Skip punches me in the shoulder, and I obviously don't perceive her as a threat, because I feel the impact. "Aidy, you're a *superhero*."

"Hardly." I have a flush of warmth at her tone, which dissolves rapidly away at the memory of the dead man at my feet, like I've been taken from sunbathing on the beach and plunged into icy water. "My powers are more an accident than anything. It's not bravery or anything, almost the opposite. I'm so scared and my body reacts to protect me."

"And modest too." Skip bats her eyelashes at me. "My actual hero."

Mélodie signs rapidly.

"We're both very impressed," Skip says. "Anyone else would be bragging, but not you."

For a moment, I actually allow myself to look at this new version of Aidy reflected in their eyes. Someone brave. *Heroic.* Who does what's necessary and is confident enough to bask in a job well done rather than seeing affirmation. It's a beautiful picture, and I'd long to step into that role, but it's too far outside reality. The truth is I was terrified and almost fell apart—not to mention that since then I've tied someone up in an abandoned shack in the forest. I'm wildly the opposite of a superhero, although I did what was necessary. People like Chatterbox and Leftie use that as an excuse all the time for terrible things. Maybe I'm not so far from them after all.

"It was one mission." My cheeks are pink like the rising dawn. "And I don't think I did a great job. I probably failed. They won't ask me to do anything else." Which isn't even true, because I heard Chatterbox and Feral talking about a new team, one with me and Leftie and Skip, but that sounds so ridiculous given the current situation, I may as well tell them a fantasy in which Leftie is the kindest, sweetest girl around.

So instead, I parcel out pieces of information about the mission as we eat at one of the outdoor tables, watching as the sky shades to a deep and saturated blue, the stars punching tiny holes in its velvet surface. Like me and my new life here, one burning fragment after another until the whole thing collapses in fire.

"I'm shattered," I admit, when the meal is finally done. I've managed to withhold the one biggest piece of news yet again. That the ghost from Leftie's past has returned, leaving both of us haunted. I could have told her in the forest and almost did. It would guarantee an island free of her, especially since I've got problems of my own. But I'd be sending her off to die and that echoes loudly enough to make me wince.

"You should sleep," Skip says. "Mél and I are going to a 'meet the newbies' night, but it'll be a lot of chatter, and I know that's not your favourite thing."

"No." I want to curl in on myself, a fern under the night sky. "All I need is sleep."

Except alone in the dorm room at eight in the evening, my mind keeps returning to Rayner up there at the mouth of the forest. In a hut that could be used for any number of reasons. Maybe it's Chatterbox's personal night-time retreat spot, or it's actually part of Cybele and I've fed Rayner to an alien goddess.

The island is far too busy in the evening for me to head up there, so I lie awake and stare at the ceiling for hours until I hear Skip fumbling at the door. I roll so my back is towards her, and focus on making my breathing soft and slow.

"Aidy!" Her whisper could barely be called one, but I ignore it anyway. She tries again a handful of times before collapsing down onto the bed with a dramatic and even louder sigh. Thankfully, it's only a few more minutes before her breathing melts into sleep, and hers is genuine.

I don't waste any time heading for the door. The corridors of the dormitory are mostly deserted. A couple is making out in a doorway, but both are far too preoccupied to notice me hustling past them.

The night outside is wild and wind-tossed, clouds draping the three-quarter moon in rags. Every tree is lost in the dance, and there are so many, many trees on Mutopia. The shadows jump too, and I am only one small fragment amongst it all, scurrying from tree to tree and doing my best to merge with the night. Nobody sees me—or if they do, I don't register them.

Any calls are whipped away from me and I reach the clifftop path to find it deserted.

I navigate by moonlight, the path picked out like a silver thread amongst all the rolling green. The forest beside me is a rustling wall of darkness, impossible to make out any individual trees in the whole. The rundown shacks are hidden so well I almost run past them. It's only that an errant shaft of moonlight glances down with a pale eye at one mossy wall.

There's no sound coming from the hut where I left Rayner. If she's dead, I don't know what I'll do. Flee the island without stopping to pack, probably. I won't have many options. My heart thumps wildly in my chest as I press my eye to a crack in the door. Something flutters inside, a moth the size of a person, iridescent wings marked with a swirling pattern of dots and loops.

Rayner, recovered from her bump on the head, but as skittish as I remember. Each time the clouds dart away from the moon, the pale light that filters in through the tiny cracks in the wooden walls send her into a fluttering frenzy, desperately thrashing towards the glow. I can't go in when she's like this, or she'll escape. I'll need to wait for her to transform back to a human before going back in with supplies. And hopefully come up with a way of explaining the situation. She lived through the Dark Year the same as I did, so hopefully she can understand the logic of a deal.

For now, there's nothing to be done but leave her.

I make my way back towards the town, my brain churning over possible opening sentences for a very difficult conversation. It's interrupted by a horrible moment of deja vu when I stumble across a pale figure. She's standing on the edge of the cliff, looking out over the sea. How is the Left Hand of Darkness always in my way?

"It's an odd habit you have of creeping around in the dark." She bats her eyelashes at me in a parody of flirtation. "Are you trying to copy me, lurking in the shadows?"

"What are you doing?" I ask her.

"Picking my moment. Making my escape." She stares into the distance. "Won't you be glad to be rid of me?"

"Of course not." I don't think either of us believes me. "People will come after you."

"They'll have to find me." Leftie scowls. "I'll make it hard for them. That Penance can find me in shadow, but who's to say that's where I'll be?"

"What if the humans kill you?"

She laughs, but it sounds more like a war cry. "Plenty of people have tried. Goodbye, little Aidy. Enjoy your peaceful life without me."

Without a further word, she steps off the cliff and dissolves into the night. As if she was never there. Like she was a dream, a night spectre that appeared in the depths of my slumber. Which is the story I'll tell anyone if they ask about this.

It takes almost no time at all for things to fall apart.

Although it's not the Rayner situation, like I feared. I wake to a sharp pressure against my foot. When I sit upright, wide-eyed and frantic, I find two small figures perched on the end of the bed. They might be aliens, but their mutant genetic lineage is still clear. Gleeful, gnomish versions of Chatterbox and Marvellous. Neither of them look pleased to see me. They creak when they move, like trees in the wind, and their eyes are very bright green.

Standing at the end of the bed, arms folded and equally disapproving, is Alyse Sefo.

"They're awake," one of the children says. "Now we're allowed to talk with them, right?"

"Yes." Alyse sounds faintly amused.

"Hello, I'm Willow." One leans over and extends a vine-covered hand. "And this is Soo-yeon."

The other arches an eyebrow and tilts their nose up. "We have a problem."

"I'm sorry to hear that!" I widen my eyes and smile like I do with the children at the school. "What can I help you with?"

Willow narrows their eyes. "You can stop talking to us like we're babies for a start. We're horrible alien monsters. That's what Leftie says, and we like her."

"Oh." Leftie's nighttime exit *and* the Rayner situation crash through my brain at the exact same time. It's like falling through multiple trap doors at once. "Leftie. I'm not sure what happened to her."

"Farsight saw you." Soo-yeon leans forward, one small finger extended. "You were on the cliffs with her last night, talking. And then poof—" She claps her hands together in front of my face, making me squeak embarrassingly. "She was gone."

Oh God. I'm scrambling. Did this Farsight see anything about Rayner, or was she more focused on Leftie? "When I say I'm not sure what happened, I mean I don't know where she went. She didn't really say. And I didn't know how to stop her. She's, you know, she's..."

"Interesting." Willow scowls. "Aunty Lys, how are we going to find her? Bonus Mum says she's not in the shadows. Then Mum and Pear both said we're not allowed off island, even though we asked them separately and told them the other one said yes."

"Bonus Mum is Penance," Alyse explains to me. "And, as you can see, we're a little worried about the Leftie situation. Aidy, can you tell us everything she said on the cliffside before she went away?"

I explain as much as I can remember. There's no point in lying, because there's not much to say. She wanted to leave, and I couldn't stop her.

"You didn't tell her, right?" Alyse's voice is hollow.

"About?" I gulp. "About the, uh, person in her past? No, of course not."

Alyse pats both children on the head. "We'll have to do some old-fashioned detective work, kiddos." She transfers her attention back to me. "Someone else has gone missing too, which is doubly odd. A girl who can transform into a moth. Arrived on the island yesterday and never checked in at her dorm. Nobody's seen her anywhere on the island. Can't see how these two things are possibly related, but did you see anything strange last night?"

I shake my head, the picture of confusion. Which I am—confused, I mean—because how am I getting away with this? Farsight didn't see what I was up to and Cybele hasn't sensed Rayner's presence in the hut. Not a single person on the island is aware that I basically mugged and kidnapped a mutant. Which I feel terrible about, but I didn't have a choice in the matter. Now everything *should* be spiralling wildly out of control except it's not. It's like my powers of protection extend further than I could have imagined. The unnerving question is how long this is going to last—and what I'll have to do to keep it going. All I can do right now is keep smiling and be this new Aidy.

"Come on." I slide my legs out of bed. "Let me get dressed, and I'll help try and figure out where Leftie could possibly have gone."

The twins exchange glances that I don't understand before Willow shrugs.

"Okay, fine. We're still mad at you for letting her go, but if you help enough then we'll forgive you. And you don't want to be on our bad side, do you, Aunty Lys?"

"No, you little menaces," she says, but her tone is unmistakably fond, and she hoists them up into her arms to snuggle into her. I cannot read this situation at all. All I know is that I'm in trouble, but I have to keep these plates spinning.

There are so many ways this could go wrong.

17

LEFTIE

I spend as little time in the shadows as possible. Penance can track me there, and I've got no idea how long I've got before the annoying Aidy raises the alarm. My destination is inspired by my unpleasant conversation with Cybele. If someone's insisting on digging up the mess I buried with Uriel, there's a location I really don't want them visiting.

It's the only situation I remotely care about, and that's only because I made the astonishingly terrible mistake of making them my problem. When I cut my way out of the Children of the Broken World, I took the actual children with me. And if anyone has messed with them, there's no power on earth or Mutopia that can hold me back from my revenge.

I realise that taking my wanted self into the children's orbit is a risk on its own, but I'll give the humans a chance to catch me first before I stumble onto their shore. When I burned the compound, I took all the money with me. And like a lot of cult assholes, that smug fuck Uriel had a lot of cash. Enough that I could literally buy a fucking island and set everyone up on it with all the shit they need. I don't tell anyone this part of the story, because then it gets gross takes like a monster with a heart of gold. And fuck that—I know what those kids went through, and this is the least of what they deserve. So they're parked up on one of the smallest Greek Islands, protected by people I pay very well with more of Uriel's money. Plus whatever cash I make from being paid to kill people I'd kill for free anyway.

I cool my heels on Mykonos first, waiting for the inevitable attack. It's already taking a worryingly long time, given how bold they've been to strike at Mutopia, plus how quick they were to shoot at me when I was with Willow and Soo-yeon. Maybe they've learned from their mistakes. That's not a fun thing to think about, especially when they can already nerf my powers and make me fight old-school. At least it'll be a workout.

So I stroll through the open-air markets and buy baklava in a little cardboard tray. I eat it on the rocks overlooking the ocean, such a dazzling blue it's like it wants me to stop and marvel at the fact it just came up with the colour on its own. A stray cat or five turn up to lick my fingers clean and it's while I'm letting one butt its head against the heel of my hand that I get that oh-shit feeling, that faint displacement of the air. I throw myself backwards and reach for shadows at the same time. There are some pooled at the base of the rocks, but they're thin and watery in my hands. It's enough to craft a shard that splits the bullet down the middle, a single, impossibly thin blade skewering it from the air. Having some paltry amount of my mutant power means the device they're using must have a range. And likely an operator as well. Time to find out who it is.

The island is bustling with people, which is another reason I chose it. It's easy to slice through the crowd, ditching my jacket, scooping a cap from a cute mother of two squalling kids and tucking my hair up underneath it. Lifting sunglasses from the back pocket of some dudebro loudly explaining to his friends shit about currency arbitrage. Wiping my lipstick off on the sleeve of my jacket. Finally, I step into the middle of a group of college-age British girls drinking premix margaritas from cans.

"Hello, darling." I throw my arms around one of them, the one whose eyes *lingered* most as I approached. "I can't *believe* I run into you here of all places."

She's completely taken aback, but she doesn't pull away. She's a few drinks in, warm from the sun, looking into dazzling blue eyes gazing at her like they've soaked up all the colour from the ocean. I'm best at bringing death to those who deserve it, but I'm not half bad at this too.

"It's me. Olivia. Olivia *Whistler*." I place my hand against my chest so my t-shirt pulls tight. "Please tell me you didn't forget me. How will my ego suffer the blow?"

She doesn't register that I haven't used *her* name, too bewitched and bewildered.

"Of course, babe. Oh my god. I would never." She enfolds me in a hug. Her lips hit the corner of my mouth, and she smells of too-sweet alcohol and sunscreen.

I put my arms around her waist and lift her into the air, spinning her around as if I'm so delighted to finally find this girl who time and circumstance had stolen from me. It lets me scan the crowd, a full three-sixty degrees and more. The girl throws her head back and laughs, her hands on my biceps, feeling the strength of them. She's lost in the moment, unguarded and beautiful, but all I have eyes for are my targets, because I've spotted them.

And fuck me, these people are amateurs. First off, they're not remotely dressed to blend in. Who wears combat gear on Mykonos? Plus they're standing in a small cluster, arguing frantically and gesturing. Pros would do it while sunbathing with their guts out and reading trashy paperbacks. Learn some fucking tradecraft, assholes. Which makes them military and not spies. Whether they're dangling from the chain of an official country who's looking to swat me like a bug, or are in the pay of some corporation doesn't entirely matter. Eventually, I'll cut the head off the snake, but right now I'm only buying time.

I cease my spinning and let the girl's feet land on the ground again. She's flushed with delight. I kiss her, my bottom lip dragging over hers, my tongue darting into her mouth like the sun flashing on the ocean. A tease, a promise. Enough to make her cling to me, her hand wrapped possessively around my arm. I wonder what story she's telling herself about me and this moment she can't remember.

"We need to celebrate." I press my mouth close to her hair, so my lips brush light against her skin. "Find a bar. Do some *shots*, babe. Just like last time. And hope the night ends the same way."

"Yes." She squeezes my hand and spins to face the group. "Shots!"

They all chorus along with her, because these are drunk British girls on holiday, and some things are practically laws of nature. They surge through the crowd, shouting and laughing, and the frothing mass of them carries me past the arguing military without them any the wiser.

Once we've looped around behind them, I press an impulsive kiss to the girl's cheek.

"I'll be back," I tell her urgently. "Left my bag on the beach. Wait for me!"

She clasps her hands to her chest as she watches me disappear. I've already forgotten her, purpose served, because now I'm where I need to be, approaching the soldiers from behind. One woman holds a long umbrella-like device, turning it in a slow arc. Trying to pick up my signal in the direction of where I was, way back when they first shot at me.

I'm almost insulted. She has such a low opinion of my capabilities.

I break upon her like a wave, lifting the knife from her waist in one smooth movement and plunging it into her chest. The second blow strikes at the hollow of her throat, but she's as forgotten as the cute girl in the crowd, because for all intents and purposes this soldier is a corpse. I lift the device from her hands, shattering it across my knee. The handle of it hooks into another soldier's throat, a blow that doesn't break the skin but crushes his Adam's apple. He's dead too, or seconds from it. At this point, everything is simple mechanics. Angles, direction of force, and points of impact. The third man I kill is clutching a device to his chest, as precious as an infant. It emits something noxious and suffocating, an infecting cloud that spills into shadows and poisons them, turning darkness weak and ineffectual. Here is the magical tool by which they render me powerless. It breaks easily beneath the heel of my shiny black boot. I make sure to collect the fragments, as one of the Mutopia scientists may be able to reassemble some logical sense from it. If I ever deign to return.

Now the shadows are back, but I only seek them for breaths at a time. I'm not sure whether this will trigger some proximity alarm for Penance, but I cannot imagine she is aware of all shadows at all times. It cannot be helped either way, since there are two further teams on this beautiful island, and I must end all their lives, stalks of wheat falling before the blade of my scythe.

My first kills are less than a minute old, but their effects are spreading amongst the crowd like drops of blood falling into a pool of crystal clear water. People scream. They run in different directions. *There was a girl here a moment ago. She stabbed a woman. She cut the throat of a man. I didn't see where she went. Look, look, the body. It's there. Oh god, there's so much blood.*

The police are summoned. They're wildly unequipped to handle this, mostly dealing with light robbery and sexual assault. Multiple bodies brutally murdered leave them clutching their heads and calling further up the chain. They try to restore order, but by this point it's a lost cause. Thousands of people have flocked here for their beautiful holiday, and now they're face to face with a gruesome reality that rarely intrudes on their lives. For most of them, that means fleeing to their hotels or somewhere else far distant.

I catch the ferry borne on another tide of people. There is screaming and crying, people clutching their phones to record something for instant internet notoriety or to make frantic calls for help. Nobody understands what's going on. They pass their fears among themselves, whispered urgently and screamed over people's heads. I lean against the railing and tilt my head back to catch the sun.

"The horror is over," I murmur to nobody. "You can return to your mundane lives."

When we reach the deep water, I dive over the side of the boat. I don't think anyone will register my departure. They are too consumed with their own fears, arranging their near-death experiences neatly to be shared and re-shared. I kick methodically down to the depths, where there is a realm of shadow through which I can pass like a figment. Penance's eye will hopefully not seek me in this darkest of places.

Even still, I am only here for minutes. I peel myself from the shadows cast by the towering pines on an island shore and splash through the shallows. The beach I've landed on is a crescent of sand below low cliffs, a small path winding upwards. I wring the water from my hair and watch a figure descend towards me. At least they're paying attention. The air's warm enough that my shirt's already drying, but my pants will remain uncomfortable for a while yet.

The guard finally reaches the beach. By this stage, she's seen it's me and her weapon swings loose at her back. I've tested her before, tested them all. If I was a threat, I'd already be dead. Martinez is a tall woman, over six feet, and it's not all for show either. I rescued her from an anti-mutant hit squad where she was beaten and tortured for refusing to follow orders.

Loyalty isn't something I put a lot of stock in given everything I've seen, but she's never given me a reason to doubt hers.

"Surprised to see you, boss."

"Don't call me boss." I frown up at the cliffs. "Am I the first unexpected arrival you've had recently?"

"Everything's been quiet. Got some chatter on the radio about an incident on Mykonos but don't know what that is yet."

I give her an extremely unimpressed look until she laughs.

"Roger that. I'll let the others know it was you. Is this a friendly visit, or should we be making plans?"

"Not sure yet. You'll know when I do. They all good?"

"Same as ever. They'll be happy to see you. I'll warn everyone else to keep on high alert in case we have company. Shit looked pretty bad on the news, boss. End of the line shit. News is that Chatterbox themself rescued you."

"Rescued." I curl my lip. "Whatever. High alert is right. Stay that way until you hear otherwise." I head up the path at a jog, leaving the guard to stare out at the ocean and wait for incoming disaster. There are another two armed guards at the top of the path, and I head past them with nothing more than a nod. I'm not here to fucking socialise. The idea that one of the kids is somehow involved with this cult situation sits in my chest like I've swallowed something poisonous. It means I made a mistake with my mercy—even worse, it means that some of Uriel's poison can't be escaped.

The path that winds between the trees has cameras and hidden weaponry able to be fired by remote. There's a bunker below the compound with more guards who watch on shifts. I hear the very faint whirr of the cameras moving. Surveillance is in place as it should be.

The path ends at two large wooden gates which swing inwards on my arrival. They open onto a courtyard in the middle of a large house, made of stone that's been painted white and blue. From the air, it looks like some rich person's hideaway nestled among the trees. Right now, it appears entirely deserted although I see the faint impression of damp footprints on the stone tiles. Children playing who've scattered on a signal. Everyone is doing what they've been trained to do over hundreds of drills.

It's Rose who sees me first. Not even feet tall, mop of fuzzy brown hair. She screams in delight and tells the others to come running.

"Oh for fuck's sake." I scowl down at her as she runs directly into me, wrapping her arms around my waist. "Do you ever listen to anything I tell you? This is not how you react to uninvited guests. What if I was an evil clone of myself or someone wearing a disguise?"

"Of course it's you." She tilts her head back to look up at me. "You're the only person who scowls at us like that."

And then there are more children, spilling from every doorway in the house, and they're all shouting and laughing and calling my name.

<h1 style="text-align:center">18</h1>

AIDY

The missing Leftie is honestly the least of my problems, but I can't tell anyone that. I promise the uncanny twins that I'll help after breakfast, which is also my chance to collect some extra food to take to Rayner. Except Skip and Mélodie are both there, waving at me frantically, so I end up sitting down with them, the pockets of my coat laden down with extra food.

"You're running in elevated circles these days." Skip shakes her head. "I would never have guessed that *my* Aidy would wake up the twins perched on their bed. Here's me trying desperately to pretend to sleep, hoping to not attract any attention."

"More Leftie drama." I try to act like it's nothing. "She left in the middle of the night. I only got involved completely randomly. I couldn't sleep, so I went for a walk when I woke up. Bumped into her way up on the cliffs and then she just... bailed. It's not like I could possibly stop her."

"Did you try?" Mélodie signs.

"Sort of, I guess." I look down at my empty plate. "I mean, it feels like it's not really my place? It wasn't really a discussion anyway. She'd made up her mind."

Mélodie sighs and puts her chin in her hands, staring out the window as if Leftie will rematerialise there and blow her a kiss.

"Someone else went missing too," I say. "One of the new arrivals is gone. Maybe Leftie ran away with her." It feels like another bold move, but throwing a rumour might help to draw attention away from anything to do with me.

"She could have run away with me," Mélodie pouts.

"I don't think leaving with Leftie right now would be a good idea for anyone." Skip stabs a fork into her bowl of neatly cut fruit. "They're trying to kill her. Governments, cults, all kinds of people. That's why people are so worried, Aidy. She's in real danger."

"I understand." I try to sound like the voice of reason. "But she's a lone wolf, you know? This is what she's been doing. All through the Dark Year and still now, even when there are other options available to mutants. Like, at some point this is her choice. We can't force her to live a tame little life on Mutopia." Oh shit, now I've gone too far. "I mean, obviously I want her to be safe! But some people aren't built for island life."

"Maybe." Skip sighs. "And it's not like we really know her. But when people kill the mutants who stand up for us it feels worse somehow. They take extra pleasure in it, like murdering Leftie stands for their desire to get rid of us all."

"The world's changing," I say weakly.

"Is it?" Skip grimaces. "You lived through the Dark Year, Aidy. That doesn't go away completely because we have an island now."

"In the refugee pods." It's only partly a lie. "But I know what you mean. And I'm *going* to help find Leftie and maybe this moth-girl too, if they left together."

"You have to tell us all about the twins," Mélodie says. "They're so fascinating."

They're more scary than fascinating to me, but I nod and promise that I'll give them every piece of gossip they long for, as soon as I get a chance. Then I scurry away from the breakfast table before I attract any more attention. I've got to deal with the Rayner situation before meeting with Alyse again.

In daylight there are more people on the island, but all I get are cheerful greetings and waves from passers-by. Most are in pairs or groups, and are more preoccupied with their friends than a lone mutant striding past them.

When I reach the abandoned huts, I spend a few minutes lurking and watching. Once I'm sure there's nobody around, I duck under the cover of the trees. Through the crack in the door I see Rayner curled on the ground—maybe sleeping, or at least barely moving. She's returned to human form so I carefully unbar the door and slip inside.

Some creak of wood or shuffle of my footsteps startles her awake. Rayner struggles to her feet and throws herself at me, hands battering uselessly against my skin, as insubstantial as moth wings. She even transforms briefly, darting around the room and fluttering around my head as if I'll flinch away and offer her an avenue of escape.

Finally, she turns back to human form, hunched against the far wall. Her gaze darts to me and away and back again, as if I'm a light she reviles but is drawn to all the same. "You can't get away with this."

"I brought you some food." I pull it out of my coat, wrapped in paper, and toss it to the ground in front of her. "I'll try to come twice a day, but that won't always be possible, so ration it out."

She shakes her head, but creeps forward to pick up the food all the same. "Finally getting to Mutopia seemed like a dream come true after everything I went through. And when I saw you, I couldn't believe it. How you could show your face after what you did."

"I did nothing." My voice is hammered flat, this repetition I told myself over and over during my time in the pods, when I began to sketch out the vision for the Aidy I became.

"Doing nothing was the problem." Rayner says. "You can pretend all you want, but I remember exactly what happened. There are only two of us left now, do you know that? So if you kill me, there will only be one person left who knows what you really are."

"Shut up." I wish I hadn't come here. "I'm not going to kill you."

"You have to do *something*." When she sneers, something flutters inside her mouth. "You can't keep me hidden here forever. Once I get out, I'm going straight to the people in charge."

"Maybe I will kill you," I blurt. "Unless you're smart enough to make a deal." After all, Leftie kills people as easily as breathing and so does Feral. I've stumbled into death before, wide eyed and unaware. Will it feel better to do it with care and attention?

Rayner's lips tremble and she returns to moth form, spiralling up to the ceiling and dancing among the motes of light that drizzle down through the slim cracks. Her wings shimmer, sunlight limning the edges like a lover's touch. Is this an invitation? She's so fragile in this form. I could crush the feathery softness of her wings against the rough wood and wipe the grit off on my trousers. There would be no blood, no real evidence. It might not even feel like murder. No need to gasp and collapse, forced to stare at the reality of death.

Even still, I can't bring myself to do it. This girl holds my future in her hands, even more fragile than her wings. She could crush it. She *will* crush it. And yet I'm still too weak to take action. I have to find a way to get her off the island without killing her. Perhaps I can use her moth form, lure her with a light in the darkness and find some place it's impossible to escape from. Lure her into some forgotten jail or isolated island cave. That's an even crueller death I suppose. It reminds me of when I was a child, and we used so-called humane traps for mice. Except we forgot to check them and the poor creatures starved to death. There is no good outcome here. I'm caught between the promise of Rayner's fanged confession, and the need to silence her permanently.

"We *can* make a deal," I insist to the fluttering moth. "There must be something you want. I know people on the island. They can get you a great location for your house, the exact job you want. There's no reason we can't both get what we need here."

Rayner turns back into human form. Her eyes are dark and soft. "What I want is for you to pay for what you did. It's all I needed from the beginning. I loved him. Did you know that?"

I shake my head. "Rayner, I didn't... None of it was meant to happen."

Her chest rises and falls, her eyelids flutter as she composes herself. "Of course it wasn't. The whole Dark Year shouldn't have happened. Michael and his angels. All of that. I understand it was a nightmare. We were all there. But *you*. What you did was different. You chose yourself. And you'll pay for that."

This is all too much. Too many bad possibilities, all reaching for me on the wings of this fluttering girl. If I'm sent away from the island, there's nowhere else in the world for me. I can't go *home*, and life out in the human world isn't known for being kind towards mutants. It's the whole reason this island exists in the first place.

All of this is Rayner's fault. If she'd accept reason, or wasn't so hung up on one mistake I made back in the past, we could make a real, practical decision and move forward in a way that would work for the two of us.

"We're both mutants," I tell her. "This island can help us both."

Her fist clenches at her side. "Rufus was a mutant too, and look what happened to him."

I lunge towards her, and she spins away to begin her transformation but I crack one heavy steel hand on the back of her neck again.

She collapses as easily as she did the first time.

"I'm sorry, Rayner." I nudge the food closer to her. "We'll figure something out, I promise."

Except as I leave the hut and barricade the door closed again, I'm well aware that this might be one of those unsolvable knots. The kind you have to cut with a sword. And if I'm not willing to use an actual weapon, I need to figure out another equally drastic approach.

Perhaps I could approach Alyse first. Tell a story very close to the truth but pinning the blame on Rayner. Then I'll deny Rayner's story, no matter what she says. I can claim that I locked her up because I was scared she'd kill me for knowing her secret. It's a terrible thing to do on so many levels, and shows the unmistakable cracks in the foundations of my Aidy persona. How can I build something new when the bones of me are my past selves?

The true Aidy thing to do would be to admit everything. To confess the shadows in my past and throw myself on the mercy of people like Alyse Sefo. The Left Hand of Darkness has done so much worse, and they welcome her poison flower into their garden. Except the problem is that Leftie's crimes are of boldness, in defence of the mutant species. Mine are of cowardice and deceit. I hardly think Chatterbox and the others will be so tolerant of those.

And that leads me back around to the beginning of my plodding circle of helpless thoughts. The loop preoccupies me all the way back to town when I bump into Alyse outside my dorms.

"Ah, there you are." She pats my arm. "Aren't you looking miserable? Is it because you're worried about Leftie? I wondered if the two of you would find your odd-couple connection in the end."

I've barely given a thought to Leftie, who's perfectly capable of looking after herself on the evidence I've seen. But again, I can't say *that* to Alyse.

"Who knows what trouble she's got herself into." I sigh, although all the misery Alyse sees is on my own behalf.

"We're planning an off-island trip to find her." Alyse looks into the distance, as if she'll be able to spot that disastrous girl. "I assume you'll want to come."

It's all I can do not to sink to my knees and wail. Of course I don't want to come. I've got a prisoner to look after! The longer I leave her, the more likely she'll figure a way to escape. Or she'll shriek and someone will hear her. Or the alien spirit in the middle of the island will finally notice the small moth in the ointment. There are a thousand reasons to stay and solve this and zero reasons to leave.

On the other hand, I can do something good here— make a decision in the name of the new Aidy rather than the shadow of the old me. It's also practical, in that it'll amass some goodwill with Alyse, Chatterbox, and those ridiculous twins. It gives a chance that they might not abandon me when the situation blows up in my face. When I get back, I'll figure out a solution one way or another.

"Of course." I smile at her, some approximation of delight. "Count me in as the shield."

19

LEFTIE

There are a lot of damn kids in this little fortress of mine. I remember all their names, but we play a game where I forget half of them. They stare into my eyes trying to psychically communicate it to me until I pretend to remember with a great flash of inspiration. It's a complete waste of time but they find it hilarious. This hidden place is my own penance of a sort. It's exactly not that I owe all these children a debt. On the contrary, some might consider the obligation to be in the opposite direction. If I had not ended Uriel and his parade of sycophants, their future would have been bleak. He cared little for anyone save himself and his God. I was considered his most precious gift, but in reality I was nothing more than a tool to force the world to break before his will. These children of his acolytes were his next generation of fools and tools.

It was me who bought them a future, although it cost the bodies and blood of their parents.

And now here they are, alone in the world aside from each other and the guards I pay to keep them safe. It is not the life I would imagine for them. I think about Willow and Soo-yeon, and the way they spoke of their sprawling family. Even though most of their aunts are deadly and many are wanted by intelligence services around the world, they are surrounded by love. These children I rescued live on an island too, but it is little more than a prison for their own protection, watched over by guards. This place is no miracle, no Mutopia, only a green rock in a beautiful blue sea.

"Someone tried to kill you," Rowan says, very seriously. She's sitting cross-legged in front of me, looking up through the blonde fringe hanging in her eyes. One of the guards is supposed to cut all the kids' hair, but they run wild most of the time.

"People always try." I shrug. "They didn't succeed."

"Father Uriel tried to kill you," Javi says from the back of the group. He's fidgeting with his hands, too shy to look at me. "But you killed him."

"He was a very bad man," Leilani says. She's one of the older girls who can remember a little bit more. "He used to hurt my Mom all the time. She'd come home crying, hiding in the bathroom and trying to keep it quiet, because my birth father would do things to her if she disrespected Father Uriel."

Fuck. I wish I'd killed all these assholes earlier.

"Has anyone come to the island? Anyone new?" I ask, looking around the faces of all the kids. If someone's co-opted the guards—or even some of the children—they won't all be able to lie to me. There are various expressions of confusion and worry, because they all know that it's very bad if someone shows up here, but everyone shakes their head. They understand that secrecy and safety are the most important things in their lives. In the beginning, it was more from the media than anyone else. The thought of those predatory fucks descending on these kids and carving them up into chunks digestible for mass consumption made me want to stab every journalist on the planet, and I already had a long enough hit list.

It's soon confirmed there's nobody on the island. This is a relief but also a concern, because it leaves me no closer to finding the people who can tamper with my powers. And that's a problem almost as deadly as I am.

"And nobody's left for any reason?"

Everyone shakes their heads again. They're even more worried now because they know the number one rule. Stay on the island. If you need something, ask a guard. But stay on the fucking island or Leftie will come down with her sharp little teeth and ask you why. In the nicest fucking possible way.

"Why are you asking all this?" Leilani asks.

I don't know how much of the truth to parcel out to them. I never have. Even from the beginning, when I came to the nursery as a revenant figure painted in gore. A trail of bloody footprints was smeared behind me, left leg limping slightly from where a guard slashed my calf open. If anyone had followed that trail it would lead to the quarters where their parents lived. Slashed lines of throats, gaping like mouths singing silent hymns to the god who abandoned them. Tangles of gory bedsheets, eyes staring at the ceiling. So many called for Uriel, but he didn't intervene to save them. Of course he couldn't. He was only a man with no power beyond his words.

"Somebody knows secrets," I tell them. "Things that should never have been told."

"We would never do that." Leilani is furious, fists clenched and eyes wild.

"Never," Jace adds. He's one of the older ones too. They have the most rage, because they remember enough of the past for it to seep into their minds. The little ones mostly know the island, which is a blessing, I think.

The chorus of confirmation spills through the whole group. Nobody's gone anywhere or said anything. Leaving me with no leads or clues.

Novikov and Martinez are the two guards at the entrance to the compound. They're both shooting me disgruntled looks like they're a little bit pissy about this line of questioning. I tell the kids that we're going to the beach and they all go racing off to change. It gives me a chance to talk to the guards properly.

"I'm not questioning your fucking diligence or loyalty or anything." I scowl at them. "I've been incommunicado. Haven't checked the dead drops on account of... complicated life shit."

They exchange glances. Novikov's mouth twitches. She's just under six foot, built like a tank, buzzed blonde hair. "Complicated like being on trial for murder, busted out by Chatterbox, and then vanishing? Presumably you've been sunning yourself in that mutant vacation hotspot."

I see-saw my hand. "That's one way to frame it. The scary part is that people came for me on that hotspot, which is very, very well protected. People wanting to dig shit up from my past, preferably post-mortem. So me being naturally suspicious, I wonder where they got their information from."

Martinez nods. "Like maybe they're getting it through one of the kids. Maybe one who's got fond memories of Daddy Uriel? Or one who doesn't know the information they're giving away?"

I glance around the compound, excited shouts drifting from open windows. "Call me a sentimental bitch, but I was hoping for the latter."

Novikov grunts. "If anyone hurt these children, I would hunt them down and tear them apart. And I would do it for free and refuse any money you tried to give me."

"Novi's sentimental too." Martinez laughs. "But I'd be right beside her. Nobody's been on the island, Left Hand. I swear it. Unless there's spooky mutant shit going on, but we're pretty locked down and none of the kids have exhibited any suspicious behaviour."

"So we're good." I crack my knuckles. "Means I'll have to look elsewhere, but I'm glad it's not one of the kids. Don't know how I'd deal with that."

"How long are you here for?" Novikov asks.

"Flying visit. These assholes are tracking me. I think I set them back a little, but it's a risk even staying this long."

"Don't go." Rose has returned in her bathing costume and throws her arms around me again. "You only just got here."

I crouch down in front of her. "It's not safe for me to stay. Bad people want to find me and I don't want them to follow me here."

"We grew up with bad people but you saved us."

"That's true." I want to take the girl in my arms but she needs love from something better than a monster. As precious as this place is, nothing here proves I'm anything more than a weapon. My mind drifts back to the twins again and their attempts to bring me into the fold. What I have here isn't family.

It's a responsibility and an obligation. If I'm fooled into regarding it as something I want or deserve, it becomes a weakness. And I can't afford weaknesses. Weapons with flaws always shatter at the worst possible time.

"Okay," I find myself saying, despite all the things I know. "I'll stay for a little longer."

The whole group of us follows the path back down to the beach I arrived from. I'm surrounded by children laughing and talking. They ask about a thousand questions, mostly about Mutopia. Most of them I can't answer, but I try my best or make up some shit. I'm acting all smiley and bubbly, being a version of myself I almost never am, but it fills me up with sadness like there's a slow leak from my heart that permeates slowly through every part of me. These kids are so wide-eyed and dazzled at the very fucking thought of Mutopia, let alone its living forests and hollow-tree buildings and all the amazing mutants tucked away in every corner. To them it's a fairy tale, because all they've known is the regimented hell of a heaven that Uriel built for them, a brief intermission of bloody freedom bought at the end of my blades, and then this idyllic prison of theirs. A series of small and circumscribed cells and I've never brought them anything brighter or sweeter.

But now we've reached the ocean, and those concerns are splashed away. I am the centre of their joy, and everyone wants to be close to me as if I bring healing rather than death. The smaller children fling themselves onto me and I hurl them into the depths, flickering through the shadows and reappearing to catch them. Their laughter is delirious, delight so cool and pure I wish I could bottle this feeling and save it for the moments when it's so desperately needed.

The older children splash me from a distance, almost shy. They remember the past too well to abandon themselves in the presence of the dark and holy chalice through which God would channel his wrath. They were raised to love me and fear me, not to see me with my hair plastered to my scalp, my clothes saturated, and my teeth bared not in fury but in laughter.

I almost miss the first warning signal, lulled as I am by the soporific joy of the day. One delicate touch on the outer edge of my awareness, prey moving featherlight to not disturb my web.

There. A displacement of air, not a bullet this time, but a person stepping out of nowhere. A broad-shouldered man behind a black mask. He stumbles, surprised to find himself up to his thighs in water, and by then I have torn out his throat with two daggers of darkness. His blood leaks into the sea, weak iron threads of it tugged by the waves.

He is not the only one. My enemies have come en masse to descend upon me. I have indulged myself too long in this beautiful place, and this is what I reap for my foolishness.

The older children have run to find driftwood on the beach, standing in a circle with their backs to one another, ready to defend themselves. It fills me with a thrilled, savage joy to know that these survivors would fight with me. But that gives way like cracking ice, plunging into the despairing realisation I have led them to this moment.

"Get them safe," I snarl, but Martinez and Novikov need no orders. They have trained for moments like these. Despite more soldiers appearing, my allies keep their focus where it should be—they gather the kids and hustle them back up the path. Novikov lays down covering fire while Pattinson and Farhat perch up on the cliff with sniper rifles, firing down at the soldiers on the beach. This is what I pay them for, but it satisfies me to see them do their jobs well.

It leaves me the freedom to dance. I led these children out of the maze of Uriel's twisted mind, and these men have used me to strike at them. When I was young, I was taught of the many hells, the honeycomb layers that descend into the earth. The great wickedness of the world had turned these hells into crowded slums that festered like boils below the surface, bringing disaster and destruction and yet more depravity. The greatest sign of this, of course, was the rise of the mutants. This was why Uriel tried to raise me up to kill Goddess and end their species. Although I cut my way free of his grip, I've never forgotten that image of an infection bubbling beneath the world, the evil of every man and woman since the beginning of time who did not understand that the world was made to be broken apart for the true children of God.

I no longer believe any part of this fantasy. Death is the snipping of a thread, nothing more. Before their birth, these men exerted no weight on the fabric of the universe, and now I lift each of their lives from the scales. The air is filled with screaming and gunshots, the wet meat sounds of impact. Around me the shallow waves froth pink. I'll have to tell Martinez to ban the kids from coming to the beach for a while, because the tide will bring in many gruesome discoveries once I am done.

What I still believe in is wickedness. And there are few I consider more evil than those who would risk the lives of traumatised children in the name of killing me and looting my corpse. Uriel formed me for the purpose of punishing others and breaking the world, and Goddess remade me to avenge those who are suffering.

Now these men bring suffering and I turn it back upon their heads. There is little joy in what I do. I am a machine, built to do this. To return to one of my more insistent and annoying metaphors, the scythe does not take pleasure in the fall of a stalk of wheat. It simply moves on and cuts down another.

"They're all dead, boss." Farhat has come down to the beach. Her hijab is spattered with blood. "You can stop stabbing that one."

"More might come." I drop the man's head into the ocean. His cheek is flayed open and his skull is scored with the force of my blow. "And don't fucking call me boss."

"Don't think anyone will be lining up for that treatment." Farhat shoulders her rifle. "But we'll stop them if they can't learn obvious lessons. You should get up top and see the kids. They'll need to know you're okay."

It takes a few moments for my breathing to return to normal, for my body to find full presence in the world. I focus on my breathing, the hummingbird song of my heart, damp cloth clinging to my back and the sun beating down.

"Thank you, Farhat." I sprint back up the hill and storm into the compound, wet hair swinging around my face. I'm furious at myself, for my weakness. For staying.

And then I see Novikov kneeling on the ground. A small figure lies prone in front of her, hair splayed around like seaweed, a trickle of blood creeping across the ground.

When it finally comes out, my voice is strangled, like I'm speaking around thorns. "Rose, no."

20

AIDY

This time the mission crew consists of Alyse Sefo, Violet Parker aka Penance, and me. Once again, I am swimming in very deep waters. I cannot understand how or why this keeps happening, but all I can do is frantically keep my head afloat and hope that I can find a way out.

"No time to plan." Violet is surprisingly small in person, petite and very pretty with a cloud of black curls that looks like she carries around her own personal thunderstorm. "We've got a lead—on Mykonos of all places."

"I always wanted to go there." This isn't the time for small talk, but I have no idea what tactical advice I can offer, so I'm trying to make nice. That's all I have.

"It's very pretty." Violet wrinkles her nose in delight. "If we ever get married, Dills and Dan and I will go somewhere like that on our honeymoon. One of the smaller islands, though. Zero tourists allowed. Although I'm not sure any of us believe in marriage—except to say fuck you to people who say that two girls can't marry a thembo—so we should probably go there on holiday instead."

Alyse snorts. "Good luck getting Dilly to take a break. Especially not while they're obsessed with their other spooky travel plans."

The two exchange looks which I'm smart enough to understand are way above my pay grade.

"How do we get to Mykonos?" I ask instead.

"The Keepaway Express." The teleporting mutant appears out of thin air, like they've been waiting for this moment. "Hello again, Aidy. How are you feeling? Alyse managed to talk you into another mission, did she?"

"It's important," I stammer, embarrassingly unconvincing.

"Aidy's very helpful." Alyse pats my shoulder. "From the very first day she turned up at the school asking if we needed anyone."

At the time, it seemed one of the most peaceful and innocuous ways to become part of life on the island, to make myself valuable. How could I have expected that would lead to the unfortunate opportunity of babysitting Leftie, and now this new madcap mission while the rest of my Mutopian life is collapsing around me?

"I'm glad I can be of use." I bob my head and give the world's most awkward smile.

"Yes, we're all helpful." Violet is quiet and focused. "Let's go find our girl."

Despite how much I dislike the phrase *our girl*, I keep my mouth shut. I'm all tense, wincing in anticipation of having myself torn apart into itty bitty fragments by Keepaway, even if I will reassemble somewhere impossibly beautiful. At least this time I have faith I won't be stranded in that in-between place, fragments swirling in the void where I could be flushed into nothingness.

When I'm reconstituted, I don't even get to focus on glorious Aegean vistas. Instead we're staring at corpses, marked off with police tape and dotted with bright yellow numbered indicators. People in uniforms stand around conversing, while others watch the crowd with guns. A helicopter buzzes overhead, three huge letters painted in a furiously bright yellow on the side.

"Fucking GIC," Alyse growls, but I can't look away from all the dead people. It's the clearest possible sign that Leftie was here. Presumably she's not still around or all these other agents would be dead too.

"How do we play this?" Violet murmurs. "Stealth or—?"

"You find where the little horrorshow went," Alyse says. "I'll do the diplomacy thing. Aidy, you're with me."

Violet disappears, like someone rapidly folding away an origami figure. I've heard a lot about Penance, one of the foremost defenders of the island, but never seen her power in action. I still haven't seen the knife part of her capabilities, and from the rumours I don't want to.

"At least if they shoot at us, we can both be invulnerable." Alyse winks at me and strides through the crowd towards the marked-off area where a cluster of GIC agents stand.

I scurry in her wake, trying to look anywhere but at the bodies. On a few occasions in my life, I've had to confront the fact that in the end we can easily be rendered into nothing but meat. This is worse than any other. It's hard to make sense of, to reassemble this jigsaw-like scene into humans.

"Good evening, all." Alyse strolls up, gleaming and chrome in her sleek blouse and tight pants, looking like a cross between a glamour model and a terminator. "I'm Moodring of Mutopia."

"We know who you are." The speaker is a middle-aged woman with short black hair, turning her visored face towards us. "And we warned you something like this would happen if you meddled with the Left Hand of Darkness."

Alyse shrugs, very casual. "You warn us of so many things. Although this situation looks like corporate security attempting to illegally render a Mutopian citizen into custody." She crosses to the tape and peers closer at the bloody ruins. "I'm not saying they deserved to die, but poor decisions tend to have poor consequences."

The GIC agents look like they'd very much like to take another Mutopian citizen into custody, but I doubt Chatterbox would take very kindly to their best friend being incarcerated. "Do you know where the Left Hand of Darkness is now?"

Alyse's mouth twitches. "If I did, I wouldn't be standing here in the sun with you, would I? I'd ask you to share leads, but you've proved stubborn about that in the past."

The woman sneers. "What leads? The girl murdered indiscriminately and then used her unnatural powers to flee. Horrible thing."

"Yes." Alyse sighs and turns her gaze on the woman. "There are a lot of horrible things in the world."

The GIC agent flinches, like seeing herself reflected in Alyse's gleaming face is a glimpse into a future where this conversation ends poorly. "It does appear they were here to capture the suspect. There were three teams, heavily armed and including some technology we haven't seen before. All rendered inoperable and missing key components."

Which seems like as good a description of the murders as any, and bile stings the back of my throat. How is it that we are still in this world, with humans and mutants in their endless, bloody dance? When I came to Mutopia, I felt hope, a tentative flowering in my heart that this island would be a place where I could plant roots and grow for the first time in my life, blossoming into something new and wonderful. Except even in the world after Goddess and the others saved it, we are still awash in violence and hatred, our tiny island struggling to stay afloat. And on top of that we have mutants like the Left Hand of Darkness finding their own horrifying ways of making the situation worse.

"No leads at all on where she went?" Alyse asks the agent, who shakes her head.

"We're waiting for the screams to point us in the direction of her next disaster. Another warning for you —if we find her again, there won't be a trial."

Alyse seems to *sharpen* as she leans forward, as if there's a blade inside her too, honed by all she's seen. "Believe me, we quite understand that the trial was a publicity stunt. Very few mutants who've vanished in your custody have been given any acknowledgement at all. But you wanted the perceived win of bringing the Left Hand of Darkness to heel. And I don't think you're *quite* foolish enough to make that mistake twice. But you keep underestimating me and my people. If you cannot hear the ice cracking beneath you, then I suggest you listen harder, agent."

During this speech, Alyse has slowly grown until she's looming over the agent, her face a bleak mask. She looks like a pitiless avatar of destruction, judging the petty works of humanity. I almost fall to my knees and beg for her forgiveness for all my own bullshit. Despite her warmth and radiance, Alyse Sefo has survived the bloody blade of mutant history, and seen the woman she loves die to save the planet. The fact she still has joy to give is a miracle I don't understand, but it's one I cling to. Because I want to be Alyse rather than Leftie, someone who chooses to turn away from death rather than embrace it.

There's a chime from Alyse's phone, and she glances down at it briefly.

"We're done here," She turns away and motions for me to follow her. The crowd parts around us and I stay in the shadow of her giant, gleaming form as we leave the crime scene. A few people follow, videoing on the phones, but they remain at a safe distance.

"Violet's found her," she mutters. "Keepaway will be here any—"

She doesn't even finish the sentence before I'm tugged haphazardly through the in-between space and onto a tiny fragment of beach. Here are yet more bodies, and I fall to my knees and retch in the shallow waves, part of a torso nudging against my side.

My eyes are streaming so much that I can barely make out what's happening up ahead. It looks like Alyse and Violet are on the sand while a huge blonde woman with a gun shouts at them. By the time I get to my feet, eyes burning from the salt, the situation seems resolved—or at least nobody's killing each other.

"I'll show the way." The woman doesn't relinquish her grip on her weapon. She gives a signal to unseen figures above before we start the steep climb up from the beach. This particular island seems to be covered by trees. I've got no idea where in the world we are, but the climate feels similar to Mykonos. This place is deserted, with no crowds of tourists and no GIC agents. It's only trees and sun and the path leading upwards.

When we reach the clifftop, another path winds its way among the trees. We follow that until we reach a large wooden house. Heavy gates bar the way, with two more armed guards outside. At our approach, they signal yet another hidden figure and the gates slowly swing inwards.

It feels like a mythical place, a hidden temple on a remote island where people are initiated in sacred mysteries. A long way from the cramped tunnels where the cult was hiding out. We enter a courtyard around which a tall house rises. It's made of stone, painted blue and white with arched windows to let the breeze through. My attention is more focused on the crowd of children all seated in concentric rings in the middle of the open space. And in the centre of them, cradling a small child in her lap, hair loose and face intent, is the Left Hand of Darkness.

An expression crosses her face—something almost a smile, but a little sharper. "So you found me after all."

"Not easily." Penance raises one hand in a wave. "And perhaps too late. Is everything okay here? Do we need to send for Doc?"

Leftie nods. "Rose had a bit of a scare, but we've bandaged her up and everything's fine. I've told her that it's never her responsibility to attack incoming soldiers."

"A tough one, huh?" Alyse makes her way through the circle and crouches down beside Leftie and the child. "And how are you doing? Looks like things got complicated out there."

Leftie's jaw clenches. "There's nothing complicated about this shit. Those fuckers came for me. *Here*. Where the children are supposed to be safe. They'll pay for that. They have to."

"More incoming?" Violet's eyes flicker to the soldiers at the compound gate.

"My guess is they're regrouping," Leftie says. "They lost a lot of people today. Along with a bunch of tech which they're probably more upset about. They'll be figuring out the best way to come at me next. So we've got a window."

"These kids," Alyse says. "You rescued them from—?"

"The Broken World." Leftie juts her chin out. "I'm sure you heard the stories about me. The Pied Piper of Death. They found nobody under sixteen at the compound. All spirited away." She waves her fingers in the air. "They deserved something far better than what they'd known. Or what I could realistically offer them. This little island is the best that I could do."

"It's everything," one of the older girls says. She's dressed in pale yellow that makes her tan skin glow. "We owe our lives, our freedom, our *true family* to the Left Hand."

The murderous assassin squirms uncomfortably. "You can call me Leftie, I told you that. And she's exaggerating. Fucking wildly."

The children all chorus their dissent, and a whole bunch of them actually hug her. It completely confuses me to see Leftie in this context. There's all the blood and bodies we've seen on Mykonos and the shore of this island, and then this, a girl with her hair down and a child in her arms.

"What's the play from here, Leftie?" Alyse asks gently. "I think they'll keep coming until they get their investment back. And there are more lives at risk than merely yours."

"I know." Leftie scowls, and it's a brief return to the fury I'm accustomed to from her. "They've crossed a line. Which means I've got a big favour to ask. And I hate this crap, fucking asking anyone for fucking anything. But it's an unavoidable situation, and so I feel like my back's against the fucking wall here."

"Leftie." Alyse laughs. "Enough dramatics. Just tell me what you need."

21

LEFTIE

I loathe being in this position. Of wanting something from another person, of *needing* someone. But I owe these children a life that's better than what they've been given so far, so I'll bow my head.

"What is your price for taking all these children to Mutopia? Including feeding and housing them, all that shit." I glare at Alyse, as if she's dragging each word up out of my throat.

The children immediately begin whispering at this surprising turn of events. I whip a glare around at them and they subside obediently.

"Price?" Alyse stares at me. "Leftie, what are you talking about?"

"They're not mutants." I stare at my knuckles. "But I want them cared for and safe. Mutopia's the best place to make that happen. As annoying as your damn *Dilly* is, they've got a family there and that's what I want for these kids."

"Leftie, you're utterly ridiculous." Alyse reaches out and takes my hand, as if I'm a person and not a weapon. "There's no price. Of course we'll take them. And we'll take you, too, if you're willing to settle down and grow roots. I know you probably want to carry on with what you've been doing, but they'd adjust better to life on the island if you were around."

"Yes to Mutopia?" I can't see who says it, but I think it's Cori, her voice ascending into a squeal. "We can have our very own houses grown by the island?"

"You can have your own little neighbourhood," Alyse says, although the kids hardly need any more encouragement. "Up in the trees, with walkways strung between them like vines."

"And Leftie will be there too," Rose says emphatically. She's still woozy, with this big puffy white bandage on the side of her head. Despite my better judgement, she's taken up residence in my lap and simply won't leave.

It's tempting to listen to her and to make promises. Those plant children and their parents have infected me with this idea of family. It's bewitching to think of the Mutopian network and my hardy little shrubs joining together into one grand flowering forest. But there's only a small step between that beautiful thought and imagining myself among them too. It's tempting to believe that caring for them doesn't have to be an obligation, but a source of connection.

Except that makes me weak and I cannot afford flaws. If I am a dull blade, then I am worthless and should be cast into the fire. I cannot be the weapon I need to be if my heart is entangled with these others. Offloading them to Mutopia soothes my conscience.

"You heard the nice mutant," I tell the children gruffly. "Go and pack your things. I want to be gone from here as soon as possible, before any bad people come back."

They scatter, squealing and shouting. Novikov and Martinez accompany them as always. I suppose I'll have to beg for them to be allowed to Mutopia too, otherwise they'll be miserable. That's where weakness gets you.

Alyse allows herself to be swept away by the children, and Penance too, until it's only me and Aidy standing in the middle of an empty courtyard.

"Something to say?" I sneer at them.

They shrug, not meeting my eyes. "It's not what I expected. Finding you here like this."

"These kids didn't deserve to die."

"Of course not." They flinch away from me. "Why would they?"

"There is darkness in all of them, same as in me. They were raised to see evil where there was none, and to shatter it in the name of a false god and his ruinous servants."

Aidy looks at me for once, eyes meeting mine and not breaking in the face of all my ice. "There's darkness in everyone."

"True enough." I smirk. "And yet these children find the good in their fragile lives and in each other. Even in me, little Aidy, believe it or not."

"Maybe there's good in everyone too." Now they stumble over the words, as if there are treacherous depths inside such an inane statement. "Do you care about them?"

I don't like that question, so I find an adjacent truth and palm it off. "I'm responsible for them. Nobody else is going to do it."

"The way they look at you." There's an odd warmth in their voice, one I find disconcerting. "They're very fond of you."

This whole interaction makes me intensely uncomfortable, so I find blackened and ruined ground to stand on instead. "I was the centre of their world, raised to destroy everything. And I murdered all their parents. My first massacre. Sixteen and standing in their doorways, soaked in the blood of their families."

"Leftie, don't."

"Why not? It's true." I want to tell them more, to rub their desperate face in the truth of me, but the first children have started to reappear, towing suitcases, some almost as big as their owners. They have enough nightmares on their own without me stepping like a ghost into their minds.

"What's your name?" Jalisa is standing right in front of Aidy, staring up into their face. On past evidence, Aidy will find this terrifying and completely overwhelming, but they manage to fumble a smile.

"I'm Aidy. I'm from Mutopia as well."

"Are you a mutant?"

"Yes I am."

"What's your power then?" This demand is echoed by multiple children, but Aidy's all shy and blushing.

"Let me show them." I take a handful of shadow cast by the tall stone walls of the house, and fashion a rudimentary club out of it. Then I swing it wildly through the air, connecting brutally with Aidy's skull.

Everyone jumps, including Aidy. They scream the loudest too.

"Invulnerable skin." I hit them again a couple of times for good measure. "Pretty cool power, huh?"

"What happens if you're shot?" Tomas asks. "Like with a machine gun or a laser."

Aidy blushes even deeper. "Bullets don't hurt me. They sort of stop dead when they hit my skin. I've never been shot by a laser, but I was set on fire and that didn't hurt me."

The kids approve of this fact very much, which admittedly does sound cooler than literally anything else about Aidy.

"When did you get set on fire?" I demand.

"Dylan," they respond, as if that explains everything rather than raising more questions. When did Aidy get dragged off with Chatterbox on a combat mission, and what was the purpose of it?

"Tell me." I aim a lazy blow at their head and then follow it up by pummelling their midsection. "I want to know everything."

"Stop it, Leftie," they say crossly. "You're being a nuisance."

This does not go down well with the kids, who understand that in theory I am only a person slash mutant but can't really wrap their heads around the concept.

"You should be grateful." Leilani tucks her hair behind her ear. "To be a colleague of the Left Hand of Darkness is a position of great privilege. And to be a *friend*."

"Aidy is not my friend." I roll my eyes theatrically. "They don't even like me very much."

"You have to love her." Rose frowns. "Everyone does. She's strong and powerful and good. She fights to save people."

This is a hell of an endorsement from some five year old with a bump on her head, but it's clear Aidy doesn't agree in part or whole.

"Will you be in charge on Mutopia?" Cori asks me.

"Fuck no." I shudder. "Chatterbox is in charge and I don't want any part of that shitshow, thank you very much."

Alyse snorts. "Ray is the President of Mutopia. Chatterbox has no official title, believe it or not. There are all kinds of committees and teams for different purposes. We all join together to keep the island running smoothly and safe. It works for the most part."

"Leftie should be in charge," Rose says. "She'll stop the bad people all the time, and everyone will be too scared to hurt mutants ever again."

It's one of those moments where inspiration scrawls something new across my synapses. A refinement of my original mission, and also a way to satisfy some of this burgeoning desire for *family*.

I will become Mutopia's new and improved weapon. Chatterbox is old and exhausted, so I can step into their shoes and give them a chance to curl up in front of the fire with their remarkably impressive girlfriends. Goddess chose me to be her instrument, and so the alien Cybele should be willing to take me into her arsenal as well. Then I can be part of the great Mutopian system, to lurk amongst the trees with the twins, and to have dinner with all their many aunts and one huncle, all crowded around the dining table.

It feels like a rare, perfect solution. The one flaw being that it involves making a deal with someone more powerful than me, a situation I find offensive in so many ways.

I've said nothing for long enough that a few of the kids have joined in chanting my name.

"Stop your nonsense," I growl, but they know I'm mostly joking. "I've talked to you before about worshipping me. What is it?"

"Fucking gross," they chorus dutifully.

"Yes. One hundred percent fucking disgusting and I won't stand for it. There are lots of very smart, very brave, very dangerous people on Mutopia. I'll help them out if they need it, just like Aidy here."

Rose still can't let one problematic concept drop. "But you have to love Leftie, Aidy."

"Nobody has to love me." I touch Rose's shoulder lightly. "In fact, it's good for me to have someone who thinks I'm a horrible asshole, because it keeps my enormous ego in check."

Aidy looks so startled that I wonder if I read that right out of their mind. "I think Leftie's a very good fighter. Brave, too, astonishingly so. And look what good care she takes of all of you."

I catch Alyse's eye, who's looking far too smug about this, like it's actually bonding and not playacting for a bunch of children who've just witnessed a massacre and are about to have their lives disrupted yet again. "We're good to go," I tell her. "Abandon ship and set sail for the mutant seas."

Her voice is soft and her smile is warm. It's easy to forget the other side of her when she appears like this. "I think you're making the right decision here."

"Pragmatism." I shrug. "I'm good at that." And a weight off my shoulders too, not to have this hanging over my head. They'll be Mutopia's responsibility now, and I can be the irresponsible aunt who shows up every now and again and showers them with presents, telling stories of my unbelievable life.

The teleporting mutant appears and takes everyone back to Mutopia one at a time. Alyse goes first to smooth the way, and then the kids one after the other like dominos falling. All the guards choose to go, even after Penance's warnings that they'll have to undergo Mutopia entry protocols. It's slightly galling that these ruthless mercenaries will happily submit themselves to the yoke of mutant life to keep on hanging around the kids. Where's their fucking pride in the work? At least I chose well, finding these protectors for them.

In the end, it's only me and Violet.

"Are you running again?" Her hand flexes restlessly, blades folding and unfolding.

I tilt my head. "Would you let me?"

"You're hard to stop, but we'll keep looking for you. It's dangerous to have you out here like this. People trying to recover whatever instrument of death lurks inside you."

"I am the instrument of death," I snap, but even I can tell it's overly dramatic.

"We're working on solving your problem." Her curls dance in the warm breeze. "If you can keep your head below the parapet until then, it'll make everyone's life a lot easier. Including these kids, who worry about you. I heard them talking when they were packing their stuff. That's the most important thing to them, above their own safety. And I know you hate that, because it's all bullshit they were fed. But it'll still mean a lot to them to know you're safe and happy."

I close my eyes briefly. Everyone wants me to be something I'm not. Something able to be tamed, to be human. "Fine. I'll return to Mutopia and from there we can make a plan."

Starting with me heading into their mysterious forest to speak to what might be far closer to a god than anything Uriel Clements ever knew.

22

AIDY

When I return to the island, I rematerialise back in my dormitory room. Nobody else is there. I collapse down on my bed for a moment, curling up into as tight a ball as I can manage. I'd really like to not get up after everything I've seen today. The idea of a single uninterrupted hour of sleep seems something carved out by the gods of a more perfect world. Except I desperately need to take more food up to Rayner and confirm the situation hasn't exploded in my absence. The uncertainty of it balls in my gut, like I've digested something heavy and metallic that's leaking toxins into my bloodstream. I can't put this off any longer. Today I have to find a solution that works.

When I crack the door to leave the room, Skip is leaning against the wall opposite, looking casual in knee-length denim shorts and a hot pink t-shirt. "Aidy." Her smile is instant, although it quickly falters as if sapped of all its power. "There you are. Ms. Sefo wants to see you."

"But we've only just come back."

Skip shrugs. "She said in her office."

The uncertainty breeds, spinning off whole new universes of dark possibility with every passing second. "Did she say what it was about?"

"I didn't exactly interrogate her." Skip's smile is barely there, her mouth an unfamiliar line. "She's Moodring."

I shake my head. This has to be Leftie-related but I can't figure out what. Hopefully she's not still focused on her ridiculous idea of starting a team based around the two of us. I'm trying to convince myself this is all totally innocuous, but then why send Skip to drag me for an audience?

If I delay too long, they'll probably send Keepaway who can pop me in there instantly. It'll look much better to show up all bright-eyed and cheerful. More like the Aidy I keep forgetting to be.

When I reach Alyse's office, I find Dylan here too. That's the first bad sign. They're perched in the windowsill, looking out at the trees like they'd rather be in the forest. Alyse is sitting behind her desk. She's changed into a pale blue shirt since the mission, and has touched up her makeup. It makes her look like a schoolteacher again rather than a superhero.

"Aidy." Her voice is too warm, too soft. That's when I know something is going to break. "We've heard an upsetting story about you. There have been some accusations laid, and we'd like to know if it's true."

I feel myself splintering, like my mind is overfull of all these different versions of myself, and I can't decide which one to offer up in justification or penance. I've never assembled a version of me worthy of love and acceptance. This Mutopian version might have been the closest I've come so far, but it was torpedoed by the spectres of my past selves. Words founder inside my mind, everything I could say in fragments, chunks of meaning dissolving into each other. There's nothing coherent, no narrative that holds true. I don't even know how I feel, let alone how to explain it.

Alyse doesn't offer any opinions one way or another. Doesn't lead me in any particular direction. The overwhelming impulse that swells in my throat is to lie, but I can't think of anything remotely plausible to say.

"Rayner," is all I say in the end.

Alyse sighs, very faintly. Dylan clicks their tongue but doesn't turn away from the view outside.

"It was impulsive," I blurt. "I was scared and made a terrible decision, and I'm so sorry." It's true. I *am* sorry that I did it. I'm also sorry I got caught, and that it happened at all. Everything swirls in my head like a nauseating spiral until I can't make sense of it.

"You assaulted her and locked her in a cabin." Alyse frowns. "Although you checked her and fed on her— not that it excuses any of it, but." She buries her head in her hands. "Fuck's sake, Aidy, what were you thinking?"

Dylan makes an odd choking sound. "People freak out and do dumb shit. God knows I've done my share."

The support from this quarter is so unexpected that I burst into tears. "She knew what I'd done before, back in the Dark Year."

"What shit?" Dylan whispers.

"In their file," Alyse says, almost irritable. "You read about it like fifteen minutes ago. Fetch wrote it all down when Aidy arrived."

"But that's Dark Year shit, Aidy." Dylan swings their legs down from the windowsill. "It's all covered by amnesty."

"I'm still someone that did something like that." My voice is raw, still hiccuping soft around unshed tears. "That's who I am. That sort of person. And I just proved it again with what I did to Rayner. I don't know how to *be* better."

"Oh, Aidy," Alyse says in this impossibly gentle tone which makes me cry harder because I don't even know what she means. All I know is that I'm wretched and I don't deserve this island. Not when it should be a home for people like Leftie's cult survivors.

Dylan sighs yet again, like I'm the most difficult problem they've got on their plate today. "Paths to self-improvement aside, we've got to figure out what the fuck action we're supposed to take in response to this. We can't do nothing."

"I'll make it easy for you." I push myself up out of my chair and stumble for the door. Neither of them make a movement to stop me, although Alyse says something that's lost as I slam the door behind me.

I'm barely aware of my surroundings as I make it back to the dormitory. I'm shaking, nauseous, replaying the conversation over and over in my head. Not only have I been caught out in my litany of crimes, I've been weak and useless when confronted. The most horrible thing is the mercenary little part of me saying I could have gotten away with all this if I'd clung to the Dark Year amnesty. But it's not about paying for what I did back then—it's about who people see me as. All I wanted was for people to see the Aidy I showed the world.

It shouldn't take me long to pack. I don't own much. But with how much I'm trembling, everything takes a long time to fold, and I keep stopping in the middle, staring into space and trying to remember what I was doing.

"Aidy, what's going on?" Skip breaks into my reverie, standing in the doorway with Mélodie. "People are telling all kinds of weird stories. That you and Leftie were in some massacre and rescued a small army of children. That you kidnapped some moth girl and locked her in a shack in the forest. And in the Dark Year you—"

"It doesn't matter." I'm practically screaming. "None of it matters. Maybe it's all true, maybe none of it's true. But you can forget about it, because you don't have to put up with me anymore."

Mélodie signs something rapidly, but Skip shakes her head vehemently without translating. "Aidy, I've got no idea what's going on, but you're obviously upset about *something*. But we're friends, like I thought we were really close? So I've got no idea what you mean about putting up with you."

"We are friends." Oh god, I'm about to cry again. "*Were* friends, whatever. But you didn't really know me and so you don't have to worry about finding out the real me anymore."

Skip frowns. "You've been pretending this whole time?"

I don't want to be in this conversation. There's no explanation that will make any of it okay, and I'd rather be left alone. "Of course it was me. But I kept a lot of parts of me hidden. The ugly parts, things nobody should have to see."

Mélodie makes an emphatic sign.

"Exactly," Skip says. "We're all icebergs. Holding a bunch of ourselves underwater for all kinds of reasons. I mean, I'm way more of a bitch than I like people to know."

"It's true," Mél says.

"I've never seen any sign of it," I whisper.

"That's because I like you a lot and I want you to like me back." Skip laughs. "Right from when we first met, I was like—this person is very cool and I want to be their friend. But now you're saying that was all fake and so you're *leaving*."

I clench my fists in the blue sweater I'm holding. "Not all fake. But yes, I'm leaving. I don't really have a choice. Dylan and Alyse made it clear there are consequences if I stay on Mutopia."

"What consequences?" Mélodie asks.

I've got no idea, so I shake my head and turn back to my suitcase. It's not even necessarily the consequences themselves, it's what people will think of me. To have every mutant on the island know the story of what I did back then, and then what I did to Rayner as well. For them to understand how despicable I am, how worthless, how—

"It's easier if I go, that's all." I focus on packing, because that's something I can actually manage. It's a solvable baggage problem.

"Easier for who?" Skip asks, and I hear her long sigh as I ignore her. "Aidy, I hate this. You won't even talk to me about it, won't even explain it in a way that makes sense."

I whirl around. "Maybe it doesn't make sense, or I don't make sense. I'm so scared all the time of being found out, of being rejected yet again, of everyone discovering exactly why they don't want me in their lives. I'm sick of running up against the limits of people's love. So I'm done. I can't do this again, can't have something this beautiful fall apart because I'm not good enough for it."

Skip fidgets. She stares at the floor, lost for words. Because this one glimpse into the heart of me and she's recoiling. "Aidy..."

"I've got too much packing to do before the ferry leaves," I snap. "So can you please let me finish?"

Mélodie takes Skip's arm and pulls her slightly towards the door. Except there's another person standing there, looking equally as confused.

"Can we have a chat before you rush off?" Alyse Sefo asks.

"Please talk some sense into them," Skip says in a low voice before allowing Mélodie to tug her from the room.

Alyse drifts over towards me. The edges of her are blurry and indistinct, like she's a watercolour sketch stepped out of her frame. "What's all this in aid of? Unintentional pun, sorry."

"I'm making things easy for you." Bitterness leaks into my voice, the ruined plumbing of me poisoning my exterior facade. "It's clear I don't deserve to be here, so I'll take myself away rather than forcing you to kick me out."

"Do you really think this is the first dispute we've had on Mutopian soil?" Alyse sits down on Skip's bed. "Mutants are people too, and a lot of them have come through some rough times. If we dealt with every conflict by kicking people off the island, there would be very few of us left. Even Dylan and I fight sometimes, you know."

"I don't deserve to be here," I mutter.

"Conversations about worth aren't helpful." She pats the bed, but I refuse to sit because it's the only dignity I have left. "There's been wrong done, and there are many ways to address it. Paths to redress and reconciliation. But honestly, Dilly and I think what you need most is a change in perspective."

There's a huge part of me that wants to automatically spurn this offer. It allows me to claw back some of my own agency. To say no, I don't need them or their island. To walk away for my own reasons. And I'm scared, too, of what this could mean. These mutants aren't only bright and shiny facades to show the world, they have awkward angles and shadows too.

"What does change in perspective mean?" I ask, sullen as a teenager.

"You talk to Cybele. In the Crown, the deepest part of the forest. Then you decide what you want to do. You're free to stay or leave, although if you stay we'll work through reconciliation with Rayner."

"Cybele." I turn towards the dormitory window, from where I can see the line of the forest marching upwards to the peaks. It's not so far from the little shack where I hid the poor moth girl, although I'd be going much deeper in. At the mercy of whatever lives there.

When my eyes blink closed, I drown in green, lost in a viridian tide. Vines snake their way through my mind, tracing my neural pathways. Flowers bloom in my cerebellum, blossoms erupting in wild abandon until I imagine myself from the outside, mouth spilling leaves and flowers sprouting from fluted holes in my skull.

I'm in the shadow of an enormous tree that towers over me. It dwarfs everything, its topmost branches disappearing into banks of dripping cloud. Under the spread of it, the strangest and most beautiful plants thrive, species with singing leaves and glowing flowers.

I am only one flower in a vast forest, all intertwined with vines that run from one to the other. I am surrounded with so many interconnected plants, but none of them are linked to me. Instead, my roots dive deep, plunging through rich soil and then into a brackish sea of toxic waste that lies below everything. This is where I get my nutrients from, while all those blooms that surround me nourish each other and draw more from what they are planted in.

As far as metaphors go, it's a little on the nose.

"Aidy." Alyse is standing beside me, holding my hand. "Are you okay? You had your eyes closed and you were humming."

"The island really is alive." I shiver, but it's more anticipation than fear. "She wants to talk to me."

Alyse nods. "That's what I'm saying. A change in perspective."

And I don't think about what any version of perfect Aidy would want, or any one of my past selves. It may be terrifying or overwhelming. The alien creature in the forest might devour me and spit out my bones.

But I say yes, without hesitation.

23

LEFTIE

I know where the forest is without looking. I'm not sure if that's something everyone here can do. Perhaps Cybele senses my dark intent and calls me to her leafy embrace. The last time I entered the forest, she gave me a vision of Uriel. That was the death of the old god, and she is the new. I will be a far better weapon in her hand than her errant children Chatterbox and Moodring. A dark star orbiting her, acting in accordance with both her will and my own.

I stay in the shadows until I reach the edge of town, melting through the cool darkness thrown by the buildings until I reach the flower-spotted field that rings the forest. The sun is low on the horizon and it makes the shadows spill long and tangled, but for some unnecessarily dramatic reason I want to approach in full sight. My feet swish through long grass that hums as I move through it. I wonder if Cybele will change me again. Maybe I will be granted some of the abilities of the plant family. Would that make me part of them in some way? I'm slightly shocked to find I do not hate the idea, but it somehow makes sense.

I never had a real family, only people who gave me to their leader like an offering. Who turned their faces away as I was thrown into the darkness and let me become infected with the seeds of apocalypse. They died just like strangers when I killed everyone. I would not be opposed to Willow and Soo-yeon regarding me as some long-distant cousin who they enjoyed seeing from time to time. And Chatterbox as some irascible parental figure I enjoy baiting. It means I should probably stop thinking about Marvellous in certain ways. No, all this is ridiculous, no matter how much they tow me back into their orbit time and time again. I am not made for connection. I am a poisonous flower that stands alone, rootless and only waiting for my spores to infect everything they touch. They would be better off staying away from me. And yet, and yet...

I sense movement to my right, and snap my head up, ready to melt into shadow. Who have they sent after me this time, to drag me back to their embrace?

It is only Aidy, head down and stumbling through the grass as if they're lost.

I ignore the shadows and watch them. They're not even aware of my presence, bumbling towards the forest, the same as I am.

"Little Aidy!"

They jolt like a shot of electricity has run through their entire body and turn to squint at me. "What are you doing here?"

"Talking to Cybele." I stride through the grass towards her. "You?"

"Same." They're frowning at me, like I'm crashing whatever grandiose plans they had for a romantic evening in the forest.

"I'm offering myself to her service." I gesture dramatically at the looming height of the trees. "A team-up, really. I don't like to serve. I assume you're here for other reasons."

Their mouth pinches tight, like they're controlling a wave of emotion from spilling out. "I'm here for a new perspective. Find the right path."

"She's not a fucking guru," I snarl, suddenly furious with this weak bullshit. Sometimes I think Aidy's pretending to be a person. Always watching wide-eyed, trying to gauge everyone else's reactions before they choose what they're going to say or do. What would an alien goddess have to say to someone like them?

"Alyse suggested it," they say, absolving themself of even the decision to be here. "But now that I'm here, the forest seems huge, doesn't it? Like it's listening."

"It's alive." I roll my eyes. "Of course it's listening."

I turn to head into the forest, but Aidy makes a croaky sound and then says "Wait."

"For what the fuck now?"

"Have you, uh, like, um, *spoken* to her before?"

"I talked to her a little last time." My brows draw down, because I don't want to share this information. I'm going to be part of this damn family, not her. "She showed me some things."

There's a tiny frown that appears and disappears in a flicker. "Did it help?"

"With what?" My scorn does not vanish so easily.

Aidy literally takes a step backwards, like they're too scared to say what's in their head. "Your, uh, deal? I guess?"

I'd like to slap them, or stab them, just eviscerate them in this field and water the ground with their blood. They're so fucking *frustrating*, so feeble and unsure. "What fucking deal? I was created to be a monster and I've got a lot of people to kill. They're a powerful being responsible for the creation of mutants. I think we can come to some accommodation."

"A team-up." They blink rapidly. "Of course. All I want is answers, really. I want to be *fixed*." They give themself a fright with that admission, I think, something too close to the truth. I'm envious too, the tiniest flicker, because they believe that fixing is even possible.

The best way to fix Aidy is probably to slit their throat and make their death fast, but let's assume Cybele knows shit I don't. Maybe she can fix that fucked up brain, stop them jumping at every goddamn shadow. It's so exhaustingly petty though, little Aidy fumbling towards their attempt at self-discovery. Some of us actually have a purpose in life, even if it's a dark one.

"I feel like Cybele has better things to do than fix one lost little mutant." It's far too easy to find my mouth forming a sneer when I talk to Aidy.

"She showed me a vision," Aidy blurts out. "When I said her name, I saw these images in my head. Of flowers and trees connecting to each other, and her being the centre of it all."

I roll my eyes. "Yes, Dilly talks a lot about that stuff. It makes a nice story for the joiners."

"Dilly?" Aidy whispers.

"You know, androgynous half-plant half-person. Dating two of the hottest women on the planet. Got a couple of weird alien kids. Likes to pretend they're not in charge of this shitshow."

Oh, how I love the irritated look on their face and the way it turns to stone. "I knew who you meant. It's very familiar, that's all. Calling them the name that their friends do. For someone who's so far above all the petty concerns of humanity."

I want to laugh in delight, because look, here is baby trying to sting me. "It's so important to them so it seems cruel not to play along. They want me to be part of their odd little family." I'm only saying this to annoy Aidy, but the words still feel wrong on my lips, like I've swallowed something I shouldn't.

Their mouth quivers. "You really are a disease. Dylan and their family are bringing you in close because they're kind and caring, but you'll only disappoint them."

"Shock horror." I mug an expression for them, and their mouth twists again. They really do dislike me. It's refreshing, actually. So much of their time is pretending. I hope it feels freeing to judge me. "I've never promised to be anything but a monster." Oh, but to be in a family of monsters, to have them love me despite my shadows and my poison fangs. That longing is far too much to admit to anyone. I can barely even hold the thought in my head before dropping it as it scalds me.

"I hope you can make a deal that benefits you to the exclusion of everyone else." They spit the words like they're bullets. "Now if you'll excuse me, I'm going into the forest to speak with Cybele. Who sent me a vision and asked me to come."

Oh, now that's a hit. Not bad, little Aidy. I've got no guarantee the thing dwelling among the trees will pay attention to me again given how last time went. But I can't let them see me flinch at all.

I step lightly across and link my arm through theirs, like we're best friends on a delightful outing in the beauty of nature. There's an immediate tension as Aidy pulls away from me, but I bat my lashes and tip my head conspiratorially in towards them. "Let's go in together. Last time she showed me such marvellous treats from my past. I wonder what she has in store for you."

And there's the evisceration I was hoping for. I feel the tremor go through their body and the way they tighten as if a thousand screws have been turned at once. It's obvious that little Aidy has some secrets of their own. I doubt they're actually interesting, but sometimes the best weapons are the ones you find lying around.

I tug them even closer, and they stumble into me, the warmth of their arm pressing against my own naturally cooler skin. The shadows always keep me a few degrees colder to the touch, as if I've stepped from an ice cave.

Aidy shudders, but sadly it's not from me. "The forest. It looks like it's moving."

"Probably is." One corner of my mouth lifts, revealing a gleaming tooth. "It's alive after all. Living things get hungry. I wonder what she feeds on. Life, memories, pain. Who knows why she called you." I'm honestly a little giddy at the thought of what might await us inside. Another chance to kill Uriel can't be something I turn my nose up at. I'll complete any trials Cybele has for me, prove that I'm the best weapon she has in her arsenal. Together, we'll make the world safe for all these people. Willow and Soo-yeon, Dylan and Dani. Alyse, Feral and Penance. Even little Aidy. It's the oddest thought of all to list those names. People I would fight for. A trick Chatterbox pulled somehow, some sleight of hand I was not expecting as I looked for more deadly attacks. I am simultaneously pissed off and in awe, dragged in by the undertow of them.

Aidy has nothing else to say as we move closer, me towing them against their subtle inclination away. Their steps get slower and skid through the damp grass. The trees are different from last time. They tower higher, and their bark is cracked and grey, oozing green sap spilling out and dripping down in lazy strands. Crooked branches form interlocking lattices that function like a wall, a crazed spider-web of wood that teems with insect life.

"Pretty." I stroll through the shadows, brushing my fingertips along the rough surface of the nearest truck. Sap clings to my fingers, stinging lightly. It smells of mint and iron, like toothpaste scented blood.

"It's not remotely pretty," Aidy croaks.

I rub the sap over my lips and resist the temptation to press a stinging kiss to Aidy's neck, just to watch them jump. It's hard to know what to do with them. It's hard to know what to do with *anyone*. Most of the time when I deal with people, I'm killing them or kissing them. Conversation without a purpose isn't something in my skill set.

"So much life." I slide my hand in between a gap in the branches and wait for something fluttering to alight on it. "It's like the forest is taunting me."

"You're not a disease." For once, Aidy's voice has something more hollow than hatred. "You're a girl who's very good at killing, that's all."

"Rude." I close my hand around the bug, slow enough that it has a chance to flutter away into the darkness of the forest. "And look, there's a path up ahead."

It's not visible exactly, but I'm aware of the subtle interplay of shadows, and I can feel the tunnel pushing into the trees like a needle puncturing the skin of the forest gloom.

We're almost at the mouth of the forest. All we need to do is step inside. Hesitation loops around my throat like a noose. I talk a good game and it's true that very few things in this world strike fear into my heart. But deep down I know there are creatures more terrifying than me, and right now I'm on the verge of one of them.

I refuse to tremble, or to bow. Whether you call me disease or death or monster, or deny I am any of them, I am a girl with fangs and heart and will. Nothing can break me. They have already tried and failed. Whatever Cybele is, I will stand before her.

And here I've still got the presence of mind enough to bring something of an insurance policy. Cybele called for Aidy, based on some logic I cannot understand. If my new god is going to speak to this breathless shadow of a mutant, I'll be there to say my piece too.

By now we have reached the forest entrance, where it swallows light entirely. It's a *threshold*, a place to cross from this world into another realm. This is different from before, when we were among the trees and I was haunted. This is breaching a barrier.

This is—

"Let's go," I say, and tug Aidy forward.

24

AIDY

This whole experience is like a fairytale. And, with the same slippery logic of stories, I am making a dreadful mistake. I am arm-in-arm with the shadow girl, standing at the entrance to the spooky forest that called me here. Something fundamental has changed about it from my previous visits. The trees don't look real, a spill of dark ink made with savage brushstrokes on a tattered canvas. Even the sky above is infected by them, wisps of darkness spiralling upward into a cloudbank that's bruised purple.

Perhaps I imagined that sense of being called by Cybele. Or maybe I am walking numbly to the fate I deserve. This is so different to the forest I saw playing behind the screens of my eyelids. I understand that vision was a metaphor, but I cannot reconcile the beautiful, spreading shade of that massive tree with this army of wood scratched out in dark and furious lines.

"Let's go." Leftie's blue eyes are alight, as if the darkness of the trees sparks something new inside them, tinder to flame. She's been deliberately goading me, giving reminders of how she's made these effortless connections on the island despite being so poisonous and ill-mannered. The way she said *Dilly* proves it. It seems monstrously unfair, that I can try so hard to shine and yet end up so dull and forgettable, while Leftie spurns the world and is adored for it.

She may want to bargain with what lurks in the forest, but my promise is more uncertain. A shift in perspective, Alyse called it, which could mean anything.

"Are you sure you want to come with me?" I'm torn between pushing her away and craving the company— even this girl.

"Don't be *scared*, little Aidy." Her voice is soft and reassuring, even though I know she's being sarcastic. It twists the knife a little deeper, watching her snarl and bite at the offered hand when I long to take it. And of course she has no fear of waltzing into something that feels more and more like a lair.

In the end, I steel myself internally, the one thing my powers cannot do for me. "Fine." I clench my fists step over the threshold, from day into darkness.

We are not inside a forest. There is no rustling of leaves, no soft churr of insects, no fresh, bright smell of things growing. Instead, we are on a street, near-identical houses stretching around a curve in the road. Recent-model cars sit in driveways. From a nearby backyard comes the sharp sounds of children arguing.

This cannot be real. It is impossible. We are in the forest, and it is *doing* this to us.

"Fuck is this?" Leftie's arm is still in mine, and in this landscape, she is the one who looks like she's been drawn in dark ink, a black-and-white portrait of a girl who burns like a fuse. Her hair whips in the breeze, like it's staining the air around her.

"Cybele did something." My voice sounds younger somehow, unbroken and more sure. "Is this not what happened to you last time?"

"Saw some ghosts." Leftie's very still, poised to fight. "But they were lurking among the trees. Nothing like this fucking surround-sound hallucination shit. Where the fuck is this boring-ass suburban hellhole though? What does it mean?"

"Me." It's hard to swallow. "It's mine. I mean, it's where I grew up."

Leftie snorts. "Fucking brilliant. We could've gone back to the creepy cult compound, but instead we're trapped in your beige fucking life." She tips her head back. "Thanks, Cybele! Appreciate the break, really."

I ignore her and stumble down the road towards number forty-two. It is exactly as I remember. The lawn is slightly overgrown. Roses in many shades fill the front garden. When I would leave the house, I would always catch brief trails of their scent. It was the one thing my mother and I agreed on. I stand at the end of the path. Last time I stood here… This is all *too* vividly realised, down to the scratch on the front door where my younger brother crashed his bike as a child learning to ride.

This is plucked right from my memory, and for what purpose?

The door bangs open, and I come out. Past me, a version of myself lying interred below memory and re-learned habits and lies. The hair of my old self is a lurid pink, and my new septum piercing is raw. I'm dressed in black, many items layered atop each other.

"Ruth-Ann Lillian Bader." The voice is an exact reproduction once again.

"It's Alex," the past me spits. "I fucking told you."

Another apparition appears in the doorway. Tall and slender and immaculate. My heart jackhammers in my chest, as if I've run a mile or my body's telling me I should be fleeing. This is the last time I saw her.

"Do not speak to me like that. It is unacceptable. And I am not calling you Alex, you ridiculous girl."

"I'm not a girl," past me screams, spittle flying, fist clenching. There's a bag dangling from that white-knuckled hand. I used that as a pillow for a long time after that day. I know every lyric written on it, every patch I painstakingly stitched to it.

Mother shifts her angle of attack. She could always do that, never so stuck in an emotional rut as me. Her body language softens, her tone changing as if she's stirred a tablespoon of sugar in. "I know you're dealing with a lot, darling."

"Use my name." I forgot how bold my past self could be. "Call me Alex."

"We can talk about all that. And about your other changes as well. I've been reading online. There are places who can help you with this." Her voice is even warmer, but I know her well enough to know the flames that heat it are made of nothing but rage. "All of your changes."

"I'll never be her again." Past Aidy juts their chin at their mother, trying desperately to scrounge up enough defiance. I still remember this, still remember how it felt to be trapped between two impossible arcs. "I never *was* her."

"You were my little girl," my mother whispers, tears rising in her eyes. Fake, always fake. I could never believe her. There was always an angle. It was always about her. She never liked having a tomboy—to have a child that might be *transgendered* as she calls it is abhorrent. The thought of other people's judgement consumes her. There is no limit to what she might do to bend me back into the shape she wishes me to be. "You're not a boy. You're not a *mutie*, Ruth-Ann. We can help you through this. You're just confused. You've read too much online, and people have gotten into your head. We'll fix this, I promise. That's what parents do."

"I don't need *fixing*." It's less of a scream than I remember. It's less final than I remember. It's almost pathetic, with mascara forming drippy curves on my cheeks. My shoulders are shaking, my fishnets are torn, and my long-sleeved shirt is stained.

"No, but you need *healing*."

I can't argue with her. I never could. I'd get backed into a corner, or have my words twisted into pretzels, or end up feeling guilty because she would be so hurt by my words or my ingratitude. So I turn and run.

It wasn't meant to be final, not really.

My past self flees, and my mother shakes her head.

"Stupid girl." She taps one hand against her thigh and then disappears into the house, closing the door behind her.

She thought I'd be back, too.

Leftie snorts again. "So dramatic, little Aidy. Probably a smart call, getting out of all *this*." She waves her hand dismissively at my house and the entire suburb and presumably my mother as well.

"What do you know about it?" I growl at her.

She laughs. "Fair point. I was the precious daughter of an apocalypse cult. Not quite the same thing as being bored to death by cookie cutter people. So is this it? Your deep dark tragedy?"

"Fuck off." I'm mad that Leftie is here for this, with her snide, sidelong glances. It's even more embarrassing that I once looked vaguely like some knockoff version of Leftie herself. "This was a long time coming."

"Shall we go in and talk to your Mom?" Leftie begins to saunter up the driveway. "Show her how delightful you've turned out to be? I could kill her for you. Make a whole production out of it, blood spurting everywhere. It might be cathartic."

"This is a memory." I try not to picture it, but my mind is spooling the images on a private reel. My mother, standing at the top of the stairs in her imperial pose. Leftie, materialising out of the shadows, that sharp-toothed smile bared and a long, cold blade in each hand. "You can't do that."

"I'm quite good at killing, didn't you know?" A shadow-knife flickers between her fingers. "Why don't we give murdering the past a try?"

"It doesn't matter." My words taste bitter, and I still have something like an electrical charge running through me at the thought. "I never saw her again."

"Maybe because I broke through into the past and stabbed her in the—"

Leftie's words are cut off as the street around us abruptly disappears, a fast cut like a movie. For a moment, we're surrounded by the looming shadows of trees before a new set slams into place.

I recognise this one too, and I want Leftie to see this even less. When I glance to my right, she's still there, tapping her foot and pursing her lips insouciantly.

"Oh cool. Episode two." She winks at me, and saunters across the damp grass towards the playground in the distance. There are two figures sitting on the swingset, moving idly back and forth. The moon pokes fingers of light through tattered clouds, as if it's clawing its bone-white face free of a shroud. I don't need the light to see who it is. It's the before-me, along with the figure of Petra, a girl who I had the most wretched and hopeless crush on.

"Leftie," I hiss, but of course she doesn't listen. She's strolling towards them, either to kill them or to eavesdrop. I don't know which is worse. I remember this all too well.

"I don't know, Alex." Petra toes the scattered bark below the swing. "I'm sorry it turned to shit with your

Mom, and I'm sorry she's a bitch, but this is way too much drama."

"I'll sleep in your garden shed," Alex-me says. "Or in your garage. Look, I don't care. I just need a *place*, that's all."

There's a silence that I knew was awkward when this happened, and now it's so embarrassing I want to snap the neck of my past self just to *end it*. I wish Leftie would do it. She's right there, half-shadow, half-girl, one side of her curious face illuminated.

"Shit." Petra throws herself clumsily out of the swing. "Like, I can't have some random girl, I mean person, show up and crash. I don't know how to explain it to my parents, and I can't just, like, *hide* you in my house or something. Sorry, but you must have family, right?"

"Yeah." I remember how my lips felt numb. "I've got family."

"I'll see you at school." She flees without even looking back, leaving the ruins of the conversation behind her.

Past me sits on the swing and tears roll down their cheeks. They stare into space for a long time.

"Is the memory frozen?" Leftie asks.

"No. I didn't know what to do. I couldn't go home and Petra was my only friend." I want to laugh at that. "Or someone I thought was my friend. I never really got on well with people. I bored them, or they bored me, and then when I came out as nonbinary a couple of people really… took offence, I guess?"

"At what?" Leftie frowns as if I'm the one at fault. "Because you're not a girl? The fuck business is it of theirs? I tried to make Uriel and the others call me a boy for a while there, but they did not like that." She grins at me. "At all. The cult was very big on the fecundity thing and the feminine mysteries of the apocalypse seed. All so I'd eventually be plundered by the keeper of the sacred penis, but there was a happy ending to *that* story at least. Not so much for the boy, but they do tend to get their own way a lot." She slings an arm around my shoulder. "It's the only thing I like about you, little Aidy, so wear it proud."

As an ironic counterpoint to Leftie's declaration, the scenery shifts a further time. Now we're in the overstuffed bedroom in my grandmother's house. It's the place I finally washed up after that night in the park. It wasn't a refuge of any kind—the only thing we had in common was a hatred of my mother. The delight taken in harbouring me against my mother's express wishes didn't stretch to tolerating anything else about me.

"Ruth-Ann." Grandmother is wiry through-and-through, clad in a tracksuit and sun visor with grey curls escaping all bouffant. "Put that damn device down and come to dinner. I got an email today about how those things are ruining everyone's mental health."

Past me obeys. I did that a lot back then. Giving up my new name, and the way I dressed, and my identity as nonbinary seemed like small things when conceded one at a time. All in the name of ease, in the name of quiet, in the name of peace. Life was simpler this way, I told myself, and I knew who I was on the inside. I was working retail and fed up with customers asking questions about *what I was* or why I dressed the way I did. Appearing normal didn't mean the same thing as being normal. It's easy to tell yourself these things, to peel slivers of yourself away and think it's not going to hurt, even when there's a whole collection of bloody fragments at your feet and you don't recognise yourself anymore.

"You make the best mac and cheese, Grandma." Past me takes my seat at the table and bows their head. "Thank you."

"Tch. It's fine. Not like it's my mutant power." She makes another dismissive noise through her teeth. "Mutants. What is the world coming to? Did you see the news? That Chatterbox is at it again. Scruffy kid trying to change the world."

Back then, Gran was obsessed with mutants. She especially claimed to hate Chatterbox, who was unruly and disrespectful. Somehow in their cold war over my status, location and life trajectory, Mom failed to inform Gran of the piece of information that could shatter my place there. I'm not sure whether it was mercy or the belief that to do so would make her own situation even worse.

"This is boring." Leftie looms over Grandmother, hands on the back of her rocking chair. "Why are we watching this? The story of your life has been very dull this far. It's time for some excitement."

"Wait." I remember this night. It's impossible not to. "I think you'll get your wish."

There's a crash from outside, and past me flinches violently. Gran doesn't blink, whether because she doesn't hear or is inured to it. Present me wants to flinch too, to turn away from this.

If this is why Cybele called me here? If this is what healing means—to watch the past unfold again with Leftie providing irritating commentary—I don't understand it. Gods might be beyond the understanding of mortals, but this seems only cruel.

"Mutie!" The chant from outside is ragged. "Get out here, mutie, and pay for what you did."

Past me stands up fast, banging their thighs against the table and making their plate clatter.

"What *now*, Ruth-Ann?" Grandmother snaps.

"Something's happening outside."

Gran cranes her head, as if she'll be able to see through the curtains.

"Don't worry." Past me is already hurrying for the door. "I'll deal with it."

Present me is standing in the middle of the dining room, unwilling to follow.

"Come on." Leftie nudges me. "I can't wait to see how you *deal with it.*"

25

LEFTIE

Finally, something is happening, and Aidy is inevitably acting skittish. The content might be boring, but I'm enjoying this virtual reality past journey Cybele is rolling out for us. I wish she had done this performance for me. It would be much more satisfying murdering a realistic memory-Uriel than some fucked up plant version of him.

Aidy is not so enthralled, despite the fact their past is predictable and dreary so far. Hardly something to induce all this angst in them. I get it's unfair to compare my own chaotic upbringing to anyone's, but please.

The old Ruth-Ann version of Aidy is fiddling around with all the locks on the front door. Someone's paranoid about something, but without any real sense to it, because if it was me—even without powers—I'd come bowling in through the window. The noise from the street outside is getting louder, and I'm surprised

Ruth-Ann is even going out there at all. There's a crash, and they flinch again. What the hell are they going to do out there? Very politely ask these shouting assholes to leave?

At least *I'm* here this time. Not sure what I can do to kill a memory, but I'm willing to try. A shadow-blade takes form in my hand as Ruth-Ann finally swings the door back.

"Leftie, don't," Aidy whispers from behind me, but I'm already leaping down the stairs and out into the street.

For all the noise, it's only four men, and they're not even here for Ruth-Ann. They're two doors down and across the street, standing outside one of those narrow brownstone houses and continuing their pointless chants about muties. The crashing sound looks to have been a trash can someone threw at the door.

"Shall I kill them?" I ask, but Aidy has their back pressed up against the door of their house. So much for anything interesting or dramatic happening.

The curtain at the door twitches, and a shadow flickers, and it sends the four dudes into a baying frenzy. I know this is a memory, but there must be a reason we're here. A chance to intervene, to try a different outcome.

The door finally cracks. There's a woman framed in it. Probably mid-twenties, wearing trousers and a blouse that both look expensive but not like fuck-you expensive. Glossy hair frames a very nice face. I'd date her. A couple of times, maybe. She looks like the type to get sick of my shit very quickly though.

Right now, she's terrified. There's a cellphone clutched in her hand.

"I've called the police." Her voice shimmers.

"Darling, we are the police." One of them holds out a badge. "Anti-mutant patrol. Clearing the neighbourhood, making it safe."

"I'll call Chatterbox." The woman's voice rises into a screech.

"Oh, please do. I'd love a chance to shut that bitch's mouth."

The woman begins scrawling a symbol on the doorframe of her house in fat black marker, but one of the cops leaps up the stairs. He smacks it out of her hand and grabs the woman by the hair before tugging her down the stairs towards the others.

Fuck it. Memory or not, I'm getting involved.

Except a bulky, angular shape stomps past me. It's moving awkwardly, crablike on distended feet, stretched out into a cross between a person and a wall.

Holy shit, it's little Aidy.

Except my version of Aidy is still huddled against the door across the street. This is the Ruth-Ann version. This is the memory. Ruth-Ann barrels into the closest cop, sending him sprawling. Then they spin around, knocking another one to the ground. Except their transformation isn't quite right—a mix of hard and soft—and when the third cop jabs an elbow into their throat, they stiffen up and collapse.

"Look at this." The third cop smiles in the sickly pool of yellow from the overhead streetlight. "We came out to catch one mutie and found ourselves another." He jabs one foot hard into Ruth-Ann's gut, but there's a clanging sound. They're still partially armoured.

The first cop woozily gets to his feet, but the other is down for the count. The last one is still hanging onto the first mutant, but recoils when she catches him a wicked scratch along his left forearm.

"Fucking b—"

I'm done with this. Fuck memory, fuck Cybele, fuck these games. I am the Left Hand of Darkness, and I exist to protect mutantkind. Whatever healing might exist for me, it does not involve turning away from that.

The street is drenched in shadow, and I gather huge drifts of it into my hands, forming it into a massive axe with a wickedly sharp blade. I've done this so many times, I barely need to think of the shape. The darkness knows what I want, and it obeys.

I swing the blade at the cop who's kicking Ruth-Ann first. It punches through his chest, but there's no bright spray of blood. There's not even any sensation of flesh giving way. He simply topples, as if I've struck him down from on high like a god.

I'm already moving to the next victim, the pattern of movements bright and clear in my mind, so I've barely registered the odd manner of the man's death when the second swing of the axe melts through the man's neck. He raises one hand to his throat, and falls too, bloodless and staring.

The others know something's happening—their fellow assholes simply falling lifeless to the ground is a dead giveaway, but they have no idea what. One looks at the original mutant, as if this is something she might be doing, but he doesn't get time to make a sound before he's dead as well.

"What are you *doing*?" Aidy has finally left the door, standing behind me with eyes wide and breath coming ragged.

" Not standing by and watching this shit," I sneer.

"This isn't how it happened."

"So? We're not here to watch a fucking movie." I let the axe dissolve back into shadow. "This is a chance to do something different. This is how we communicate with Cybele."

In the street, the first mutant has fallen to her knees trying to rouse Ruth-Ann, who's doing a classic Aidy, all curled in on themselves and whimpering.

My Aidy only stands and stares, like they're watching an alternate version.

"It was bad, huh?" I ask.

"Very." Their voice is husky, hollowed out so only the edges hold sound. "In the real world, that woman died. I was... it took a long time for me to recover from seeing that so close. From being unable to protect her."

I kick one of the dead cops in the face and feel his bones shatter. He caves in like he's hollow, fragile as a bird's egg. "Isn't this better then?"

Their face shutters. "You can't just kill your problems, Left Hand."

"Fucking watch me." I stamp on another skull and feel it shatter, leaking brain matter on the ground around in a grey puddle.

"We can play this out a thousand different ways, but it doesn't change the reality." Aidy's voice ratchets higher. "I failed to save her. They beat me until I could barely breathe. My Gran didn't even want to pay for me once she found out what I was. She spat on me while I was lying on the stretcher, clinging to life by a thread. It was a mutant charity that paid for my medical bills and kept me alive."

"Then why do you *give a fuck?*" I lean in towards them, teeth bared. "Why are we here, little Aidy?"

"Stop calling me little Aidy." Their hand reaches out and shoves me in the chest.

I reach out and catch their wrist, more on autopilot than anything else, twisting their arm away from me. "Why does it matter? Are you Ruth-Ann or Aidy or someone else?"

"None of it matters." Their lip looks raw where their teeth have gnawed it. "All of those versions of me are bullshit, worthless assholes. I've never been worth anything. You were right about that from the beginning. Now you've had a front row seat to my shitty memories. You saw that my mother didn't want me, and nobody else did either. I ended up with my grandmother because she hated my mother, not because she loved me. I didn't come out here to help that poor woman. It was because I was terrified and wanted them to stop screaming mutie so my Gran wouldn't know what was going on."

It's a hell of a tirade. I almost rock back on my heels from the weight of all this mundane drama. I have a dizzying shift of perspective, where I realise that to Aidy, all this is as monumental as what happened to me in the darkness beneath the compound. These are the formative experiences, where they learned to hate themselves, to apologise for their existence in the world.

"So why did Cybele bring you here?" I ask.

That throws a spanner in their internal workings. Their eyebrows shoot up and they lose that pensive look. "I'm not sure." Their teeth scrape their bottom lip again. "Was she showing me or you?"

"I don't give a fuck about this." I roll my eyes. "I killed those men for fun. I'm tired of seeing assholes pushing mutants around, memory or not."

"But you're right. Why did Cybele choose these moments?"

At least they're fucking thinking rather than wallowing. It's a good start. Why I care about their emotional state is a question that occurs to me oddly late.

"They showed moments of rejection in my life. Moments where I lost relationships and found myself alone. But it only makes me feel worse."

I spread my arms wide, a dagger in each hand. More for comfort than anything else. There might be something to stab, and at least I can kill things in these damn memories. Maybe I should walk back into Gran's house and slit her fucking throat for the lack of healthcare shit. There I go, caring about Aidy again.

"No opinions, Leftie?" Now they're glaring at me. "For once in your life?"

"Cybele showed me things from my past. So I killed them, and then she was talking about finding a different option than killing."

Aidy stares daggers at the blades in my hand, and I shrug.

"These aren't my memories. Maybe she's telling you to do something different too. Maybe for you it's not being scared and stabbing someone instead."

"You've seen it all." They do the chin-jutting thing, which seems to be their shorthand for defiance. "What do you really think?"

"I was raised in darkness. I had no parents. Only a Father who was distant and cold, and watched me like a monster being grown in a cage. He loved me, desired me, and wished me to destroy the world. Then we'd usher in a new reality where he ruled with me by his side. That was my fucking life."

"Oh," Aidy says.

"So I see this shit, and I don't understand it. You wanted your mother to recognise you are more complex than a naive distinction between male and female. It seems a very small thing, as opposed to infecting a child with the trigger for an apocalyptic event."

"It never felt small," Aidy whispers.

"The same to sleep in a garage on a shitty fold-out couch, or to sit at a table and not be misgendered or criticised for a genetic mutation you could not control." I find myself biting out the words. "It seems petty to me, almost laughably so, except I find myself equally furious at them. I want to spill their blood as I murdered my parents, and the Father, and every other person who wished me to be their monster."

Aidy is wide-eyed. "I'm sorry."

I gesture irritably, my blade dissolving again. "Don't fucking apologise. I received my own justice. To me, murder was healing. You'd probably say it's because I'm irredeemably fucked up. That's what you get when you raise a kid in the dark and tell her she'll destroy the world. But fuck it, it's what it is. Maybe we'll change that, maybe we won't. But what does healing look like for you?" The words pour out of me as if they're scalding. I've rarely been this honest with anyone. Maybe the plant kids or Chatterbox, I got close.

Aidy shakes their head, like I'm overwhelming them. All these little cuts have left them so fragile, a person who all the fight bled out of long ago. So much for my words of reassurance. I've never really needed them before, which might be lucky given they've failed here. I honestly wish I could help her, but all I've ever been good at was a tool and a weapon.

"There's something else." Their voice hitches. "Something worse."

"I've got a really low tolerance for bullies."

"It's not that." They're shaking as if they're going to fly apart in fragments. "I think, I think. What she's doing is showing me. I try to hide everything, try to cover it up. Cybele's making sure I remember. She wants me to see it. See it all."

The street and the bodies and the houses all disappear around us. For almost a full minute we stand in the dark and silent forest, breathing the damp air. I'm about to open my mouth and say it's all over.

Then the world changes again.

26

AIDY

Of course we would end up here. Cybele is forcing me to confront my past—that shift in perspective the mutants promised me. The past I have hidden away, or papered over, or built an entire construction of false memories and wishful thinking atop. The goddess is tearing my walls down, laying my kingdom to waste and forcing me to confront the wreckage. Even more insulting, she's doing it with Leftie at my side. Who hasn't been entirely terrible, to be fair. The stabbing was unnecessary, since it played out in my mind either way. My body's still saturated in adrenaline and emotion. I think in her own clumsy way, she's trying to help.

I can't help wishing it was Skip—or anyone but her. Even her compassion is cold, like an android regarding a tortoise lying on its back in the desert, kicking its feeble legs. If someone is going to witness the disaster that is me, I'd rather have someone who might understand.

"The fuck is this now?" Leftie is far too cheerful.

I try to answer, but the words stick in my mouth. When the Dark Year began and most mutants fled, those left behind had to make other plans. Many of them ran to the safety of Goddess and the Cute Mutants, but I didn't. When the first big migration happened, I was stuck in hospital. I was high on pain medication, feeling too thoroughly sorry for myself to even scrawl the logo on the wall above my hospital bed. I thought about it so many times, but I imagined an entrance examination where they'd discover I'd let a mutant die on the street, beaten to death by off-duty cops.

By the time I was discharged, shaking and withdrawn, the mutants were in retreat. Most people in the cities had accepted Michael into their hearts and become nodes in his network. It was not a good time to be a mutant.

I found refuge quite by accident. I'd been intending to leave the city. It was difficult to buy things without being part of Michael, and in my wretched state I thought it would be better to risk life out in the wastes.

It was in the markets, surreptitiously trying to barter for a gate pass, that I found Lara, who took pity on me and brought me back to a three-storey apartment where fourteen other people lived. Mutants, all of them, and not a single one happy about it.

"It was somewhere safe," I tell Leftie, as I trace my fingers over the walls. There are names here, whole sprawling trees drawn in many colours of marker. People remembering where they came from, trying to stake their claim to humanity. We were hiding in the city waiting for a cure, a chance to step from the shackles of mutantkind and return to where we came from. None of us ever asked to be mutants—it was something forced upon us by tricksters and chance. One day, this poison gift might be taken away, and we'd be first in line to free ourselves from the curse. "Somewhere I had friends."

"Real safe." Leftie's poised beneath the main doorway, looking up at the words *No More Mutants* painted across it in jagged red lines. "I found a place like this once, somewhere in London. Went in there intending to kill them all, but they were too pathetic. No threat to anyone but themselves. Please sir, can I have a cure?"

"What else were we supposed to do?" I ask. "Fight against the inevitable?"

Leftie laughs, but for once it's not cruel—more surprised at how different two people can be. "That's *exactly* what you're supposed to do, not roll over and show your belly."

As we stand here, the ghosts of the past drift into the room. I know every single one of their names. This building wasn't a comfortable place to live, sleeping in the grime-spotted bath on the second floor where the water didn't work. But it's the first place I ever found something that felt like acceptance.

Cybele doesn't show me any of the moments that gave me warmth, like when we all ate in a circle on the floor. Where people laughed, and forgot about the curse of being mutant, and the cold world that awaited us outside. As much as we could, at least.

I'm glad we don't see the night before this, when everyone fought. It started with everyone against three, and ended with all against one. An argument over this city, over mutants and humans, and the hideous limbo we found ourselves in.

Leftie and I have arrived here in time for a much worse moment. A banging sound coming from the door. An amplified voice, impossibly calm and reasonable.

"They're outside," Marcus says. He's veiled to hide as much of his mutation as possible, although when he turns his head, I see flashes of light from his compound eyes.

"How many?" Angelique's snakelike tongue flickers as she talks.

"Four. All constructs."

"Why? What brought them here?" Rayner flutters at the window, a moth-like girl seeking the light.

"Someone did something." Marcus fidgets with the long sleeves of his robe. "They know we're here. They let us live. What changed?"

"Nobody would do anything." Rayner bangs on the glass, leaving damp streaks. "It's got to be someone from outside. Lying about us. Selling us out."

Past-me lurks in the doorway, silent and still.

"Is this a guilty conscience?" Leftie whispers loudly, pointing at me.

"Shut up," I hiss, as the thumping at the door intensifies. From one of the upper floors, Lara wails, and Pierre thrashes in his tank. The wet sound of tentacles comes from the basement. Xia does not wish to show herself. There are certain mutants that the more dangerous constructs will execute on sight.

"Get the door," Angelique hisses.

Marcus tugs his veil tighter. "I cannot. They might..."

Constructs are electronic servants that work for the Michael AI that runs the cities and most of their world. They take the form of angels, but they are anything but. Their programming can be rigid when it comes to mutants. The people we've made the deal with for this cure house were Quietus adepts, working for the local node of Michael's throne. To them, redeeming mutants back into humans is a noble and worthwhile aim. To a construct, we're simply better off dead.

"I'll do it." Rufus can pass as human better than most here, except for past-me, who's still frozen in the doorway. I remember how suspicion tightened around my chest and in my throat.

"What could it be?" Angelique asks fretfully.

"I'll go too," past-me says and scuttles awkwardly after Rufus. The front hallway is dark, because nobody's bothered to replace the bulb. Going out into the world is not something most of us do unless it's absolutely necessary. We've got subdermal identifiers that flag us as mutants, and some particularly devout types like to get proactive.

Through the milky glass pane on the front door, golden light pours in. Past-me is only a few steps behind Rufus, with Leftie and I shadowing invisibly behind. Rufus fumbles with the locks and swings it open.

Standing in a triangle formation on the doorstep are three angelic constructs. Their bodies glow, and white light pours from their eyes in narrow beams. Halos of fire flare out behind them. Even now I am intimidated. It's clear the constructs have not arrived for any kind purpose.

"Residents of Cure House AN3104. It has come to our attention that one of your residents is culpable in a crime."

"Crime?" Rufus' voice comes out in a high-pitched whistle.

Past-me is stalled behind him, one hand splayed on the hallway wall.

"I killed a lot of these fucks in my day," Leftie says cheerfully.

"Kill these ones," I demand. "Do it now." This is the only way we can stop this playing out.

"Shh. Let's see what happens." She nudges me, as if this is an exciting televisual romp we're on, rather than the worst moment of my life.

"—at nine fourteen pm," the construct is saying. "An illegal and forbidden symbol—namely the logo of a notorious terrorist group—was placed on a wall in the market quarter. Seventeen minutes and forty two seconds later, a contingent of mutant radicals arrived. In the ensuing battle, four hundred and forty one angelic constructs were destroyed, eighty seven Quietus agents were killed, and a number of Michael nodes were incapacitated."

"We love to see it," Leftie mutters.

"Symbol." Rufus looks around wildly. "Nobody made a symbol."

"The symbol was placed. We have footage. Based on our analysis, we determined it was drawn by a hooded figure, who returned through the streets on a remarkably inefficient trajectory—presumably in an ill-conceived attempt to fool the onlooking monitor cameras—and arrived at this location."

"We wouldn't do that." Rufus spins, and sees past me. "Tell them, Alex. None of us would risk what we have here. We're *safe*."

Even back then, I knew this last statement was a joke. Safety was impossible for mutants. Even their stronghold was under constant attack from Michael. Chatterbox and Marvellous were dead, and Goddess was in hiding, lashing out occasionally to keep Michael at bay. We existed in the city like rats in the walls, scurrying and hiding and waiting for the exterminators to arrive.

It's the reason why I drew the symbol on the wall. I wanted Quietus and the angels to suffer a fraction of what we suffered. And I naively thought I could escape their surveillance.

"I haven't been out of the house in weeks." Past-me's voice is flat. It's a lie, but only barely. "Who went to the market last?"

"I was at the market on that date, but it wasn't *me*." Rufus doesn't know what to do. He turns back towards the constructs and prostrates himself on the ground. "I would never turn away from the light of Michael's love. We live under his sufferance."

"Mutants are faithless liars." A second construct speaks up. "You cannot trust this one, brother. Analysis of the surveillance footage shows the size of the miscreant was within margin of error from this one here."

"I agree we should not trust this one." The first construct's eye-beams play over the flattened figure of Rufus. "He is a mutant, and therefore inherently untrustworthy. We are in accord, brother. He was at the market and matches the surveillance profile."

This is the moment. The single point on which everything hangs. Here is my opportunity to speak. To admit my guilt and suffer the consequences. I knew exactly what was about to happen, although I can pretend I didn't.

"Execution approved," the third construct says. "In accordance with Michael's law."

Past-me continues to say nothing. I remember the relief I felt, coursing through me in wave after wave. I had no idea what else to do. Flee deeper into the building and risk the lives of all the mutants here? There was guilt under the surface, but at that moment I couldn't access it. Mutants died. It's what they did, especially in those days. Rufus dying *now* was a mere accident of time—maybe a difference of hours, maybe weeks, maybe a year.

Leftie watches me, even as the construct takes aim and vaporises Rufus. It is a single beam of light, erupting from its right eye, the one that allegedly gazes on the glory of the Lord. It overrides my optic nerve, like staring into the sun. The wash of brightness fades, dancing globes of light dissolving until I can see there's nothing left of Rufus but a dark grey powder and a thin, gleaming smear of fatty tissue.

"It was you," Leftie says.

I ignore her and walk slowly back down the hallway. I'm following past-me, who is screaming about what happened to Rufus. The constructs ignore me. Their work is done, their justice meted out.

Except Rayner has been listening, and she agrees with Leftie. "It was you, Alex. You're the one who drew the symbol."

"It was Rufus." Past-me is flat against the wall beside the door. "The construct said so."

"Rufus wouldn't." Rayner's wings beat the air furiously, fluttering in front of me and sending a drift of soft particulate dust towards me. "He loved Michael and hated being a mutant. He never would have called those monsters down."

"You're right." Angelique won't even look at me. "You heard Alex last night. All that stuff about the random stops, about the attacks, about *everything*."

"Well, it's bullshit," past-me spits. "It all is, but I didn't draw the damn symbol."

"I saw you come home." Rayner's eyes are soft and wet. "Only a few minutes before Rufus did. You weren't supposed to be out of the house, but you were."

"They hate us. We've done nothing to them. We've bent the knee and kept out of sight, but they'll still hate us. For what? An accident? Some cosmic joke? We can't do anything to make them forget what we are."

"Call the constructs." Marcus's eyes flash red. "Tell them it was Alex."

These are fragile friendships that I've nurtured like tiny flames on a cold and windy night. I've gently grown them in those most inhospitable of places until they bloomed with the tiniest flowers. Now the frost has come and everything is shattered by the cold. This is all because I went out in a red-hot fury and did something reckless. Called down fire from the mutant Goddess. And she smote Michael's servants hard, and yet it was still not enough. We're still barricaded up in this rat-trap of a house. And now one friend is dead, and the others turn against me.

"No." Angelique's voice is cold. "We can't risk it. Who knows how they'll choose to respond. They might kill all of us, all because of what Alex did."

"That's my point." Past-me starts gasping with laughter. "They might choose to randomly kill us, and we've got no choice but to lie down and die."

"Or let Rufus die in your place." Rayner darts closer to my past self. "That's what you did. You said nothing, and now he's gone."

"Because none of it matters. We'll all die soon. Why not him?"

"Why not you?" Rayner lashes out with the tip of one wing, scoring a bloody line down one check. "He was always better than what you are—a coward even among cowards."

"Get out of here, Alex." Marcus sounds exhausted.

"We don't want you." For once, Angelique sounds confident in a decision.

Past-me is still laughing, doubled over with one hand pressed to the wall as if it can anchor me here somehow. This last, fragile refuge falling around me. My selfishness, my fear, my failure—it has all coalesced into something cold and vile that's now revealed for all to see. Who would want me when they know what I am? And then more feeling swells inside me, like an orchestra tuning up for a concerto of self-pity.

I still remember all these feelings, each one is etched into the deepest bedrock part of me. Lost again, adrift again, unwanted again. I washed up here and didn't leave because everywhere else was worse. Unexpectedly, I found friends. I found warmth. Now I would be out again, with nowhere else to go.

It's the first time it occurs to me. The problem isn't everyone else in my life. I cannot blame my mother, or Gran, or this group of friends I made in this place. I am the common thread. I'm the one who ruins everything. It's not a problem with everyone who rejects me. It's something in me that pushes them away. There's something about me that's fundamentally unlovable.

"Don't make us force you," Rayner hisses. "You've got five minutes to pack, or else we start making it very unpleasant."

Past-me scurries for the door, and Leftie slings an arm around present-me.

"Pretty dick move there, little Aidy."

"I know." I look up at her, my eyes streaming. "I had a long time to think about it. Somehow, I bought my way into one of those refugee pods that they strung under the ocean. Forty-five mutants survived the Dark Year like that, and I was one of them. Almost two-hundred days of being suspended in the dark, thinking about what a toxic person I was. Deciding to build someone new. But it doesn't work, does it? Underneath it all, I'm still Ruth-Ann, still Alex. No matter what, Aidy is a pretty house built on top of a reservoir of shit."

Leftie opens her mouth but disappears before she can speak.

I'm left alone to watch past-me walk out of their room, laden down with a duffel bag containing all my possessions in the world. Not one of my friends says a word to me as I leave.

Not one.

27

LEFTIE

I find myself alone in the forest. Aidy and the parade of their sad fucking life is gone. There's a flicker of movement among the trees and I turn towards it, darkness forming in my hands.

"There is no need for that." Cybele steps out of the shadows, as comfortably as I do. Her skin is rough and dark, and her eyes flare like two green stars lighting the night sky. "You have nothing to fear from me."

"Does Aidy?"

Cybele's mouth turns downward. It's a remarkably human expression. "You cannot move forward without confronting your past. Aidy hides from theirs, and you embrace yours too much."

It's my turn to look sour. "Do I really?"

"You draw lessons that were not intended."

"I think you're the blind one." I lean forward, the daggers gleaming in my hands. "All these years of life, all this time suffocating on the brink of death and no lessons learned. You still hold a flame in a cupped hand, as winds howl around you."

"Your suggestion?" She has dissolved into the night as if she has become one with the trees, and it's them that speak to me.

"Stop the winds from blowing. They come from somewhere, after all." I grimace. "Sorry, my analogy is falling apart. Let me be blunt. There are many clear and present dangers to mutantkind, and only one of us here has been doing something permanent to solve that problem."

Wind blows through the trees and stirs my hair into a dancing frenzy. Cybele's form is gone, but the trees loom higher, and motes of red light dance between them. This may be closer to her true form, if there is such a thing.

"And what would you have me do, Left Hand of Darkness?"

"Use me for the purpose I was intended for. When I was born for the second time, the cult put a seed inside me. It flowered as I did, but I ended them all before it was time for me to fully bloom. I burned everything of theirs to ash, so I am not sure of the exact mechanisms. But you are a true god, and if anyone can divine my secrets, it is you."

The window howls louder, a hellish shriek, and then dies away as if someone clapped a hand over her mouth. In the silence, her voice is very young, an echo of mine long ago. "What would you have me do?"

I stand with a shadow dagger pressed against my heart. "It is time to open me up. To pour out my wrath upon the world. The seed of the apocalypse in furious flower. With my mutant powers, plus what the cult bestowed upon me, none of our enemies will be able to stand."

"It all comes back to death." The voice is a sigh this time, some entwining of mine and the exhausted breath of the wind stirring the leaves.

"By design. Dylan and Dani died to be reborn as your weapons, didn't they? It is the great churning cycle of existence. Life and death and life, the endless turning of the wheel. This is what they taught in the darkness, and not all they said was lies."

"There is potential in death, yes, but waste too."

"We will not kill *all* of them. You will weigh their hearts and decide who is worthy, and I will be your instrument to pluck out those who do not."

The only sound is the wind in the trees, and I cannot make out any words. I wait. I have always been good at waiting.

"What did you think of what you saw in Aidy's heart?" Cybele has taken form again. She walks close to me and looks into my eyes.

"Very little." I sigh. "An object lesson in how each individual sees their narrative as a grandiose tale, no matter how petty and narrow it is."

"You have no sympathy for them?"

"What good would that do?" My fist clenches around the dagger's hilt. "We are entirely different worlds. I cannot understand a person who would stand by and let a friend die."

"Perhaps they cannot either."

I incline my head, because she is correct. The thing with death is it cannot be undone. When Aidy let that boy be killed, it was a decision they could never take back. In the same way, I cannot resurrect any of the people I have executed. If my dark touch has laid upon even one innocent, that is something I cannot fix. So I have always looked forward, rather than backward.

The past is dark and full of murder.

"So that is your answer then," I say finally. "We cannot do this because of the chance we might be wrong. So instead, we will let them attack us and hope we are strong enough to weather the storm."

"There are other ways to fight," Cybele says. "Quiet ways, subtle ways. We are already fighting a battle on multiple fronts."

I bare my teeth at her. "Fuck quiet and subtle. I am not made for that."

"No, you are made to unleash an apocalypse. And let us hope that only the good and just are standing once your dark flower has bloomed, shall we?"

I know it is the wrong thing to do to put a shadow-blade into the hissing heart of this god that stands before me, but I want to. Partly because I know she's right, but mostly because it's yet another death to leave in my wake.

"I'll go for the obviously evil people in the beginning. That'd be a damn good place to start."

Cybele takes a single step back. The trees seem flat and lifeless, like a backdrop. "I refuse to be a tomb carrying billions of dead. An empty, poisonous rock spinning emptily around a star. We will find another path, and my children will survive, as they have always done."

"Willow and Soo-yeon," I blurt. My eyes are hot, as the fluid in them is threatening to rush out of invisible puncture wounds. "Who will protect them?"

"You have met them." Cybele smiles. "I think you'll agree they're quite capable of protecting themselves. And they have their many aunts and one huncle as well. And you, I think, who would perform all manner of terrible acts in their defence."

"I would like a world where they did not have to defend themselves." I wipe at my eyes, which continue to bleed moisture. I inspect my fingertips, but there is no blood, only a clear, salty fluid. "That does not seem too much to ask."

"Yes, love is difficult. It is hard to conceive of a world where your children may suffer. You want to lash out against all dark possibilities. For most, that is impossible. It is worse for you, because you have the capability to tear the world apart. And now I ask you to show mercy, which is the cruellest thing of all."

"Love." The word tastes wrong. "I love nobody."

"You love those children that you rescued, and the twins too. I see the connections that bind you together."

"I will sever them." I slash outwards with twin swords, as if my shadows could part these unwanted entanglements. "I will cut myself off. You do not wish to help me, Cybele. I will find my own path. What did Goddess give me these powers for, if not to defend her children with whatever force I have within me?"

Green fire flares in the depths of Cybele's eyes, and something like antlers erupt from her forehead. Her limbs are craggy, clawing things and her breath rasps in and out like a fire. "Goddess was a desperate woman fighting a terrible war, and she saved humanity every day. You have no idea what it cost her to keep balance, when everything was on the verge of collapse. She carved out time at impossible cost to herself. If you were part of her plan, you were the smallest fraction of it, a sliver of darkness and not some doomsday device."

I gather shadows around me in my own carapace, fade back into them so they weave around me in my own forest of grasping hands and bared teeth. "Perhaps you know her less than you think. You were in your death throes while she did your job. The darkness in her heart was greater than you think. I *spoke* with her."

There's a long, drawn out moment, the shadows of the forest enfolding me as I stand against them, unbowed and unafraid. Every leaf in the forest trembles as we two stand at odds. And then it passes, and Cybele is simply a dark-skinned and slender girl.

"Perhaps. I was not fully there. My mind was elsewhere, as you say. Perhaps you should speak with the one who loved her most, and was by her side through it all."

My shadows dissolve in wisps around me, a haloed haze that reveals me. Darkness in the shape of a person. A hole in the world. A bomb that was never allowed to detonate. And helpless, despite it all.

"Who are you talking about?" I ask.

"The woman called Moodring. Alyse Sefo. The one beloved of Goddess, before her ascension, during it all, and up to the moment of her death."

My eyes are mysteriously wounded again. It is an impossibility to me, that the Goddess I sensed when I changed could have ever passed from this world. Nothing has ever burned so bright. It also confuses me on some level that Alyse was the one chosen. She is beautiful and strong, but it is still like those myths of the Greek gods coming down to consort with humanity. But before all that—and perhaps the entire time, although it's an idea that I cannot fully understand—Emmaline Jing Hall was a girl.

"So you will not take me as your weapon." I am angry, but I'm also exhausted, bone-deep weariness that permeates right down to every shadowed part of me. "Despite everything you have seen of the world since its beginning."

"I understand, Leftie." This god reaches out and touches me, consorting with mutantkind after all, or whatever lesser being I am. "In my darker moments, I dream of it too. But we have to do it the slower way, the better way. Change the world increment by increment."

I try to imagine what that looks like, but I cannot. All I have ever been is the promise of death, and I cannot see anything but death for my people, or me as the bulwark who forestalls it all.

"Then you are useless too," I tell her. "And I am alone as always. Just like Aidy. Perhaps that was your lesson. We are alone in the end."

"Oh, my sweet child. How can you take the precise wrong lesson from all this? Think of what Goddess did, how she found love and friendship and family. That is her legacy, and it begins on this island. It is a place full of connections, and her future is this network expanded across the world to encompass all who wish it."

It is a pretty image if it is true. In my mind, I see a green planet, a sprawling network of forest habitats and undersea bubble worlds thriving amongst vast oceanic jungles. Vines trailing everywhere, an instantaneous communication network, and everyone, both mutant and human with a green spark in their eyes.

It could be beautiful or horrifying, but either way there is no place for me. I am darkness, and I am built for death. Their beautiful new world will be something I am destined to die to protect.

"I should go." I raise my shadows again, a cloak against feeling.

"Leftie, speak to Alyse," Cybele says. "Please."

I am already fleeing the forest, running in my easy, loping gait. I can run a long way, but the island is small and I can already feel the ocean hemming me in. The shadows are inviting, and I spin myself into them, ascending upwards through the silken slick of night until I am miles above. Below, the few lights of Emmaline make it look like a tiny constellation among an unbroken sea of black. A single pixel marks the cottage where Dylan and the others make their home. Where they carved out space for me, an ungrateful shadow.

Aidy is lost in their memories, no doubt berating themselves for all their failures. Even a little life can have its own tragedies, I suppose. Mine was grandiose but at the end of it all, I'm still here, in my feelings five miles up and sifting through my life for a single connection.

"It's very emo," a voice says from the air.

"I *told* you she was sulking." Willow spins themself out of shadow, a thing of leaf and blade dancing in the air. "She went to see Green Mum, and they got in a tizzy. I felt it in the vines."

"I felt it too." Soo-yeon reaches out their vines and weaves a cradle for me in the air. "I think everyone did. Bad dreams tonight. Lots of people are sleeping restless."

"Did you know Goddess?" I ask them.

"No." Willow shakes their head. "We were born a year after she died. We see her in Cybele's dreams, but that's not the same."

Soo-yeon nestles into their sibling. "We know her from the hole she left behind. Trace her memory in silence and sadness."

"Now who's emo," Willow smirks.

"They miss her so much, Will."

"I know." The two of them swing together, entangled. Giving each other comfort.

There's a long silence.

"Do you need a hug, Leftie?" I can't tell which twin asks.

"I've never needed a hug in my life," I tell them haughtily.

There's a rustling of vines and leafy limbs. "Well, *I* need a hug," Willow says.

"I'm giving you a hug," Soo-yeon says.

"For fuck's sake, Soo, you're supposed to be the smart one."

There's a giggle, and then I'm enfolded by four leafy arms.

I suppose it isn't the worst feeling in the world.

28

AIDY

Cybele does not force me to watch my time in the refugee pods. She doesn't need to. Part of me will always remain there, my feelings turning slow and sour. In desperation, it's where I came to the conclusion that if I ever surfaced, I would become someone else. A person who was bright, who oriented themself towards others. Someone who used their powers for good if given the chance. Someone who gave aid to those who needed it. Hence the name.

There are proverbs about good intentions for a reason.

However, it has become apparent I cannot escape myself. When they asked me to actually be part of a superhero team, to *aid* others, the corpse of my true self came bobbing to the surface of the lake, evidence of all my past crimes. To be around these beacons of righteousness made me even more bitter. Alyse said we were all made up of layers of ourselves, and it was meant to be reassuring, but all it did was prove to me that I could never escape this. I am a noose around my own neck, a weight dragging me down.

When I return to the forest, I am alone. Leftie is gone, presumably in disgust at what I am. Right now, she must be with Skip and Mélodie, spilling all my secrets through her sharp little teeth and smeared-red lips. I wonder if they'll be surprised, or if they'll bend their heads together and whisper that they knew it all along. My true nature is too apparent to be disguised.

"What now?" I ask the forest, but the only reply is the sighing of wind among the leaves.

The sad thing is I have nowhere else to go. I suppose I could leave the island. I can pass as human, although most countries have taken advantage of the existence of Mutopia to introduce variously draconian mutant identification laws. I am sure there are some where we're tolerated, or at least ignored. A quiet life by the seaside, where almost nobody knows me. That was my inevitable end, I suppose, to wash up somewhere far away where nobody can know me. This time on Mutopia was a lovely dream I came up with in the dark, which I clung to for too long on awakening.

It's time to say goodbye.

"I think I shall abandon this healing vision quest business." The voice from behind me is snappish and crackling. "I have been singularly unsuccessful with both of you. It is tempting to place the blame at the feet of you and Leftie, given your internal stubbornness and refusal to shift, but perhaps I understand the human heart and mind less than I hoped."

When I turn to see Cybele, she is a gnarled and twisted form, as if exhaustion has aged her. "I don't know what you mean." I am numb inside and out. Feelings bounce off me like I'm protected against them too. It should be a relief, but I am still drowning in my past.

"You pretend you are making yourself somebody new, but you cannot truly avoid this damage you carry around. The past is held deep within you, but it's like a bruise. All you wish to do is touch the edges of, press it over and over to see if it still causes you pain. I cannot understand why you would rather do this than embrace it as part of yourself, and let it fade."

Her words press on my chest like an invisible weight that makes every breath an effort. It isn't so much that I touch it to see if it still hurts. It's that it's at the core of me, so much of who I am. In many ways, I am the bruise in her analogy, and the pain it gives me is the only sign I'm still alive.

"I'm sorry." It's the only thing I can think of to say. I don't even know what I'm apologising for. For being me, for being unlovable, for a lifetime of selfish decisions, curling around myself to protect the wounded core of me. I don't know where it started. I can't remember the first hurt. But uncurling to stand and be unafraid is impossible.

"My sweet Aidy." Cybele stands and enfolds me in her arms. She smells exactly like the trees, dizzyingly fresh. "I hoped seeing your past in such detail would make you realise it is one story among thousands. We are all bruised, even me. In my fear and pain, I created the monster Heart of a Flower who nearly damned the world to nightmare. I used Dylan and Dani as weapons with little regard for the cost to them. My crimes are so much greater than yours. Except I still reach out, and now look at the world we have. It blooms so much brighter than I dreamed. This is what I wanted the lesson to be. You are not irredeemable. Your story explains you. It is the soil from which you grow, but you can reach out to others. You can connect to them and borrow their strength, their community."

It is a beautiful story, but only a story.

"Thank you." My words are mechanical, and my body angles away from her involuntarily.

Cybele shivers. "Reach out to your friends. Build your forest. Even one with the Left Hand of Darkness."

My cheeks burn hot and red. Leftie, who has never liked me. Who saw my weakness, I suspect, in some instinctive way and understood how broken I was. To her, I am proof of some theorem where all others are failures. I cannot say she's wrong.

I came here for a change in perspective, but all I found was proof of what I've known all along. So I flee the forest, stumbling along the path until I breach the treeline and am back in the wide meadow. I still don't know where to go. The night is warm, and the moon is full, turning the grass into a rippling silver sea.

And ahead of me on the cliff's edge yet again is the very last person I ever wanted to see.

"Little Aidy." She sketches a mocking bow.

"The Left Hand of Darkness." My lips are still numb, as if I've ingested poison. Or, more accurately, it's boiled up from inside me. "Are you feeling especially smug now?"

She tilts her head, as if she's shocked to hear the venom. "And why would that be?"

"You've seen what I am."

Her laugh is much higher than her speaking voice, and I scour it for traces of mockery, but it seems to hold more surprise than anything. "You're an ordinary person who did something shitty. A tour through anyone else's life would show the same."

"I let him die." My voice hits the last syllable and shatters, a head-on collision that leaves me gasping.

"Imagine if you confessed and were killed instead. Maybe he'd have mourned you and spent all this time beating himself up for not intervening. He probably would've died, though. Those constructs are no fucking joke, and I've seen them smack down mutants for nothing more than existing."

"He's still dead, Leftie." I want to step forward and into her arms, and I don't know why. It's the only circle nearby, I suppose. "And it was my fault."

"You made a mistake, and you've been hiding from it. That's your problem, the hiding. See, I am what I am. A murderous creature, raised in darkness and set upon a throne. I've done more shitty things than you can possibly whip yourself to death over. You think that cute little friend of yours never did anything shitty?"

"I don't know." I can't imagine Skip letting someone else take the fall for her.

"If you're all pretending you're better than you are, and hiding all your shitty parts, how can you be sure you actually like each other?" Her blue eyes look like meltwater, and the curve of her lips is almost soft.

"Everyone in my life has hated me." I'm dissolving in front of this awful girl, and it's insult added to insult.

"Little Aidy, I don't hate you."

"You do so," I snuffle.

Leftie laughs again. "I think you're annoying, but I don't hate you. Not even a little bit."

"But you're so horrible to me!"

"I'm like that with everyone." She raises one pale shoulder. "Blame it on being a pampered cult princess who had a date with Goddess. And maybe I did hate you in the beginning. But we're all carrying our own shit, aren't we?"

"I hated you," I howl.

"Most people do." She winks. "But you don't catch me making a big production out of it."

"I don't anymore. You stabbed those cops for me, and you call me little Aidy."

"Yes, but that's supposed to be annoying." Leftie steps forward and wraps her arms around me.

It feels slightly awkward, as if we've both had hugs explained to us differently by disinterested observers, and neither of us are getting it right. Her skin is cooler than mine, as if she's stepped out of a freezer, and her chin digs into my shoulder. Even still, I don't hate it. Not even a little.

When we disentangle, the awkwardness descends in full. I don't know what to say. Thank you seems both inadequate and unnecessary, and any more words would tangle themselves in knots inside my mouth.

"I should find the others," I say.

"Yeah, me too." Leftie simply steps into shadow and disappears.

It's not so easy for me. I have to walk the long way back across the fields and into Emmaline. It gives me time to try and understand this new Leftie, the moonstruck one that descended from the sky. She said she didn't hate me, and she put her arms around me. I wonder if I stepped out of Cybele's realm into a parallel universe. It's the most reasonable explanation.

In this universe, perhaps this Aidy can talk to Skip and Mélodie, even to Alyse and Dylan. Explain everything. Tell the story as Leftie saw it unfold in my mind. Be honest about who and what I am. And they'll understand, like Leftie did. They'll take me in their arms, one after the other, and tell me that none of this matters. That I'm still worth something, a person adrift in their own life, who'd stand by and watch a friend die. Parallel universe Aidy is stronger and braver than I am. I'm not sure where she gets it from. Perhaps some of it leached from Leftie during that long, strange hug.

I go back to the dormitories first. It's hard to figure out any other option, even though it means Skip will be the first one I'll tell. That's if she'll even talk to me after how odd and rude I was before dashing off into the forest.

When I reach our room, I find Skip curled up on her bed, watching something on her phone. Mélodie is sprawled asleep on top of my bed, one arm flung up over her head. The instant she hears my footsteps,

Skip leaps from the bed. Her face lights up and it's so beautiful to see.

"You're okay." Her arms go around my neck and I feel her body pressed tightly against mine. My hands pat feebly against her back. This is a much warmer response than I was expecting.

"Yes, yes, I'm fine. Are you okay?"

Skip has hold of one of my hands, tugging on it as if I'm a doll that'll be activated that way. "You went off to Cybele's forest, and didn't come out. It's been three days."

"What?" It's my turn to be wide-eyed. "Three days? How?"

"You tell us." Her face is very close to mine. "What happened in there?"

"Leftie was there too?" Mélodie is up now too, although her hug is briefer.

"Yes, it was me and Leftie. It was…" Here is the moment. The point at which I explain my story, step through it moment by moment. From Ruth-Ann to Alex to Aidy. The suburbs to the city to the hospital to the cure house to the refugee pods. To shuffle the layers of me and present them as a whole, full person. For them to see me as I am, and decide if they still love me.

But this is not a parallel universe, and I am the same Aidy I've always been. The same Alex, the same

Ruth-Ann.

A coward. Unlovable. Adrift.

"I don't really remember." I open my eyes as wide as I can. "It was sort of trippy, I think, lots of visions of forest and vines. Connections growing. Like a weird nature film on drugs. I think it did something though? Reset some things in my brain. I feel a lot better."

Skip is looking at me, a slight crease in her brows. "You look the same."

"Of course I'm the same." I smile, and I know it's too forced, but I hold it there all the same. "Why would I be any different?"

"I'm glad you came back." There's hesitancy back on her face, like the joy of seeing me has already evaporated, and she's remembering all the other stuff.

I'm going to need to figure out a story to tell her, to explain all the rumours. One that's close enough to true. I imagine Leftie's disappointed face when she sees my shift in perspective wasn't a revelation after all, but another missed opportunity. I'll find her, and I'll figure out something that she'll go along with. Assuming she hasn't already fled the island to stab people.

"I'm happy to be back too," I tell Skip, and pull her back into a hug, because then I don't have to look into her eyes.

29

LEFTIE

I approach the house on the tip of the island in the most roundabout way possible, as if it's a mission target. Alyse probably isn't home. Even if she is, I doubt I can make her talk about the exact topic everyone's warned me against.

Don't mention Goddess.

But Cybele gave me this advice, so it's awkward. I'm not made for situations like this. If someone had asked me to stab Alyse, it would be…

Also impossible. How did this happen? These *entanglements*, becoming part of this metaphorical forest. This root structure that joins me to the others undeniably exists. I am not as versed in self-denial as little Aidy. And, despite everything that I was made to be, I find myself unwilling to sever these ties.

I step out of shadow a half-mile from the hut where I live. Moonlight smears a silver arrow across the ground, and I follow obediently. I trace the shape of the shadows ahead, and become aware of a figure before I can even see them. They stand on the headland like a sentinel, a figure watching for danger. It seems as if they've been there a very long time, something ancient and pitted with time.

"Leftie," they say as I approach, and they are no longer a decrepit and eroding statue, but a woman with shadows under her eyes and her hair twisted into a complex braid. "How was the forest?"

"Inconclusive." It's as good a word as any.

"Dilly and the twins were bouncing off the walls. I sent them away to give them something to do. Otherwise they get insufferable."

"I did bump into the twins afterwards." I can't bring myself to admit anything about the hug.

"Yes. They were excited about *something* happening in the forest."

I click my tongue irritably. "I argue with Aidy. That's all. And then Cybele got fed up with me and said I should talk with you."

Her smile is broad, as if she loves this idea more than any idea that's occurred to a person in the history of the world. "I'm always here to talk." She pauses, and the smile gets even wider. "Little Leftie."

I hesitate for a moment, not because of little Leftie, which might be a tiny bit appealing to me at some cellular level I don't want to investigate too deeply. Because of what I'm about to say next. "It's about Goddess."

There's a physical flinch, as if I've reached out and jabbed two fingers into a wound."Of course." Her voice melts into the night, soft as the grass at my feet. "Let's talk inside."

The house where Dylan and the others live is mysteriously empty, as if everyone scattered when they heard me coming. Even in the shadows, I sense no sign of eavesdroppers. Alyse busies herself with making tea.

"I argued with Cybele about what Goddess would want." I have no time for niceties. This is something I need to know. "When I changed and became a mutant, I saw your Emma. I spoke to her. She made me a thing of shadow, a weapon to defend her beloved mutants with. It is not a task I can lay aside."

Alyse turns to me, a mug in each hand. "I made you one without asking, sorry. You don't have to drink it." She offers it to me, and I take it. "This was Emma's favourite."

I hold it to my lips and inhale the steam. It smells as if woodsmoke was emptied into the cup. The first, tentative sip is delicious, as if I'm standing beside something that gently burns for me.

"It's good," I whisper, and she smiles.

"I won't say your story isn't true, but I can't imagine Emma asking you to be the sole defender of mutantkind, alone out there in the dark. We knew each other impossibly well, the two of us. You can't spend so much time in each other's head without it. Although towards the end I felt like a teacup bobbing around in a planet-sized storm, so it's possible she kept some savage part of herself tucked away. She did show me a lot of her nightmares. Someone had to witness the things she went through." Alyse's fingertips are white against the scuffed black ceramic of the mug. She forces a smile, and if I had a heart, it would have split neatly in two inside my chest at the sight of it. "You should tell me what you remember though. Nobody can truly know a person completely."

"Oh." I fold myself into the nearest armchair. "Sure, I can do that. I don't know exactly where they got Emma's blood from. Something about a penitent in a laboratory once owned by a company called Jinteki."

"Ah." Alyse takes her own seat and settles back into it. She takes a sip of tea and tilts her head back. "Interesting. I've wondered how that came about. The missing sample of Emma's blood. One of those dangling plot threads."

"Uriel explained that by drinking the blood of Goddess, I would ascend and gain the power to destroy her. Thereby assuring the breaking of the world. It seemed a wild swerve to the plan, even to me..."

Uriel stands over me, flanked by acolytes. Their faces are invisible behind their blank masks, so I see only the Father. I hate him, so deep and unyielding, it's like a river bubbling up from the Underworld and taking all souls with it.

"This is the moment of your true ascension." His breath is too loud, as always.

"What prophecy mentions this?" I tilt my head.

This is a poor question, as he rattles off a series of verses from the Bible and from his own witless ravings. Squinted at in poor light and with no regard for logic, they could possibly construe an argument. In reality, he stumbled upon this opportunity and it is too good to pass up. Mutants are evil according to the Father's teachings, but to harness the power in the person of their chained teenage servant...

I do not know what to think. I lack context to make the decision. If it is my death, then it is an escape. If it gives me the slightest advantage, I will lunge for it regardless of the consequences.

"The world shall break." I lower my eyes from the Father's face. "And we shall rise."

The blood tastes no different to mine, when I bite the inside of my cheek in a frenzy, fighting the acolytes in one of my many bids for freedom. It's unpleasantly warm, as if they've heated it slightly too much, and it clings tarry to the inside of my throat.

I swallow, again and again. I retch and my eyes close, wet with tears.

When I open them again, I am in a wide open space. It looks scoured clean, a great circle of bone white sand. Above me, the sky is a dark vortex, bruised into an inverted funnel. At the centre of this ruptured sky sits a figure with tan skin and long, dark hair.

"Shadows." Her voice echoes and warps. "An appropriate power, it seems, given where you come from."

I can feel them pressing all around me, the weird light from the sky laying them delicately against my skin like wet cloths. They are a refuge and something to hold. My left hand reaches out and brushes the contour of the closest one. I take a handful and sharpen it into a rough blade. It moves easily, as if it wants to take this form.

"I am meant to kill you," I tell the woman in the sky.

"Yes, I thought you might be." She is sitting cross-legged in the meditation position, and a kaleidoscope of her rotates above me, fanning outwards in a dizzying mandala of replicated forms. "You can try if you wish."

"I have no desire to end your life." I let the shadow I hold dissolve back into darkness. "If I did, your name would be at the end of a very long list."

There is only one of her now, standing in front of me. She looks terribly young, barely older than me. Her lips are chapped and she worries at the edge of one with white teeth. "There is so much to do, and most of it is ugly and painful. Yet here you are, a defender."

I frown. "A defender? I was made to break the world."

Goddess waves one hand dismissively. "Breaking the world is easy. I need someone to safeguard it. To ensure my people persist through the storms."

I have never seen the point of worship—not the Father, not the God he preaches to me, not myself in the glorious vision of the future they promise. Nobody is worth it. Yet here, standing before a Chinese girl with supernovas in her eyes, I understand what it would be to serve someone.

"I will do it." I do not bow my head or my knee, but only because I don't think she wants or needs it.

"I wish I could free you, but you will have to free yourself. Then help anyone you can. Whatever it takes. The world is dark today, and I would see someone carve some light from it before this ends one way or another."

The sky buckles and pours violet light. The shadows stretch and swirl over the ground. It is an involuntary motion to reach out my hands and take hold of two blades.

Darkness falls like a veil, and when it lifts, I am back in the compound.

Acolytes lean over me. One is pushing rhythmically at my chest, counting under his breath.

His shadow, when it falls over me, is cold enough that it almost burns my hand.

I smile.

"Uh, yeah." I blink away the memory and look at the ground. "It got messy after that."

"I remember that day," Alyse says. "We lost Abby, and both Roxy and Oni were grieving. I was the only one they'd listen to. In their eyes I was the closest thing to Dilly. It was a really bad day for everyone, Leftie."

"It was a good day for me." I'm not lying. It was the best day of my life.

"After Roxy died, Ems disappeared for a while. I was worried, but there were a million other things to worry about. Then she came back and she told me where she'd been." She pauses, and I hear her breath hitch. Her hand trembles and she touches it to her lips as if she's remembering a kiss. "You know, I never connected these two things together until now." Alyse smiles, and I've never seen anything as beautiful as love viewed from the other side of loss. "She said she found a girl in a hole. That she couldn't do much more than give you a way to escape, but she hoped you'd find your way home."

"The girl was me?"

Alyse's eyes overflow with tears. She's transformed into someone foggy and indistinct. "She cared so much. Trying to not fuck everything up, to somehow hold a disintegrating world together. And she'd still taken the time to reach out to you, a broken, angry girl hiding in the dark."

My hand is trembling. I want to wreath it in shadow, to still it. "What did she mean by home?"

"To her, to us. She wasn't sure if you would. You reminded her of Dylan, except lost so far away. She wanted to guide you, but it was so, so dark and there were few lights in the world."

There's something painful in my throat, like a tiny animal burrowing its way out of me. Something heaves in my chest, like the stone heart of me has been threaded through with tiny hairline fractures and is on the verge of shattering. I want to flee before it does, but there's one more question I have to ask.

"Would she have been happy to see me in her forest?"

Alyse can't speak. She fans her face, as if that will dry her tears. "So much, Leftie. You have no idea."

She holds out her arms, and despite the trickles of water eroding the walls that encircle my heart, that keep it safe, that barricade it against all intrusions—

I step inside.

Alyse Sefo holds me like I'm a lifeline. She's indistinct and drenched in salt, a shipwreck of a person beaching herself in my arms as if it's the only shore for miles.

"I'm sorry she's gone," I say, and each word breaches me. "I wish I could have met her again."

And then I'm crying, or I assume that's what it is. It feels like a tempest, like I am caught up in something larger than myself. I am a mote in a whirlwind, a shadow cast by something far larger than me, everything I have tucked away inside myself exploding outwards into a vast penumbra.

I mourn Goddess, and all the other mutants who've been lost, for the struggles of those left behind. I cry for myself, and my life in the dark. For my foolish parents, who handed me to the man who chained me. I don't cry for the lives I took, because on balance most of them deserved it. I do cry over the fact that I'm wanted, that I'm needed for nothing more than my presence.

Alyse holds me while I sag in her arms, wrung out and wretched.

"Um," a new voice says. "Hi. I was looking for Leftie, to check that everything's okay."

I spin around, wiping my eyes, and see Aidy lurking in the doorway, wishing for all the world they were a shadow. "It looks like Cybele broke me after all," I say.

"Healing sometimes looks like being broken." Alyse pats me on the back.

"Is everything okay?" Aidy asks.

"I'm fine." I step away, trying to regain my composure. My balance feels slightly off, as if the ballast that weighed me down has gone and I need to relearn what it feels like to move through the world. "Just having a chat about old times."

Aidy frowns slightly, that little wrinkle of jealousy crossing their face. It makes sense a little more now, the way they are. Now that I've seen the pages of their life from the inside.

"But I guess I'm sticking around." I am unable to stay deadpan at this. Home. It is a strange feeling, as if there are so many more arms to hold me. A network of connections spreading outwards. Something new to learn.

"That's great!" Aidy's smile is wide, but there are shadows in their expression, faint ones I cannot tease any more than strands from. "Everyone will be so pleased."

"Does this mean we're friends?" It is very hard not to make a joke about friends being shot dead by constructs, but I am trying to make a good impression for Alyse.

"Of course." There's still the same smile plastered on their face, and I wonder if they learned anything at all from their past. There are many different kinds of shadow, and some are harder to escape than others.

30

AIDY

So Leftie isn't going anywhere—at least based on the little tableau that I've walked in on. Which means whatever life I find on the island, she'll be part of it. Someone who's seen far too much of me to be comfortable. Who cares little for the attention of others, but still has it showered upon them. Light is attracted to this shadow girl, where I am always left scrounging for every glimmer I can find. And the worst part is how she's decided to casually dispensing her favour towards me. It feels like pity.

"Why don't you go find Dilly?" Alyse asks. "They'll be delighted to hear your decision."

Leftie snorts. "I guess they've won. Bet they'll be insufferable." She flashes her sharp-toothed smile and sidles for the door. For a moment, she is limned in light, then she gives an awkward wave before disappearing into the dark.

"Tea?" Alyse leans over the bench and turns on the kettle.

I shake my head.

"Did it help? Whatever Cybele showed you in there?"

I could tell my story here—in my own words, not what she's heard from others. This is a good test, in a way. Who better to confess to than the permanently kind Alyse Sefo? Someone who will listen and not judge me, simply reach out and bring me into her sprawling network of friends and family without question. Like Leftie did, bizarrely enough.

Except seeing my life play out before my eyes—not in a flash, but in a grim parade of misery—has shown me a truth it's hard to hold. I am not worth forgiving, no superhero whose crimes are granted absolution in order to bring me to their side as a glistening weapon. Instead, I'm a crumpled shield who broke when it mattered.

"I'm just really tired." I don a brave grimace, the expression of someone who's been sorely tried. "I'll feel a lot better tomorrow, I think."

"That's a good idea." Her mouth purses, but she lets any further words drop. Willing to grant me grace and time to process my shift in perspective. Cybele offered me no punishment, nothing I can do to atone. Instead, she gave me the harder task of finding change within myself. Something I'm unable to do, an empty well whose bright water drained out years ago.

"Goodnight." I hustle for the door, and make my way back to town. Frustration spins like cogs in my brain, chewing on my thoughts until they sting. There's a painful gap between wanting things to be fixed and being willing to change, especially since I don't even know how to start. If there was a guidebook I could follow, or a series of steps to tick off, then I could begin. Instead I am a wilderness where nothing good grows. I can no longer realistically picture what a perfect me would look like.

Skip and Mélodie are both gone when I get back to the dormitories. Fled to avoid me, no doubt. I end up taking my own fake advice and tumbling into bed. My dreams are of Rufus disintegrating beneath a construct's eye-beams, and Leftie watching from the shadows, swinging her legs and smiling her sharp-toothed red smile. I watch him vaporise, smell the charred, hot-meat smell. The blank face of the construct turns towards me, the multiple eyes recording my every reaction. Did they measure my relief? Did it mean anything to them?

I wake tangled in the sheets, legs slick with sweat. My chest hurts and I swing half-out of bed, the night air prickling cool against my skin. The clock's glowing numbers show me there's little chance of getting more sleep, so I cross to the window and look out. Dawn smears the horizon with a golden finger, and the buildings all around sprout new leaves in the burgeoning day. Images linger in my mind, smears of blood dragged across the border between dreams and waking. The ashen smear of Rufus, the trail of gore left behind from the man I bludgeoned in the tunnels.

When breakfast rolls around, I sit at a table alone, drinking coffee. There are few people up with me, each consumed by their own business, even though they smile and nod in greeting. How many of them will notice if I depart? My experience with Cybele held no answers, at least none that I can understand.

In the end, I seek out Alyse. She's not in her office and so I drift through the corridors until I reach the wide chamber where we first met the Left Hand of Darkness. Who's there once again, this time with Skip and Mélodie.

"Aidy, finally!" Skip's look of delight seems genuine, and the others are smiling too. "We've been waiting since dawn. Have you heard the news yet?"

"News?"

"Alyse and Dylan want to form a new team. With *us* on it. You and me and Mél and Leftie. Probably more in time, but we're the first four. Isn't that amazing?"

It is, to the point of being unbelievable. Too good to be true. Possibly a trap, something to catch me out, to force me into revealing myself. I can have all this if I stay, if I change, if I open myself up. A carrot of belonging to pair with the stick of isolation.

Mélodie opens her mouth sending bright bubbles from between her lips that burst and spill the joyous tones of her voice. "So happy/this team/all of us/and Leftie too."

And Leftie too with her perfect face in an unreadable expression. "We've already been training. Skippy, you want to show them what we can do?"

"This is amazing, Aidy, you have to see this." Skip's expression is so full of delight it's both hard to look at and hard to look away. The nickname *Skippy* reverberates in my head like a voice shouted at the mountains.

Leftie takes her hand, and my stomach twists. Then the two of them disappear together and reappear partway around the room, for the barest fraction of a second before vanishing again. They blur in the air, the barest suggestion of two beautiful forms and then I can't see them anymore.

They're gone for less a minute, but during that time my fist clenches along with each beat of my heart. When they return, Skip is practically glowing. Her smile is so wide you could curl up in it.

Leftie beams at her. "That was perfect. It's like your namesake. A stone skipping across the water. You only touch the world for the merest fraction, and then leap again. It essentially turns your small jumps into one long one."

"That's brilliant." Skip's eyes are bright. "We went all the way to the cliffs and back."

"It's how I cross the waves." Leftie looks impossibly good. The outlines of her muscles show against her skin, the faintest sheen of sweat making them glisten. Skip is standing very close, and their hands are still entwined together from where they've been dancing together with their powers.

I've never felt so *angry* before. Leftie won't be satisfied until she's taken everything. Waltzing into this island and nestling herself at the heart of it to wring every drop of goodness from it. My jaw aches from the way my teeth are clenched. At least when Leftie was in her cult everyone loved her. You could see it in the eyes of those children, who adore her *still* even after she butchered their families. And then she comes to Mutopia, and sways Chatterbox and their family to her side. And now, and now—

"You're obviously not broken, little Leftie," I say.

She stills slightly. It would be barely noticeable to anyone else, but I register it. "What do you mean?"

"What you were saying to Alyse last night, about being broken. I'm glad to see it's not true."

"I'm confused." This is a lie. Her eyes are the broken ice shards I remember from the first time we met.

"Oh." I let colour flare in my cheeks, as if I'm embarrassed. "Last night. You were crying like your heart was broken. It was sweet to see you like that."

"You're mistaken." There's a fleck of blood on one of her teeth. I wonder where it came from.

"God, I'm so sorry. I didn't realise it was a private moment. It was nothing."

"Leftie can cry?" Mél signs.

"Aidy's mistaken. They were obviously overwhelmed by their ordeal."

"Yes." I widen my eyes, shoot a sidelong glance at the others. "I imagined the whole thing."

"Leftie, it's no big deal," Skip says earnestly.

Mélodie steps alongside Leftie's other side, arm extended as if she wishes to complete a circuit.

Except Leftie breaks the connection, dropping Skip's hand and taking a single step towards me.

"Betraying people is a nasty habit." The ice in her eyes holds dark water beneath. "*Little* Aidy."

I want her gone. I want this island to be safe. Leftie is a threat, who knows too much, and so I fear the truths she holds and the violence of her gaze. My fury at her founders on the rocks of my inevitable failure. I don't know what to do. Adrift once again.

"I'm not…" My heart stutters, and my teeth chatter in time. "I was confused, I'm not—"

"Now I know how Rufus felt." Her teeth scrape thin lines of blood across the corner of one lip as she gnaws on it. "When he looked into those construct's eyes and saw his death."

"What are you talking about?" I try to lean on derision, but the ground is fragmenting under me, and I'm tumbling through this conversation as if it's broken glass.

"Who the hell is Rufus?" Skip asks. "Can you two stop talking in riddles?"

"Don't you all tell each other everything? Rufus was a… friend, would you call it? Of Aidy's, back in the day."

"I don't know what you're talking about." I shore up a framework of lies and perch atop it. "I never knew anyone called Rufus. You're obviously confused after everything in the forest but we're here for you, Leftie." I inject honeyed warmth in my tone, copying the way Alyse talks. "It'll be hard to feel part of the team, but we really do want to help. Even if it's emotional sometimes."

"We're here for you," Mélodie signs.

"I don't know what's going on," Skip says. "Aidy, things have been really weird the last few days and I wish you'd just explain. We're going to be a team and we need to trust each other."

"Yeah." A smirk crosses Leftie's face like a shadow cast from somewhere else. "A team. That's exactly how this feels." She takes two steps towards me, until we're almost touching. Her voice is low as she places her mouth right beside my ear. "You know, I did genuinely feel sad for you, if you can believe that. But it's that shitty story about the frog and the scorpion, isn't it? Never though I'd be the fucking frog, but here we are. It's who you are. You don't mean to be cruel."

Adrift, adrift. That's all I can think of. This is the same pattern playing out once again in real time. No matter what I do, it's inevitable like a law of the universe. I'm not made for people. The ironic thing is that Leftie acts like she's the one set apart, the flawless monster, when in reality it's me. I close my eyes and press my fingertips against the back of my eyelids. The colours that bloom there are a tangled network of lines, eerily reminiscent of Cybele's web. I pull my fingers away and open my eyes, ignoring the fading flowers that linger.

"I need some air," I say, and rush from the room.

The dorms are the only place I can go. Cybele is in the forest, and hiding in the shack where Rayner was locked away seems like a terrible idea. Curling up in bed with my back to the door isn't exactly a hiding place, but who'd be looking for me anyway?

"Aidy." Skip's voice is soft from the doorway. "Can we please talk? I don't understand."

I am trapped. My heart flutters in my chest like a bird escaping a cage. I want to lash out, but I don't want to hurt Skip. I've already hurt Leftie, who took the first step only for me to slap it back in her face. Why can't I do this? Why is it so hard to just *be a person*?

I roll over and look at her. The sadness is back on her face, like she keeps the ghost of it at bay until it overwhelms her. And here I am, ready to show her more darkness.

"I'm scared," I tell her, because it's the only admission I can make right now.

"Of what?"

"Losing everything again." There's the truth, a crumb of it at least, offered up.

"I'm not going anywhere, Aidy. I'm confused, because I thought we were…" She sighs. "Friends, at the very least. And yet you won't explain anything, so now I feel, I don't know, adrift, I guess?"

Adrift. How did she know to use that word? I want to collapse in the face of it, but there's the weight of so many rejections dragging me down. Leftie didn't witness them all, only some of the worst ones, the most desperate ones, the ones that resulted in parts of me being sheared away. There are hundreds of them, small to large, layered into a vast refuse pile that fills me.

"It's hard," I offer, because that small step feels like the beginning of something.

Skip runs a hand through short curls that bounce back into place. "Let me make it easier on you. I'll be friends with you either way. You can tell me you're a secret Quietus agent here to infiltrate us and kill us all—"

"I'm not," I squeak. "I swear."

"That's a relief." For a moment, she smiles like her old self. "It would've made things awkward. But I'd be your friend even then. I like you a lot, like a lot a lot, but I wanted to feel connected with you." Her breath rasps, like all these words are exercise. "But do you like *me* enough to tell me the truth?"

I like you a lot. Those beautiful words. Once I would have gloried in under other circumstances, but not here. Not with the ruins of my life sinking below the waves, and the memory of Leftie's pitiless gaze.

"Yes. And you deserve the truth. You really do." I'm teetering on the edge of a precipice. Once I say this, I can't take it back. Skip will forever know all the broken pieces of me, and see me as I am, not as how I wish to be. It could be either destruction or construction, and I cannot know until I do it.

It's time to take the risk.

So I tell her everything, all that Leftie saw and more besides. My voice comes out flat and dead for most of it, except where it wavers and dissolves. Skip listens and holds my hand during the entire thing. At the end, she pulls me into another hug.

"It sounds horrible. The Dark Year was so awful. I'll trade you my stories sometime. And what you did to Rufus was bad, but like... Aidy, I have seen some shit, believe me and you were protecting yourself in a situation with no happy ending. You would've died if you opened your mouth. The hardest thing is living with yourself afterwards, but we can help with that. Almost everyone on Mutopia has a story."

Relief courses through me and finally the tears flood out of me, like the ocean in my body won't be satisfied until it's all spilled in tribute to my sins.

"Oh, Aidy." Skip takes me in her arms and we hug for a long, long time. It's nice to be together like this, comfort running through me like a current. Then my eyes blink open and Leftie is in the doorway. She sees me looking and ducks out of view, but I can sense her there. The shadow of her, lurking. I've managed to cling onto Skip by offering up all my ugliness, but for how long? Now she knows the truth, I'll look even worse in comparison to Leftie. Not that it's a competition, but it's not exactly the opposite either. You choose who you're closest to, and who would pick me when there's someone like the Left

Hand of Darkness? All I can do for now is try to act normal.

"A team then." I let out a long breath. "That'll be an interesting group."

"And you and Leftie can be cool?" Skip asks.

"Yeah, I think so. But I doubt she's going to stay on the island forever."

"Why not?"

The words appear in my mouth, ready to spill. This will be a betrayal, another terrible act, but I'll make it the last one. The final severing line between the old Aidy and the new. Something to rearrange this garden into somewhere I can bloom, rather than choked out by the wildest of flowers. I know that I should choke them back down, swallow them into the dark heart of me, but they're falling from my lips before I can stop them. "As soon as Leftie finds out that Uriel's still alive, she'll be gone."

"Uriel?" Skip's eyes widen. "Isn't that—?"

"The head of the cult. The man Leftie killed to escape. You can't tell anyone about it, Dylan made me promise to keep it a secret. But I've told you everything, so why not this?"

"I won't tell anyone." Skip hugs me again.

And when we come back out into the corridor, Leftie is gone.

31

LEFTIE

None of this can be real. I killed Uriel Clements. His death is etched in my mind. It's the only thing I've taken any real pleasure in, at least until recently. And I saw Aidy glance in my direction before they spilled their little secret to Skip. They knew what they were saying. I'm not sure if it was a favour or an attempt to send me away from the island. Either way, if there's any chance it could be true, then I have to follow it. If that man is alive—*has been* alive this entire fucking time—then I have to find him and end him. There is no alternative.

It cannot be true and yet it makes too much sense. Whoever has been attacking me knows me well enough to inhibit my powers. They understand what I am. And they crave what lurks inside me, Uriel's apocalypse seed. He wants to take back what he considers is rightfully his. Chatterbox wanted to solve my problem for me. I'm furious at them for intervening, but I also understand their motives. The truth is that I will dash myself against him with no regard for how it shatters me.

The Father of the Broken World must be removed from the world with no chance of return. And I would rather pay with my own life than Chatterbox or anyone else's. This has always been my war, my revenge, and I am the only blade that should finish it. He chained me, he set me on a throne, he made me his instrument, and now he has made a fool of me. Escaping the death I wrought for him.

This time, he will have no chance of escape.

But there is a whole world where he could hide, and I have no intelligence. I dance across the waves, shadow to shadow. They have found me before, and presumably will find me again. I will find a high profile target, make a production of it. Execute someone from the Global Intelligence Committee, or some fanatically anti-mutant preacher. Make it easy for him to reach out and close his hand around me, and then he shall find all my hidden blades. I will break his world once more and it shall—

The scenery change is abrupt. The ocean is gone. A sterile white ceiling dazzles me with light. I can't move. Not in shadow, not in light. I'm a flat numb thing, a two-dimensional shape that can't affect the world around me. There are no goddamn *shadows*. How can there be none? It's waves upon waves of light and in them is no darkness at all.

"It's been a long, long time." The voice comes through speakers, slightly distorted. I don't recognise it. This is some flunky, and not Uriel himself. Which doesn't make my current physical state any better. I try to grit my teeth around words, but all that comes out is a dull, choking gasp. My anger has nowhere to go, so I let it burn inside me. Sometime, somehow, it will explode. It's the only constant in my life.

There's a hiss and clunk. A door opening. I can't even turn my head to see, simply have to wait for something to drift into my eyeline. A face eventually does. Pallid skin, brown eyes, a mouth that wriggles as if it's holding back a torrent of bullshit.

"You have been brought low, Worldbreaker."

I'd love to respond, but I'll have to settle for glaring. Blood will come later. It always does.

"The Father was more cunning than you realise. There were contingencies if he was killed, although he did not imagine you would be the instrument. He knew his death was the greatest risk to the holy work. And still it has been rather difficult laying hands on you, despite the many strings we have pulled."

"Where is that asshole Uriel?" I snarl. "Tell him to show his fucking face."

"I am preparing you for him. He will not be fooled a second time. The Lord has a plan, and the world remains unbroken. Sin flourishes, and the mutant plague grows unabated. The Goddess gambit failed, and the Father understands he was led astray by the devil in that regard. A mistake we shall remedy when we split your body open and grow death from the garden of your corpse."

Fuck's sake, why do assholes like this love the sound of their own voice so much? I try to move even the tiniest part of me, and nothing responds. I'm completely immobile. I think angrily in Cybele's direction, and there is no response. So much for all these connections binding me to the island. Once again, I am alone.

The man hovers the flat of his hand above me. I can only see it in my peripheral vision. "The seed is still inside you. We shall release it, and the world shall finally shatter in glory." There's the barest suggestion of a shadow from his hand, and I can sense it fluttering like a moth just out of reach, but I still cannot *touch* it. Where is the shadow of his body? Has he positioned the lights perfectly to blot it out? This all speaks of vast and intricate planning, and I feel a deeper flickering of worry. Worse than I've felt in a long, long time.

It's possible I am fucked.

They're going to dig around in me and pull out the damn apocalypse seed. The problem is I don't even know what the fuck that means. Nobody was ever specific about what it actually did. It was always spoken about in the most flowery language, peeking coyly out from between an intricate wall of metaphors. There was much spoken about the what—the world would break, or one of a host of other synonyms. The wicked would be swept away, glory would be revealed, and in the aftermath the Children would reign in God's light for some significant fraction of eternity. At one stage I thought it was a metaphor, but I have seen the proof of its existence.

I was performing a hit in a hospital on a high-level member of an anti-mutant militia and took the opportunity to indulge my curiosity. It's there, a dark spot connected to my heart. A device, networked into me with tiny tendrils.

The man from the cult is still rambling, more to himself than to me, I think. "—in the dark for so long, and now my faith is rewarded, Lord. I am simply a faithful vessel, an outworking of your great plan. Help me terminate this creature, so the Father can be revealed in his glory and all his children stolen from us by this wicked apostate."

The story was always that after the seed flowered, I'd be resurrected at the right hand of the Father. It was in every tale they told, a promise of my eventual ascension to kneel at Uriel's feet, presumably some creepy wish-fulfilment on his part. It's clear I will no longer walk out of this. My blood will be shed to destroy the world.

I can't let this happen. The problem is I'm tied to a stretcher, I can't move, and the shadows are so gossamer-thin and distant I cannot even weave them together into a fucking shank. I can't even unclench my jaw to bite at this asshole's fingers if he gets too close.

He's gone from my peripheral vision, but I can hear clanking sounds nearby. Words still dribble from his mouth, nonsensical promises of the future. More flickers of shadow dart across me, generated by his mysterious actions. I try to extend myself, beg them to melt and swirl towards me, delicate filigree threads of darkness like an unravelling tapestry.

Not even a single soft and reassuring droplet solidifies for me. I remain an immobile angel waiting for—

The man has returned. He stands over me, a mask obscuring his mouth and nose. His watery eyes gaze down at me, beatific like he's about to pronounce a blessing. Except the only offering he holds is the silver blade in his hand.

Wonderful.

My body won't respond. The shadows are inert.

Above me, the mask crinkles as he breathes faster. He's going to enjoy this.

The tip of the scalpel presses against my naked flesh, digging into the hollow of my throat. I feel a cold sting, the pain flaring through my nerves as he drags it downwards. Layers of flesh part eagerly at the touch. Blood trickles warm, pools at my throat and spills in rivulets down my neck.

He wants me to feel pain. I refuse to give him the satisfaction of any reaction, but tears pool unbidden in my eyes and spill across my skin too, slightly cooler than my blood. The movement of the blade is delicate and slow, as if he is painting with it. I am split open in wave after wave of pain. My mouth creaks open, like a mausoleum door, barely enough to let a moan escape.

And yet, the scalpel casts a shadow, and the raised lip of flesh around the cut has a shadow of its own, raggedly drawn and dark enough to take form. They finally obey me, but sluggish, trickling up my body like thick tar. My hands are still immobile, so I inhale them into my mouth. I can work my jaw in painful increments and the hot meat of my tongue thrashes around them. Shadows fill the small cavity, cool and numbing.

The scalpel has descended below my breasts and another tool is brought behind it, digging into my chest, cracking me open like I am a seafood treat. The pain is white-hot, and I lose focus. My jaw swings wider, like an echo of what's happening to my body. I almost choke on shadows, but my throat closes obediently and spits them back up.

I shred the inside of my mouth to ribbons forming them into a series of razor-edged blades. I swallow blood mixed with fragments of darkness. My body feels dipped in fire. There's been more than enough pain in my life, but this is something new. I shouldn't have the ability to process this, yet there is a single thread in my mind that's connected to something else. It seems as if it travels the miles between the unknown here and the island I wish to be my home.

A connection to my new family, my new friends.

Enough to keep me coherent through this, to lend me the focus to fill my mouth with edged shadows despite my body going into catastrophic shutdown.

The man's attention is fixed on what he's doing, his eyes alight as he follows the path of the blade. Breath coming faster at the sound of me cracking apart.

I spit the first blade into his left eye.

The second two perforate the mask.

The fourth enters right below his Adam's apple.

The last three are unnecessary because he's already dropping. His eye weeps tears and blood. His mask is a wet red smear. His throat is a torn ruin. When his forehead impacts my cheek, it feels like a punch but one I'm glad to take.

My last blade I shoot towards one of the lights. It shatters in a whirlwind of glass, but it interrupts the interlocking shield of lights and causes sharper shadows to form. Through the pain, I gather as much as I can.

Now comes the uncomfortable part.

Weaving with my teeth, I use thin lines of shadow to try and stitch myself back together. The pain is sickening, waves upon waves I cannot dance on. At some point, sobbing and breathless, movement returns to my fingertips, and I can clumsily tighten this network of lines that is holding me together.

Through it all, I desperately cling to the imaginary line that leads back to Mutopia. The dream of Goddess and Cybele, to be part of this network of theirs. I imagine it plumbed into my brainstem, winding down my spine and bursting with flowers.

I am their child after all.

There is enough shadow to spare clumsy projectiles. I break more lights until I am awash in shadow, using clumps to staunch the bleeding. The pain is so intense that I almost black out when I pull my clumsy stitches tighter.

Pain means I'm alive. Fucking barely, and in the worst shape I've ever been in, but I'm here. And if I can get back to the damn island, there's healing as well as home. There's just one little task to do first. I've got to see a man about a murder.

I wish I could tug on the thread in my mind, but it's imaginary, so I'll have to find my own way back. The problem is, I've still barely got any mobility.

There's enough shadow here that I could fold myself into it, but I don't want to lose consciousness inside there and be stuck in darkness, unable to climb out.

Let's do this the ugly way.

I grab a massive handful of shadow like a lifeline. I haul myself off the stretcher and collapse onto the ground. More shadows, more shadows, until I'm the centre of a web that suspends me in the room. By pulling this way and that and releasing certain strands, I can slowly and clumsily navigate myself to the door.

This is going to be unpleasant. I almost wish someone was here to bear witness. The Left Hand of Darkness, drenched in blood and shadow. Quite possibly a walking ghost, steps away from death.

"Still fucking alive," I croak in my ruin of a voice. "I'm coming for you, Uriel."

32

AIDY

When we go back out into the corridor, Leftie is gone. This isn't absolute confirmation, but it's likely she heard what I said about Uriel. And if that's true, I've basically fired her like a bullet from a gun, directly into certain danger. Which I can almost convince myself she can handle, given that she's the Left Hand of Darkness, but they've already proven they can inhibit her powers. And that makes me responsible for anything that happens to her. Like I stood aside once again and let the blade fall on someone else when I could have stopped it.

"Are you going to tell the others your story?" Skip asks.

"Leftie was in the forest with me. She got a front seat to all my worst moments. But I guess I'll tell Mél, although the idea makes me feel sick all over again."

"I can promise you she won't be awful." Skip pats my hand. "What did Leftie say?"

"She was sweet, that's the thing." I fidget with my cuffs. "Unnervingly so, like she's trying to be a real girl rather than a blade. Which means she's part of our lives, and part of the *team* with you and me." I shrug helplessly, because there's too much emotion below the surface and I can't let it out.

"But isn't that a good thing?" Skip asks. "Especially if she's trying to be more human and less murder robot. It'll be nice to get to know her, and even nicer to get to know you better."

Her lips curve into a smile, but something heaves inside me. A messy chunk of myself, stuck in my gut and refusing to be digested. "Who would want me when Leftie's around?"

Skip frowns. "Aidy, this is one of these thought processes that doesn't relate to reality. Nobody's choosing between you and Leftie. In fact, we want both of you on the team. The four of us together."

My thoughts spin in a nauseated spiral, soaked in regrets like I'm pickling myself. I can think of a thousand better ways I could have handled the situation, but none of them matter. This was the one I chose. Of course unburdening myself wasn't a magical transformation into a pretty guardian, ready to be the shiny person I long to be. It's step one on a journey. Most likely a difficult and painful one, where I have to make the choices over and over.

"I think I did something terrible," I tell Skip.

"I'm sure it's not as bad as you think." She shakes her head with a small smile. "You have a habit of assuming the worst about—"

"When I told you about Uriel, I think Leftie heard me. Like I deliberately dangled it in front of her and it's not because I have noble intentions of letting her choose her own destiny."

"Oh, Aidy." Skip wipes her hands over her face. "That's not good."

"No, I'm a jealous asshole like I told you. But I'm going to make it right. I don't know how, but I'm going to raise the alarm and then I'll rescue her."

"But—" Skip doesn't get to finish the sentence, because a bedraggled leaf creature crashes in through the window beside us.

"I speak on behalf of Cybele." Her voice is distant, as if it's funnelled through from somewhere else. "Who is currently... occupied. We have received a distress signal from the mutant known as the Left Hand of Darkness."

"Where is she?" I feel myself beginning to transform, my skin hardening in preparation. We'll have to go back into a place like those cult tunnels. There will be people with guns and fire, but this is how I take another real step towards being a better version of myself. "We'll go in and get her."

"We have an approximate location," the messenger says. "She was never fully assimilated into the island, and is wounded, so we have limited... telemetry? I think that is the word."

"Find the Cute Mutants," Skip says. "Chatterbox and Marvellous. They'll know what to do."

"Those mutants are no longer... accessible via any known network," the tree-woman says. "All are offline. Those known as Weapon UwU are on the network, but I am forbidden from accessing them."

"Skip, I'm doing it." I don't allow any time for second guessing. So many times I've let cowardice trip me up. I've only been on my previous missions because I was too scared to stand up to other people. This time, I'll do it because I want to. Because it's the right thing to do. "She's wounded, and it's my fault she's gone. I'm invulnerable, remember? So I'm going to use my powers and save her."

"How bad is it?" Skip asks.

"We can detect nothing but screaming." Leaves drift down as the tree-woman shakes. "We have attempted to communicate reassurance through our connection, but, as previously stated, it is limited."

I can't focus on the guilt, or how this is all my fault. That can come later. Right now it's time to be invulnerable, to make decisions. First, we need transport. I know about the magical house that lives on the island, which can open doors all around the world. I've never been inside, but we can't exactly go on foot or by plane. "We need to find One Thorn. Cybele? Can you communicate with the house?"

"Oh, yes. We grow throughout the house and it carries our seeds to far-off lands. They are part of the network, fully assimilated. They comprise multiple nodes themself, in fact. This is all to say that I can communicate your desired location to them."

"Please," I say firmly. "That's what we need."

The woman nods, and then climbs back out the window, leaving only a scattering soil and a scattering of petals and leaves.

"That was Cybele," Skip says faintly. "Part of her."

I forget that not everyone sees what I have. "The real her is... intense. But that's one more story for another time. We need to get going."

"Are you sure?" Skip holds out her hand, shows me how much it's trembling. "This is intense. I know you've flicked into action hero mode but we're talking about a mission into actual danger, Aidy. The two of us alone."

"Someone died because I was scared," I tell her. "I stood by and did nothing. I let it happen because everything was fucked, but mostly because I was a coward. And now it's happening again, because once again I let my hurt be in charge. But I'm not doing that anymore." I feel a flush creeping up my cheeks, because I've said way too much, blurted up a bunch of viscera and pain. "As of now, at least. We're going to get Leftie back." I think about how she held me after the forest, about the forgiveness she offered me, gifts I was too folded in on myself to take. "Our friend."

"I think I like this version of you," Skip says. "Coward and brave all at once."

"Oh." That's all I can think of to say.

"I like knowing the bad parts of you too."

I choke on whatever my brain was offering up as a response to this, probably a string of nonsense syllables.

"Okay." A smile hitches up one corner of her mouth. "Let's go and do this wild thing, before I lose all my nerve." She extends one hand, as if she's reaching for me, as if she can draw strength from this new Aidy, stumbling towards disaster to be born. I have nothing except what I am, the entire messy incoherent structure of me, but I take her hand anyway.

"Now let's go find One Thorn."

We run through the cool of the night, hand in hand. There are a few people out on the streets, clustered in small groups, and they turn to watch us go. Nobody stops us, which is good, because I don't want to lose my nerve. I am no longer adrift, but a boat with wind billowing its sails, skimming across the surface to somewhere new, somewhere better. A place called home.

One Thorn's door is ajar when we reach it, and warm yellow light spills from the crack, making a blade of brightness through the shadow. I wish I could collect it, take it as a weapon wherever Leftie is, as if I was a mirror to her powers.

"Welcome," the house says as I push the door open. Its voice comes from the walls, as if there are hidden speakers everywhere. Skip's hand is warm and sweat-slick. My heart is still thumping as I step inside. The room is small and well-lit, with a small wooden table and six chairs scattered around it. There's still three coffee mugs scattered on it, as if a meeting was interrupted.

"A late night adventure awaits, I hear."

"We need to find Leftie," I blurt. And then: "Hello, One Thorn. I hope you are well."

"Manners. How delightful. And yes, the active nodes of Cybele and I are attempting to pinpoint Leftie's location. We are having unexpected difficulties. Please stand by."

After our headlong rush, it feels awkward to have to stand and wait. Skip shows no inclination to disentangle her fingers from mine. If anything, she shuffles closer.

"Nervous," she whispers.

"Me too." Because I am, but I'm not letting it stop me. I'm not going to paper over all the other parts of me anymore. I'll build something new from the shattered pieces. Someone who knows what it is to be lost and then found. Someone who'll find people. "But we can do this. I'm a shield, she's a weapon, and you're our emergency escape plan."

"Skip like a stone over the water," she whispers.

I squeeze her hand. "Exactly."

The door slams shut behind us and the light snaps off with a sharp pop. There's a lurch, as if the entire house is dropping like an elevator in freefall. I barely have time to scream before it's over. When we stop, sunlight streams through a massive bay window that wasn't there before. The inside of the house is transfigured into an indoor garden, plants spidering from hundreds of pots swinging from the ceiling. The foliage makes a giant net over our heads, but the light from outside wanes swiftly, turning from the brightness of day to a malevolent purple dusk. The plants are gone, replaced by the skeleton of some enormous snake looped on itself, except instead of swallowing its tail it has two duelling mouths.

The purple light vanishes too and we're in the dark again. The falling sensation returns, this time even more intense. I imagine numbers of an elevator display flickering wildly, showing incomprehensible symbols and cries for help. Skip is still holding onto me, but her skin feels dry and leathery, as if she's been substituted for a monster without me noticing.

For one terrifying moment I'm weightless, and then the lights come back on.

Skip is herself again, and the room around us is back to its dull self, coffee cups undisturbed.

"Dimensional equilibrium restored," the house says calmly. "Apologies for any disturbance, but your urgency required some shortcuts. Hopefully this is acceptable. While we were unable to precisely pinpoint your friend's location due to her unique powerset affecting the coordinate system, she is somewhere in this underground facility."

"Somewhere?" My voice is shaking again. "It doesn't matter. We'll find her. Follow the sound of screaming. Right, Skip? You can bounce us around."

"Definitely." Her worried eyes meet mine. As I look into them, they become steady, as if ripples in the surface of a placid pool have been smoothed away. As if we're sharing what little strength we have between us. "We'll find her."

The door behind us bangs open, as if someone is urgently forcing their way in.

When we turn, there's nothing there. Only a corridor, walls painted an institutional white. The lights overhead are dimmed to preserve power.

"No screaming yet." Skip inhales sharply. "Is that a good sign?"

"Maybe she's killed everyone already," I say, but then the converse occurs to me. What if we're too late? Leftie could be dead anywhere in this place, and we don't even know how big it is.

"Like a stone." Skip squeezes my hand and *jumps*. We're halfway down the corridor, the door to One Thorn distant behind us. There's still no sign of anything, no sound. The facility appears entirely deserted. I don't even hear a thrum of machinery.

It takes us fourteen jumps before we hear it.

The sound of someone begging for help. A wet gurgle. A thwack.

Then the sound of obliterating gunfire that refuses to stop.

33

LEFTIE

The good news: I am not dead yet. The bad news: death stalks me like a fucking predatory asshole, just out of reach. I can hear its breath hissing like Uriel's. Pale snakelike fuck. Eager little eyes, damp hands. I'm so goddamn sore, puppeting myself around within this tangled rig of shadows. Still losing blood, despite being stuffed with a bunch of darkness. It's not the best bandage, as it turns out.

More good news: pain is giving me motivation to build some fucking amazing shadow constructions. I might be half-delirious, but I've got rotating wheels of shadow knives spinning around me like a fucked up mediaeval halo. Should give me some defence mechanism, because I'm a shitty slow mess. Fuck that guy for cutting me up. This is all his fault. I'd like to go back and kill him again, but it's hard enough *moving*. Darkness is probably cursing its luck right now being stuck with me as its left hand, all busted knuckles and missing a finger, barely able to hold a goddamn dagger.

Still more good news: this facility might be a huge maze of corridors, but at least it's quiet. Almost peaceful, really. Me on a nice little stroll, trying not to collapse and die. Resting in the arms of shadow for a little while.

I turn a corner, and my good news evaporates fast. There's a woman in camouflage, wearing a visor and with a gun slung around her. Her attention is on the phone in her hand, but some flicker of my movement snags at her, and she's alert in seconds. Probably seeing a dark cloud flailing like a really pissed-off inkblot will do that.

My arms still aren't working quite right, but I manage to shear off a chunk of shadow into a makeshift scythe and lunge at the guard with it. Unfortunately, I tangle myself in the net of shadows that's keeping me mobile, and I'm half-strangled. My body flops around inside the arrangement of shadows like a fish on a hook.

Which gives the guard enough time to fucking shoot me.

I've been shot a lot, but this one pisses me off extra. The impact knocks me backwards, and all the shadow lines holding me up yank really hard on all the points I've connected them to my skin, which doesn't break but does feel like someone is sticking a whole bunch of red-hot knives into me. I'm running out of metaphors for pain, wallowing in the oceanic extent of it. Luckily I'm not an amateur, so I manage to slap another ugly mess of sharp-edged shadows together and hurl it.

It takes her in the wrist and hip, more from luck than judgement. She fumbles for her gun and drops it, the hand not working right. Not bad for being cut open and near death, huh, little soldier girl? Except she uses her non-fucked hand to draw a knife cross-body and lunges at me with it.

Well, shit. I wasn't expecting that.

She hits me hard and I swing back through the shadows. This time, I detach some lines so it doesn't shred my skin all over again. I slam onto the ground, knocking my back and head as well as jarring the whole mess of stitches holding me together. She lands on top of me, which for some reason I find fucking hilarious. She's bleeding, I'm bleeding, it's a whole fucking bloodbath.

She's trying to get the knife in, but she's snagged in shadow, panting and drooling, thrashing her legs. I wrap shadow lines around her neck and when she starts turning purple, I jam a bunch of shadow blades down her gasping throat.

Not that I'm such a fucking badass. It takes me a whole forty-four count to get enough energy to drag her corpse off me, and then another hundred and fifteen to get back on my feet. Which is a poor euphemism given that I'm only upright because I'm dangling from shadow like the puppet Uriel always thought I was.

It's a sad comedown from how I was when I first changed. Moving through the acolytes like a threshing blade through grain. Like the hand of a furious god reaching down to touch humanity and saying *not you* over and over again. Truth be told, I barely remember killing my parents amongst all that. It's not like I would have spared them, but I might have paused to ask why. Maybe they'd have found an answer to spare them the blade. Instead, I made my way through the compound, killing every single person older than me.

It was all a lead-up to Uriel. I wanted him to watch every star in his galaxy wink out, before I came to plunge the furnace of his sun into my extinguishing dark.

I've got a lot of memories of blood in my short life, but this is my favourite. But somehow, somewhere it went wrong. I failed to end his life, and now he's back. I'll have to ensure I don't make the same mistake again.

What did I do wrong the last time?

"Worldbreaker," he says, when I materialise out of the shadows.

"Uriel." I am saturated in blood. I can't look human. A monster carved from a gory nightmare and set loose upon the world.

"You'll address me as Father."

"Not anymore."

"Do not presume to think you have ascended already, child. Covering yourself with the blood of the Goddess is only a means to an end."

I smile at that. My regular teeth, before I sharpened them. "This is not her blood."

This is the first sign of panic, blooming on his face like paper absorbing ink. "What have you done, Eleanor?"

"Who is that?" I spread my arms. "I am not Eleanor, not Worldbreaker, not your future bride perched at your right hand."

"You are all those things, you petulant child, and if you have harmed even a single hair on the head of one of my children, I shall—"

"I am the Left Hand of Darkness. You have no children anymore. I have murdered all save the young ones, and I will rescue those from your grasp."

"This cannot be true." The breath that used to rasp when he watched me has changed to something high *and urgent. "You are lying. This is madness, some unintended consequence of the mutant change. The acolytes bid me to leave as they tried to resuscitate you. I could not bear to watch the future of our people at risk."*

I tilt my head. "They did not save me. I woke up and killed all of them."

"No, no, no." He reaches out to me, but some instinct stops him. "This cannot be true."

"Then come and see." I hold out my blood-streaked hand.

He takes it. I am slightly surprised by this, but he still believes this must be some unfathomable lie. I lead him to the door, and he stumbles slightly at the threshold, because he's already seen the first body. One of his precious handmaid guards, women that are the protectors and servants of his body. They are victims too, I understand this, but I did not have the time or the patience to weigh out degrees of guilt. If you serve Uriel, you die. This is the price they must pay. They could have fought, too. Any of one of them could have defeated him in the night and drawn their silver blades across his throat. And if they had banded together, they would have been formidable indeed.

When Uriel sees the decapitated body, he screams, a single high-pitched sound that sustains itself far longer than I would have expected him to have breath for.

"Do not waste your grief," I tell him. "Not when there is so much more screaming to be done."

There is a cluster of bodies at the entrance to his quarters. I did them the courtesy of leaning them against the wall and closing their eyes. They are a bizarre honour guard for him, each throat opened with a single blade.

"No." He falls to his knees.

"It seems pointless to deny it." I stand over him, a death god revealed. The hand of darkness. I shall leave this place, and be the hand of the Goddess to protect her kind. But first, there is one more death to give.

"You could have ruled at my side," he says.

"I'd drown the whole world in blood to spite you. To steal your promised land and bury you beneath it once you have seen me raze it to the ground."

"The world will break." He clasps his hands, white-knuckle in prayer. "The sinners will pay for their sins, and the faithful will inherit the earth. God spoke to me. I believe it. It will come to pass."

I crouch beside him, one hand placed on his shoulder. The other draws a slender blade from the air.

"I think there was a missed translation somewhere, Uriel."

"What do you mean?" He looks at me pleading, as if there's a hope this is all a grotesque lie.

"To all the people in this compound, you are the sun in the sky. The glorious Father, shepherding them into their future destiny."

"Yes, yes. This is the true and revealed word of God. So why would—"

"To me, you were the world. You were the only thing I was ever allowed to know. Do you understand, Uriel? You are my world. So it is you who breaks."

I incline the blade in towards his throat. He coughs and he chokes and he sobs.

"Did you ever ask what I wanted?" I ask him.

His mouth works. He is at the moment of death and he is bereft. "What did you want?"

"To have a family. To have a home."

Then I draw the blade across his throat, because I do not want to hear what lies he holds on his tongue any longer.

I'd forgotten I said the last part. After that, there was so much work to do, and I lost myself in it. The darkness can be comforting, and there is so much evil in the world.

I did some good, didn't I? People lived because of me. I did my part to keep mutantkind safe, and bring them some semblance of a future. I might have come to the end of my story, but others will still be told.

Fuck it. There's still a goddamn chance. I'm the deadliest woman alive. Maybe. Depends how scary Penance really is. Either way, I'm going to drag my ass out of here, three steps past completely fucked, and I'm going to yank on this goddamn cord to Cybele until someone answers. Preferably one of those little plant brats who apparently like me so much. Then I'm going to get healed, and I'm going to lie on the beach a bunch, make out with a pretty girl, and be normal. Say sorry to Aidy for fucking with them. Be the bigger person for a change, not just the bigger badass.

It sounds like a plan.

First things first. Get out of this place. Back to using these shadow-threads to swing my broken body along down these endless goddamn corridors. It's fine. I'm fine. There's still so much goddamn blood. Some of it's from the soldier, I'm pretty sure. Otherwise I'd be a completely incoherent mess, drowning in memories.

That's a joke. I think.

I turn a corner. Another fucking corridor. This one's got an elevator at the end of it. Seems promising. Back on the good news train at least.

The numbers above the door are moving.

Thanks, shitty dying brain. Jinxing me at the last minute.

I fumble the shadow-threads, trying to figure out how to move backwards.

The elevator dings. A shrill sound that echoes off the long, narrow walls like an alarm. I pull on all the shadow lines once, hitching my body up through the air so I'm closer to the ceiling and at less obvious attacking height.

The doors clunk and slide open. Inside, there are men with guns.

I hurl as many jagged pieces of shadow in their direction as I can. Some of them are still attached. My body twitches with each one, like I've been shot. Blood's dripping from about forty different places in me, forming abstract slicks on the floor.

There's blood in the elevator too. One man is impaled through the stomach and twitching. Another trying to hold his throat together. It's not enough. There are too many of them. The world is drowned out with the sound of gunfire. Bullets impact my flesh. Healing powers, time to come in clutch. I've been in a lot of shitty situations, but I think bad luck has finally caught up with me.

My story's a strange, dark one. I thought I always knew where it was destined to go, but lately I've stumbled across new chapters, written in a different hand. But in the end it's a plot twist that didn't go anywhere, and now we're back on track. This is my darkest moment—carved up, tangled up in a shadow, bleeding to death, waiting for the inevitable.

Then Uriel steps out of the darkness. Even paler than I remember, fish-belly face gazing. Black suit hanging off him like funeral clothes. The flat hard line of his mouth twitches in satisfaction.

Oh, how I fucking hate him.

"At last you return," he says. "A broken girl to break the world."

"Fuck you." I spit blood down my front. "I'll kill you again, you fucking sadistic prick."

"Oh, Eleanor. You're not capable of killing anything right now. You're clinging to life from pure stubbornness and spite, same as you ever were. Such a poor choice, in hindsight. They say God never makes mistakes, but he did with you."

"I'd stab God too if he was real. For his shitty taste in servants if nothing else."

He shakes his head. "It's so tempting to end your life right here. You tried to kill me, Eleanor. The man who made you. You destroyed all my works and broke my world. And so I shall break you, piece by piece, until there's only the smallest possible fragment left to watch the world die. To see your failed rebellion fall. Long enough to watch me slit the throat of every single one of those children you stole from me."

"Fucking die." I can't talk properly around the blood in my throat. I'm choking on it, my eyes filling with shadow. Hard to make anything out aside from blurry movements. I think this fuck is shit out of luck. He's not going to be able to keep me alive long enough to see the promised apocalypse. At least my death will piss him off.

Fuck that. There's still the slenderest thread to cling to. If it's the last thing I do, Uriel Clements is going to die. All I need is to hold on long enough to do it. Then I can rest.

Finally.

34

AIDY

I have a moment of panic, of regret, of wanting to flee. Gunfire has that effect on me. Except this is why we're here. I press my mouth against Skip's ear, tell her what we're going to do. Me, Aidy, someone with a plan. I hope I survive this to tell the story. If I'm going to embrace all my worst moments, it'll be good to add one where I'm the hero instead.

Skip takes two fast teleporting steps towards a corner, pulling me along with her. The wall is pocked with bulletholes that shred it to splinters. We bounce around the corner and stop dead. We're inside into an elevator that looks like an abattoir. In front of us there's only one man left alive. He's tall and slender with pale skin, something unearthed half-formed from the ground and shrouded in dark clothes as a portent. This can only be Uriel. In one hand he holds a gun, and in the other a slender device shaped like a cross.

Hunched in the corner is a swirl of shadow, a confused tangle of darkness that oozes blood onto the ground. Holy shit, is that Leftie? I think it means she's alive, but we're cutting it fine.

I grab Skip's arm. "Get behind me." All the panic and fear flowing through me is something I can use to make myself bigger and stronger—a shield to protect my friend. I lurch forward out of the lift.

"—your miserable failure," Uriel is saying, his voice still clear and strong. "I will see you brought low, see you kneel, watch you—"

"Uriel!" My voice comes out high and breathy, but he turns all the same.

The gun in his hand is pointed right at me. I'm waiting for Leftie to come bursting out of the shadows and destroy him, but there's no flicker of movement, only the darkness swelling like a bruise.

The preacher fires at me. I'm still not used to my own powers, and I'm breathless before the impact. One that I don't even feel, the bullet mashing itself into my chest. I wasn't always this good with my powers, but practice and certainty are helping. Sharpening my focus, giving me clarity. I am the shield who will defend.

The preacher pulls the trigger again and again. He's screaming for his guards. Crackles of static come over the radio. This was supposed to be his moment of glory, where he lorded his triumph over Leftie. And here I am to interrupt his shining moment.

From what I know of Leftie, she'll definitely want to kill him herself. I probably owe her that. But he won't stop shooting me, so I take him by the head and slam him gently into the wall. He collapses onto the floor. There are no more words coming from his mouth. His chest still rises and falls so I don't think I've accidentally killed anyone this time. I make sure to step on the arm holding the cross device. That seems ominous, like it might trigger an apocalypse seed. The bones crunch under the armoured bulk of me, flesh splitting and blood gushing red across the floor. Skip reaches down and takes the device, breaking it over her knee in a tangle of circuitry.

We look down together at the prone figure of Uriel.

"Sorry," I tell the shadow. "I think he's still alive though, if you want to stab him a lot."

"You saved him for me?" Leftie's rough, deep voice emanates from the darkness, like a monster who hides in the closet.

"Yes." I'm shaking, but I manage to pull a smile together. "Call it my apology. Or the beginning of one."

"Oh good. It's a nice apology." There's a wet cough. "Not wanting to sound ungrateful, but are you two the entirety of the rescue party?"

"A bunch of people are away, and I sort of panicked when I heard you were in trouble. Given that it's mostly my fault."

"Aidy was very brave," Skip says. "They totally took charge."

"Very flattered." Leftie coughs again. "The thing is, I've got myself a teensy-tiny bit wounded."

The cloud of darkness dissipates a little to reveal her. It's horrifying. She's mostly naked and covered in blood, smeared with shreds of shadow. There's a brutal cut that looks like an autopsy wound right down her middle, held together with a thick crust of darkness.

"It's worse than it looks." She grins down at us, except the effect is ruined when she coughs a spray of blood. "Mostly. Okay, let me figure this out." Her face screws up and her limbs flail jerkily. "Fuck. I hate this, it's so goddamn embarrassing. Can you hold Uriel up for me?"

"Sure." I pull him to his feet. I'm stronger in this form too.

His eyelids flutter as he dangles from my grip. I don't think it's possible for him to be whiter, but his face is sheened in sweat. The ruin of his shattered arm dangles, shards of bone jutting through the skin. "You cannot kill me. God has blessed me and will raise me above you."

"Only slit your throat before." Leftie tries to smile. "This time..."

Shadows erupt from her in a furious tangle, an oncoming storm front blotting out the sky. They wreathe Uriel's head in darkness, a choking, stinging cloud. He shrieks and bucks in my grip, blood dripping down to soak the sleeve of the horribly inappropriate pink hoodie I'm wearing. There's the wet sound of knives going in and out of flesh, a buzzsaw whine of metal meeting bone.

The darkness recedes from his head, waves pulling back from the shore to show what gory wreckage is left behind. Uriel Clements is unrecognisable as human, but Leftie doesn't look much better.

"Can you crush him for me?" Leftie asks. "Head and heart, like he's a fucking zombie vampire piece of shit. I know it's gross, but I'd really like to make sure he's all the way dead this time."

"Sure." I swallow hard. "Whatever you need."

This is the other thing my invulnerable strong form is good for, apparently. Rendering a man into chunks of meat and shards of bone. I was never the biggest fan of superheroes, but I don't think this is what comic books are like. But then we're not heroes, not really. We're rescuing our friend from an evil man who'd kill her and try to murder millions of people because of his warped religious ideas. I've seen so many times in my life how people with these ideas can ruin lives.

Once it's done, I need to pause to throw up. Skip looks away, but Leftie dangles in her cradle of shadows and watches me dispassionately.

"Better out than in," is all she says when I'm finally done.

"We need to get out of here," Skip says. "Preacher man was calling for guards, which means they're going to be coming. Got a plan for our escape, Aidy?"

"Teleport," I say confidently. "Just bounce, bounce, bounce until we're free and clear."

"It can be rough on people." Skip flushes. "I've tried to teleport someone wounded once before and it, uh, didn't work well. And Leftie's not exactly fighting fit."

I take a deep breath. "Okay then. We'll have to go back out via One Thorn. It's only five floors, and we've got the elevator."

Skip nods. "Plan. Leftie, how do we get you down?"

"I can move on my own," she says scornfully. "How do you think I've been getting around?" She unspools a thin reel of shadow and flings it at the direction of the elevator. Except when she reaches for it, she falls on his face in a sprawl of blood and darkness.

I crouch beside her. "Let me carry you."

"Give me a second," she gasps. "I'll get my strength back."

"No. I'm taking you to the elevator first. We've wasted enough time."

It's only a few steps back to the elevator, where Skip hits the button for the floor where we left One Thorn. It creaks alarmingly, as if it's damaged somehow, but it slowly begins to ascend.

"Can you do recon?" I ask Skip. "To make sure the way is clear?"

"Good idea." Her hand is shaky when it touches mine. "Look at you with the tactics. You'll be okay with Leftie?"

"We're fine." Leftie's breath gurgles. "For an indeterminate amount of time."

"Go."

Skip nods, and then disappears. The elevator creaks down to the floor below and I hit the emergency stop button. Better to wait until Skip gets back and confirms things. We're so close and I don't want to risk—

"Aidy, it's bad." Skip reappears a foot in the air and crashes down onto the floor. "There are a whole group of soldiers trying to break through the door to One Thorn. It's bad."

"Shit." I tip my head backwards and bang it against the elevator wall lightly. "Shit, shit. We need another exit strategy."

"You're going to the top of the building," Skip says. "You're going to parachute away with Leftie, and I'll teleport."

"Parachute," I squeak.

"That's one of your forms, right?"

"Yes, but I haven't done it in years and it was an accident when I did! And what will you be doing?"

She glances up at me. "There are some soldiers in your way. I'll take care of them." She fumbles at the bodies of the soldiers on the ground. "With these."

"Grenades? Skip, you—"

"Aidy, listen to me."

"It's too dangerous and I haven't told you everything yet. We haven't even—"

She steps in close, one hand wrapping around the back of my neck. Her skin is hot, and her face is very close to mine. I can't focus on it all at once. "We'll have time."

She presses her lips to mine, hard and urgent. It only lasts a handful of seconds, but it stops my heart for that entire time.

Then she takes a step back and disappears.

"There you go," Leftie gurgles from the ground. "You get your romantic ending."

I cancel the emergency stop and hit the button for the top floor. The lift wheezes into life and I collapse down on the floor beside Leftie.

"What happens if she dies?" I ask.

"That'd be a shit ending." She tips her pale, blood-streaked face towards me. "Finish the goddamn apology by rescuing my ass properly, and stop your fucking whining."

Then she falls silent, and her head lolls. I'm no expert, but I think this is bad, so I take her face in my hand and shake her lightly. Her cheeks are chilled and tacky with blood.

"Leftie."

"Can't a girl sleep? Hard day's killing."

"Stay awake a little longer." I gently poke the area around her bullet wound.

Her eyes snap open, the pupils huge, rimmed with a moat of fragile, frozen blue. "I'll try. Keep me conscious. Get the fuck out." She does something with the strands of shadow and drags her body upright so it dangles like a ghost tangled in a shroud.

The numbers on the elevator tick upwards, almost at the top.

"I'll carry you from here," I tell her. "You'll have to let go of the shadows."

"Trust you." Her mouth twists, and I think she's being sarcastic, but the darkness disappears as if the light has been turned up to maximum. She slumps forward into my arms, and I wrap them tight around her. "Little Aidy."

"Call me Rescue."

"Oh." She coughs wetly against my neck. "Cool hero name."

"Yeah." I bring my other arm up under her legs and swing her into my arms. One hand clutches a fistful of my shirt. "And that's what I'm about to do."

The elevator dings. There's a second and then the doors slide open, revealing a corridor stretching out before us.

A corridor full of soldiers, all with guns pointed at us.

"Oh shit," I promptly transform into a wall, shoving Leftie back behind me.

The gunfire is deafening. It stings me in a thousand places, but I grit my teeth and hold my form. My eyes are recessed too far to make out much, but I do see a dark-skinned figure appear, only for a moment, in the middle of the soldiers.

"Three," Skip says, appearing behind the wall.

The explosion is far louder than the gunfire. I feel flames lick against my exterior, like the top layer of my skin is being methodically peeled away by an eager sadist with a hot spatula. Then it fades, along with all the sound.

I don't think my ears are working right, but it looks as if the corridor is gone, and a sizable chunk of the building along with it.

"Now that's what I call Rescue." Leftie lets out a bark of laughter that tails into a cough.

"We've got to get her to Doc as soon as possible. I'll get back to Mutopia and try and rouse someone to come and get us." Skip presses a kiss against my cheek. "Good job, Rescue."

Then she's gone, and it's only Leftie and me, standing on the edge of a ruined building. I'm on the precipice of something terrifying once again, but this time I don't stop to think. I don't allow myself to be tangled in the web of self-doubt and hesitation. I simply drop off the edge of the building, trusting my protective powers to save me. It's worked once before, right?

For a horrible, heart-stopping moment I think nothing is happening. Leftie and I are going to plummet to our very quick deaths. But my panic kicks some internal process into gear and I become a billowing vastness, huge wings catching the air and slowing our descent.

Which leaves the next problem being Leftie in my arms.

"Stay awake," I tell her firmly.

"Apology accepted." Her voice is deeper than ever, slurred in a way I don't like.

"You've got to live." Tears roll down my cheeks.

"Fucking good effort. Look. Pretty."

The vista in front of us truly is gorgeous, as if the sky is putting on a grandiose extravaganza in honour of our mission. The sun immolates itself in a bank of clouds, streaky finger-smears of cloud wiped across the horizon.

"It really is," I whisper.

"No. *That.*" One of Leftie's hands paws at my cheek, turning the direction of my gaze the way we came. Past the extent of my billowing parachute form, I can see the building we left burning like a candle. One of the lower levels explodes outwards, sending glass to earth in a glittering waterfall.

"Yes, Leftie. It's very pretty."

She gives a cackle of laughter. "Always liked you. From the start."

"You did *not.*"

"Respected the way. You hated me."

"I was awful," I tell her. "But you know that. And you know I'm a horrible person. You saw everything."

Leftie gasps her words out a chunk at a time, twitching restlessly in my grip. "Holding onto that. One sad story. Is a credit. To your self-loathing. You don't. Deserve to die. Wouldn't kill you."

"Is that supposed to be a compliment?"

"Sort of. I get why. Never had a home. Until now. Helps me understand."

It feels both embarrassing and freeing to have myself laid bare like this. I drift in silence for a few minutes, trying to assemble words that will sum me up better. I don't find any, so I opt for the truth instead. "I'm sorry, though. For everything, but especially for trying to make it about you versus me."

"This island. Ain't big enough. For both of us," she croaks.

"Except it is."

"I'm an. Asshole too. Monster. Black hole. For a heart. Don't want. People crushed."

This is so frustratingly misguided I almost drop her. "Leftie, everyone likes you, maybe despite yourself."

"Don't know me," she says, and I can't help laughing because it's such a strange mirror of my thoughts.

"I wanted to be a pink sparkle heart," I tell her. "When I came here, that's what I planned to do. That's what I *did*. Happy, charming Aidy who liked everyone and was nice to everyone. Except deep down I had a black hole for a heart too. It crushed myself and almost everyone else.”

“Saved my ass,” Leftie said. “Now I feel. Pink and sparkly.”

“Leftie, you have never been pink and sparkly in your life.”

“Right now. Almost dying. Maybe this. Bridal carry.”

“This is *not* a bridal carry,” My voice is even more panicked than being peppered by gunfire. There is zero part of me that wants any kind of romance with The Left Hand of Darkness.

“Calm down. Not hitting. On you. Skip’s job.”

“You’re delirious,” I say flatly.

“Completely. I am. Pink. Sparkly. Delirious. Still your friend. Still your team. If you want.”

“Why do you think I came to rescue you?” I ask.

“Guilty.”

“Shut up, Leftie. I’m trying to be pink and sparkly too.”

She starts laughing at this, but it tails off into a groan.

“Leftie!” I shout at her over and over, but she doesn’t respond. I shake her face again, but she’s limp in my arms. Her heartbeat is sluggish. We’re drifting above a silent city, one of the old Michael strongholds that has been left empty while legal proceedings drag on.

There's nobody around.

My friend is dying in my arms.

This isn't how our story is supposed to end.

35

LEFTIE

When I wake again, I'm surrounded by people. The plant kids are perched on the end of the bed, and Dylan snores faintly in an armchair. Dani perches on the arm beside them and strokes their forehead. Moodring and Feral sit at a table, playing cards.

And sitting right beside me with flushed cheeks and eyes that dance is...

"Little Aidy." My mouth feels swollen. "I had the most fucked up dream. And you were there." I point at her, then loll my head in Dylan's direction. "But you weren't, and you weren't, and you weren't."

"There was an *emergency*," Willow says. "But we're sorry. We would have come if we could. You're supposed to *know* that." Their eyes fill with tears and they clutch onto their sibling.

"Shit, it's okay. I was only being a brat. I'm the one who always said I could do it on my own. Now stop crying and come here."

The two plant kids leap up the bed and wrap their arms around me. I'm left to peer over their heads at Aidy.

"You're looking very pink and sparkly," I tell them.

"I'm very glad to see you up and around. It was touch and go for a while there."

"We're friends with Aidy now, too," Soo-yeon informs me. "Not *only* because they saved you. We've been in here with them every day, looking after you."

This is the first thing to alarm me about the whole situation. "Every day?"

"It's been a week." Alyse looks up from her card game and fixes me with a stare. "After you went running off from the island at the worst possible time. We're very, very lucky that Aidy and Skip went after you, and that you'd forged enough of a connection to Cybele that she could identify your location."

"Connections." I meet her eyes. "I remember someone rambling on to me about those."

As if summoned, Dylan wakes with a start. They wipe drool from their mouth, and their eyes settle immediately on me. "Oh look, the princess has awakened."

"Don't pretend to be so gruff." Dani laughs, and looks at me. "Dilly's been by your side almost as much as the twins."

"Can we do the present thing now?" Willow asks. "Please?"

"Present." I frown. Nobody has ever given me a gift before, aside from Goddess and that was somewhat unintentional. "What do you mean?"

"We grew you something." Willow waves their arms. "Aidy, go get it. Please?"

There's some fumbling about out of view, and then the twins swing off the bed. Aidy's standing at the end, holding a single flower in a rough clay pot. It's a luminous green, with a single blue flower that has an intricate spiral of petals.

"Pretty." The frown must be evident in my voice, because Soo-yeon sighs.

"The flower isn't important. It's the seed inside."

I press my fingertips to my chest. The gruesome red line that split me in two is gone. I can't even feel the scar of it there, although I imagine it's etched deeper in me, on tissue that won't fully heal. "A seed?"

"Yes." Soo-yeon looks as if they're going to burst with pride. "It'll mean they can't take your powers again, just like with Pear."

"Wait, really?" My gaze skates over Alyse and stops on Dylan, who's giving me an ironic smile. "You trust me with that? Not being able to nerf me?"

"Believe it or not, yes. You're in the network now. Part of the family. You run away, you deal with us. And these two, who are far worse." They reach out and ruffle Willow's hair.

"And me," Aidy says firmly. "You know I'll fetch you back, and be insufferable about it."

I flop back onto the pillows. "The problem is I've already got a seed inside me, and it's a bad one. Can you take that out of me?"

There's a bunch of concerned glances, like it's very clear they've already talked about this and the news isn't good. "We did talk to Cy about that," Dylan says. "Like, a lot. Consensus is that it'd kill you. But this seed of Will and Soo's isn't going to affect it."

I want to claw at my skin, dig at it with blades of shadow until I can tear out the worldbreaker seed by the roots. But my hand stills against the off-white of the sheet, and I stare down at it. "So I live with destruction inside of me," I whisper. "Like a curse."

"Something like that." Dylan stands beside me. "Lucky you're such a fucking badass and can handle that."

"And you've got friends who will help you," Aidy says. "Lots of them."

"You're the pinkest and sparkliest." I laugh, and it feels easy. "Okay, give me this magic seed of yours, kids."

"Magic seed." Soo-yeon snorts, and takes the flower gently in their hands. "It took a lot of work to grow this, I'll have you know. Cybele was very impressed with our cleverness, wasn't she, Will?"

"We like you, Leftie." Willow's eyes are very intent. "We want you to be okay."

For some reason, after everything, these are the words that make me start crying. I didn't like crying the first time, and I don't particularly like it this time either, but it's not something I have control over. I shake and blubber and gross fluids drip out of me. It's a bit like dying in a way. I've seen so many people die. Except the whole time I'm bawling, I'm surrounded by all these people, who reach out for me, this network of connections that entangles me. With my eyes squeezed close, I can sense Cybele humming underneath it all, a song of satisfaction and intricate nested harmonies. All her many children connected.

"Enough." My voice still shakes a little. "Let's do this."

Soo-yeon parts the petals delicately with vines extruded from the tips of their fingers. There's a single pale green seed nestled inside.

"Yum." I blink at the twins.

"Mum, can you make Leftie eat her vegetables?" Willow smirks.

"I can eat it just fine." I reach out my hand, and the seed is placed inside. It smells like rosemary and wet grass. When I roll it between my fingers, it feels spongy. I place it to my lips and swallow it down before I can question anything. It dissolves in the back of my throat, and there's a tickle down inside me as it descends. A seed of destruction and a seed of protection. Perhaps I'll always be poised between these two possibilities, or maybe I'll find a way to choose one.

Willow and Soo-yeon look at each other, and there's a flicker of green in their eyes. Then they smile and nestle their heads in against me.

"Thank you," I whisper.

"You're family now," Willow says. "A tiny bit plant."

"Oh." I hadn't considered that part. That connection I felt to Cybele when I was trapped in the laboratory flares into life again, this time brighter and stronger, like a constantly burning fuse. I feel like if I closed my eyes, I could see other tendrils spiralling into everyone in this room, even Aidy.

Especially Aidy, I think. Growing up in the dark, poised between the claws of monsters, meant I learned not to fear those things. And when I carved my way free of my cage, my relentless mission pushed me on and on, with no time to feel the cold around me.

Aidy's heart was colder than mine ever was, drowning in fears and rejections. Yet they still came to find me. Even to give an apology to a girl who might well have slapped them in the face for it.

Stubborn asshole. I like them.

Sometime later, when the kids are sprawled in leafy slumber, I untangle myself from them and get out of the bed. My legs feel steady, and I feel strong. It's good to move again. My fingers trace a line down where my scar should be, pausing where I imagine the seed hums inside me, changing me increment by increment.

I reach the door and swing it open. There's a figure sprawled in a chair, feet kicked up against the wall. It can't possibly be comfortable. Chatterbox. They look up from their phone, and a smile spills across their face like the sunrise.

"Hey, brat. Finally got sick of sitting around on your ass?"

"I'm not much for sitting back and doing nothing. And now Uriel's out of the way, it frees me up for any work you might have lying around. Like this new team of yours."

"What if that's all rescue operations and shit?"

I shrug. "Maybe it's a waste of my talents, but maybe I'd like it. Saving people like the Broken World kids. Might get used to being a superhero. Seems like a way to meet cute girls."

"Leftie, you have no fucking idea." They laugh, and hold out their hand. "Let's go do something cool and save some people."

I take it, and we walk outside into the sunlight.

It's a beautiful day.

36

AIDY

Skip and I have a lot of conversations when we get back, while Leftie is in bed recuperating. I tell her everything this time. The boring parts and the sad parts and the ugly parts. All the little moments that make up a life, all the small wounds that make up who I am.

When I'm finished I lie back on the grass and look up at the trees. "Please put me out of my misery."

She rolls over to look at me. "I thought you were so charmed when I first met you. This person who seemed so buoyant, I was surprised you didn't float a foot off the ground."

I can't help but laugh at this. "My disguise was really that good?"

"Apparently." She gives a gurgle of laughter. "Or I'm not that perceptive. I was like here is this person, confident in themself, confident in their body, in their lack of gender. And here I am, Skip the mess."

"That's ridiculous."

"Not so much. Do you want to hear my story now?" Her eyes are serious, and her body angles away from mine. I recognise the body language.

"I do." I know what this means, for someone to offer this.

Her story is almost as long as mine, and it's sadder in places, too. She crafts each story one by one and sails it between our hearts, and they find safe harbour there. Afterwards, we don't kiss, but we lie side by side with the backs of our hands touching, as if we need that contact to keep the connection going, to bleed off all the tension of our ruptured, shedding selves into each other, vessels to hold and be held.

"I like you, Aidy," she says. "But I don't know I'll ever be a person who *loves*. My power is to leap away, and I don't know how good I am at coming back over and over again. I'm going to try, but I don't want to promise you anything."

I think about the kiss we shared in the elevator, and how hot and urgent it was. Moments before she leapt away. I wonder if she thought about not coming back.

"My power is to rescue," I tell her. "So as long as you need, I'll be here."

Her hand turns and takes hold of mine. "You're one of the good ones, Aidy. No matter what you've thought for so long."

She plants another kiss on my cheek, just as impulsive as the first. I feel the hardness of her teeth behind them.

Then she's gone.

I stay on the grass, and watch the clouds scud across the sky. The trees bend over me, as if they're watching. I place this new rejection in a line with all the others, and admire it from all angles. So many of them weren't about me. Just like with Skip, it's about the person leaving, the person who can't stay, the person who refuses to change. I'm still me, this mutant made up of past selves, all melting together into something uncomfortable and new.

I don't know what my shape might be, but—

"Feeling maudlin, little Aidy?" Leftie stands in the shadows, but her voice holds light.

"Yeah." I tilt my head toward her. "Sometimes it's shitty, isn't it?"

"Quite a lot of the time, yeah. And then sometimes it's not."

"So profound, little Leftie."

She lowers herself to the ground beside me carefully. Her dark hair spills around her like a fan. In the dusk, her skin is ghost-pale, aside from the red slash of her lips and her eyes which reflect the guttering day in revenant blue.

"I like when you call me that," she says.

"Yeah?"

"It's like we match."

I snort. Yes, the two of us, mirror images.

"I asked Mélodie on a date," she tells me. "I don't know what I was thinking. Dylan said something about being a superhero helping you meet girls, and so I got myself all over excited because she gives me these *looks*."

"Oh yeah." I grin at Leftie. "She's definitely interested. So how did it go?"

"She said I have to *date* her. So I took her into the forest, to show her that it's not that creepy, and she said I didn't understand romance. So now I need another idea."

I try to hold back laughter, but I can't. "You took her into Cybele's lair?"

"It's pretty in there!"

"Your aesthetic is hopelessly warped."

"How?" She levers herself up on one elbow to look down at me with the haughtiest look on her face, the disdain of a cult princess brought up to break the world.

"There's like a hundred romantic places on the island. They're *everywhere*. What was your next plan, to knock on One Thorn's door and try and find a terrifying little abattoir room to have dinner in?"

"One Thorn's not a bad idea," Leftie says thoughtfully.

"You're hopeless."

"What? How? They could take us to Paris, you know, that's supposed to be romantic. We could have dinner in the catacombs. Or a pretty tropical island. One of those ones where you can find one of those big old alien skeletons."

"Are you doing this on purpose?" I honestly can't tell, but it keeps making me laugh.

"I'm suggesting *interesting* places." She wrinkles her nose. "Oh God. Is Mél boring?"

"No." I roll my eyes. "Honestly. You just have to think about the other person, though. Like do the pretty island thing, and *then* tell her about the skeleton."

"People are hard," she sighs.

"They are."

We both lie on our backs, staring up as the Milky Way brightens above us in incandescent strokes.

"Aidy?"

"Yeah?"

"You're my friend, right? You didn't only come to rescue me as an apology?"

I think about what Alyse said, about the Ballad of Dilly and Lys being as important as anything to do with romance.

"I'm your friend," I whisper. "The Ballad of Aidy and Leftie will slap, as long as someone tells it right. But, strictly speaking, I think you owe me a rescue."

"Oh, so we're keeping score now?"

"No." I smile in the darkness. "I'm just saying."

"Fine. I'll kill anyone you want. Any ten people you want. A hundred. Fuck, there's no upper limit, little Aidy. Give me a goddamn list, and I'll prove my friendship to you in blood."

"There's nobody I need dead. It's nice that you offered though."

Her hand finds mine, but instead of holding it, she travels up and pokes me hard in the armpit so that I squawk.

"I'll fucking *save* someone for you. How about that? I'll spare someone's life even if I think they really deserve it, just on your say-so. That's much harder for me than doing an execution."

"You're terrible," I say, but I'm smiling so wide I think I must've grown extra teeth.

"The Ballad of Aidy and Leftie. How does that go, then?"

"Half the verses are me singing sad boi shit feeling sorry for myself, and the others are you doing funky R&B about the joy of stabbing."

"That sounds legitimately terrible." She cackles, wild and unhinged.

"I don't know. It's something Alyse said, about her and Dylan."

"Does it ever scare you?" Leftie's voice is abruptly quiet, as if she changed the settings. "The shit those two have been through? When I spoke to Alyse the other day, I saw this gulf in her, one you can't see the bottom of. Dilly too, I think. Except they hold each other up, like some magic trick where you'd think they'd both sink but they float instead. Not just them, but the whole goddamn operation. Dani and Feral and Penance and all of them."

I imagine it in my head, just like I saw it in Cybele's dream. The sprawling forest with her in the centre, that network of connections, lit up and glowing. And here's me, the dead sapling extending one trembling limb to touch Leftie. The bark of her tree is dark as if it's covered in candle wax from a thousand black masses, but the blossoms are a blinding pink, that sparkle bright enough to be seen from miles around.

The connection to her is enough for me to sputter with light, the beginnings of blossom budding along my skin. This is only the first. I'll grow stronger too.

"I'm scared of everything," I tell her. "But a lot less now that I've got you."

I expect her to laugh, or to mock me, but instead she moves closer. Her hand cups mine, and her head moves so it's pressed against my shoulder.

And together, we lie side by side on the island, in the rustling shadow of the forest, and we watch the stars.

Acknowledgments

First off, thanks to my family, who support me to follow my own dream.

Then to my beta readers who help me keep things together. In particular, thanks to Melo who helped me figure out why my original plot wasn't working, and Monica who once again helped me to clarify confusion and fine-tune the sticky parts. As always, thank you to my support crew: Andy, Crystal, Leah, Mallory, Michelle, Nat, Nina, SinJ, SoftJ, Shannon, Rosa, Charlotte, Mary, E.M., Hsinju, Andy, Art, and Andee.

And finally, thank you once again to the readers, who helped this Universe get dreamed into being.

About the Author

SJ Whitby writes books. They're nonbinary and they live in New Zealand. That's about all you need to know, and they would kindly request not to be perceived at this time.

 twitter.com/sjwhitbywrites

 instagram.com/sjwhitbywrites

 patreon.com/sjwhitby

www.ingramcontent.com/pod-product-compliance
Lightning Source LLC
Chambersburg PA
CBHW050854210726
48290CB00004B/1221